To Lyss H,

THUMBS
UP!

DENISE LUTZ

RABBIT HOUSE PRESS
Versailles, KY 40383
www.Rabbithousepress.com

Copyright © 2022 by Denise Lutz
Published in the United States by Rabbit House Press, September 2022.
Printed in the United States of America.

ISBN: 978-0-578-98617-3

All rights reserved. No part of this book may be reproduced in any form or by any electronic or mechanical means, including information storage and retrieval systems, without permission in writing from the author, except by a reviewer who may quote brief passages in review with attribution.

This is a work of fiction. Names, characters, places, and incidents are either the product of the author's imagination or are used fictitiously. Any resemblance to actual persons, living or dead, events or locales is entirely coincidental.

Cover Art and Interior Design: Corbyn Keys
Editor: Patrick LoBrutto
For inquiries about author appearances and/or volume orders contact:
Rabbithousepress@gmail.com

"Here's all you gotta know about men and women: women are crazy, men are stupid. And the main reason women are crazy is that men are stupid."

−George Carlin

THUMBS is dedicated to my wonderful family, those here and not, that will live forever in my heart. To Uncle Paul, a circus acrobat and professional poker and golf course gambler, who regaled me as a child with colorful accounts of the racetrack backside; and to the quintessential lady, my lovely, supportive mother, who was respected in our family for many things, among them, her command of proper English; and to my dear father, who made me laugh until whole fat milk flew out my nose.

In 1972, George Carlin shared his edgy "Seven Words You Can Never Say on Television" and his mom washed his mouth out with soap. Decades later, the F-bomb got a further boost in school locker rooms when an "Indian schoolteacher" informed his "students" on its versatility as a noun, adjective, transitive and intransitive verb or adverb. Since then, certain four-letter words have become commonplace on TV and radio, the internet and in movies (new unspeakable words have replaced those, Mom). May you gentle readers, and my mother's eyebrow, forgive THUMBS's bad guys for their liberal use.

It's the unexpected turn in a joke that makes me laugh, and in the case of a thriller, jump from my seat. My favorite characters are the bumbling, vain and supercilious neurotic ones, blissfully ignorant of their flaws. There is a special place in my head for authors: Carl Hiaasen, H. Allen Smith, Janet Evanovich, and Elmore Leonard; and in film and television, the quirky characters created by actors: John Cleese, Don Knotts, Harvey Korman, Carol Burnett, Peter Sellers; and the old Saturday Night Live crowd: Dan Aykroyd, John Belushi, Chevy Chase, Jane Curtin, Garrett Morris, Laraine Newman, Bill Murray, Michael O'Donoghue, Gilda Radner, Lily Tomlin, Steve Martin. Old Baby Boomer stuff.

I would like to thank my talented editor, Patrick LoBrutto and my energetic publisher and fellow author, Erin Chandler; our dedicated book designer Corbyn Keys; my very funny ex-husband, Ken, for his fine proof-reading skills and our son, Elliott, who has been a wealth of knowledge on the guy stuff; as well as my dear and personal friends who have struggled through many drafts in the making of this book.

I hope you will like reading THUMBS as much as I have enjoyed writing it.

Denise

FIFTH GRADE

So far, fifth grade had not gone well for Catherine Kowalski, especially gym. The Maidenformed madonnas nailed her shoulders to her locker, 30 AA, an unfortunate number. Determined to unscrew her little tits, they ravaged her Fruit of the Loom undershirt, roaring with joy.

The bad girls laughed and hollered, "Twister!"

"Help!" Cathy cried out in pain, lashing back.

Their gym teacher, on her smoke break, couldn't hear a word.

"Carpenter's dream," taunted Ginny Whitehead, also known as Zitface. She hated her because she didn't have pimples and was flat, ugly, and stupid.

Zitface slammed her locker closed and shoved the others out of the way, hissing. "My turn." Cathy flinched from experience. The big girl danced in like a boxer, coming close enough to spray in her face. "Women," she announced, "can you believe the Polack's new rack?"

The satin falsies had been stashed under Mom's nylons in her sachet-scented underwear drawer. Safety-pinning them to her undershirt had seemed like a good idea, but the hyenas were ripping them off with most of her undershirt and playing keep-away.

"They're my mom's," Cathy cried as her secret cheaters sailed over the nearby john stall and splashed in the toilet clogged with her sweat socks from last week. The mean girls howled with joy.

"Score," shouted the loud one who smelled like grape gum and BO, "two points, our side." Cathy hated grape gum, and them—and herself.

Miss Wasserman was still in the lounge enjoying her Winston.

Cathy's eyes were pouring tear drops, "I'm telling, you losers."

"Aww, she'll tell the kielbasa packer, her daddy. I say, let's give it to her, women!"

In her final act of self-defense, Cathy flapped her hands and huffed liverwurst sandwich breath on Zithead's pimples and shouted, "Crater face!"

It was Hell until the bell.

FIFTH AVENUE

Christmastime on Fifth Avenue, and Jack was five. He remembered it well. It was snowing hard and getting dark, and he and his mother were late for his pediatrician's appointment. His mother's driver had dropped them curbside, half a block from FAO Schwarz and was now circling in their 1937 Duesenberg through the slow, heavy traffic.

The smell of roasted chestnuts and grilled sausages made his mouth water. He tried to wrestle away from his mink-stole mother. A Salvation Army bell ringer who might have been Santa, but probably wasn't, nodded understandingly and shook his brass hand bell. Snowflakes stuck to his red hat and everywhere. She'd promised him, young Jacky, a brand-new lead soldier with a small quid pro quo: All he had to do was cooperate and accept his whooping cough booster without spitting on Dr. Wade or Nurse Muriel like the last time.

As it was December, the sidewalk congestion was intense. Jacky and his mother had different destinations. She pecked along the salt-encrusted sidewalk in her delicate patent leather pumps, swinging him up by his gauze-bandaged thumbs, hoping to keep his shiny Buster Browns dry while he struggled to carve "icebreaker" channels through the slush with his heels.

His meltdown, he fondly recalled, occurred in front of the famous toy store's North Pole windows when he spotted Santa's magical elves in their colorful blinking train. He dug in, his feet cemented to the ice and snow and for a moment Mumsy couldn't budge him. Embarrassed and harried and begging, she was finally able to drag him in short hops as he screamed and screamed, toward the doctor's building.

"I'm not going!" he shouted, drawing a small, amused crowd. "He's going to cut them off, Mumsy—like you said!"

"Ahh…you have been sucking them," Mumsy said. True, and the iodine-soaked gauze tasted bad. She lost her grip and down he went, collapsing in his corduroy trousers on the sloppy cold sidewalk, where he made furious snow angels while looking up her skirt.

It was a win-win. Mumsy gave in and took him back to the elves and bought him the toy. And by the time they'd made it through the endless checkout line, Dr. Wade had left for Connecticut.

1
BAD SEEDS

On an otherwise beautiful St. Louis morning, the usual
Save the Earth demonstrators littered the shady
Soulard Street sidewalk outside the Henniger Chemical
Tower. Catherine K. Henniger, in her mid-forties and
feeling it, was seated next to her husband of twelve years
in his chauffeured new 2011 Lincoln Navigator. She was
about to launch a protest of her own. The next stop was
her long overdue postnuptial planning appointment just
five blocks away, but the traffic was heavy.

As the Navigator inched to a stop through the shouting
activists and their *Poison Popcorn* banners, she nudged
the elderly man with his name on the building. A cigar
drooped from his tight, skinny lips, as his thumbs flew like
gnat wings on his state-of-the art BlackBerry.

She felt like cutting them off.

A furious provocateur in full dental braces and a Green-
Please hoody flung himself and a *Cram Your Cobs* sign in
front of the brilliantly polished SUV. Jack's driver jolted
to a stop, rocking them in their belts and nearly martyring

the young man. Her trust proposal flew from her lap to the floor as the riotous pack scrambled to the aid of their comrade.

The aggressive ones swarmed them, drumming their fists on the hood and kicking at the quarter panels. She peeked at her watch, ten after nine. Jack was still unflinchingly absorbed with his phone.

Had the white-haired founder of the great pesticide firm glanced up, he would have seen his driver calmly hoist himself out and wade through the furious bodies to his door, where he stood as straight as the building with one hand on the bulge in his suit coat.

Jack's suit was a handsome dark gray which bespoke of Saville Row. He was also wearing his favorite faux-leather shoes, one of each color.

She cleared her throat. "Your plastic ones again, Jack?"

"They're waterproof, Catherine. It's going to rain." His thumbs were still a blur above the tiny keyboard. He was, after all, getting ready to chair his 9:00 a.m. Executive Meeting. He ordered the footwear from a catalog, in both brown and black, during their two-for-one sale. "No one knows they're not leather," he liked to boast.

But her mind was on her future. She squeezed her toes inside her own pumps. She dreaded being late, but often was, and hated this about herself.

"See you at the gala tonight," she said, picking at a hangnail. She hoped he would wear the matching black shoes with his tux. She knew she was Jack's flunkey blonde, and no Betty Crocker, like his last wife—the perfect one with her name still on his trust, which was what she wanted to change. All she could do was try her best. Gerte, the German housekeeper, had forgotten the dry cleaning again, but tonight's dress, except for some tiny red wine spots, was pristine enough for its second evening out this week. The parties were aging her fast. They were lovefests for Jack, but endless nightmares to her.

A Greenie pressed his bearded face to the glass, peering in. Jack's driver grabbed and tossed him back into the crowd just as her husband, satisfied with his email, holstered his BlackBerry, nodding it was time. She motioned to his items on the floor.

"Don't forget these," she said, watching the frothing environmentalists climb over the hood and begin to rock their car with passion.

Jack reached down for something. "Later," he said, "Be on time, for a change." The door opened and he struggled out in a cloud of gray smoke. The driver took his aging boss by the arm, kicking bodies out of the way, and escorted him toward the revolving door of his tall bronze building and headed back. Her fingers swept the backseat's floor feeling for her legal file…feeling nothing but a small paper sack. She gulped. Instead of his lunch, he had nabbed her own draft of the trust and postnuptial— the ultra-confidential one that she was about to go over with her lawyers. "My trust stays the same unless you drop your childishness. Steinhart crafted the postnup, carefully, to protect us both in the unlikely case of divorce." She should never have signed the skimpy agreement, but it had been their wedding day and Jack was having one of his tantrums. Her pulse quickened. If she moved fast enough, she could beat him to the door and make the swap before he saw her file.

She leaped from the vehicle and elbowed her way through the crowd, stumbling once and nearly losing his lunch bag while the driver, pushing away protesters, began to polish their handprints off Jack's gleaming new luxury model.

"Jack!" she shouted, her voice swallowed by the protest, though some in the crowd did hear, and hooted.

He didn't turn. His hand was on his beautiful bronze door.

"Jack!" she yelled again, alarmed. She had become the crowd's new interest. She had to reach that door. Jack was already inside, pecking calmly again at his BlackBerry— her future tucked under his arm.

A Greenie's hand pinched her shoulder painfully. Another tore at her clothes. She shook them off and in ten long strides, made it safely inside. But someone had beaten her in, a huge, wild–eyed activist wielding a large metal meat mallet and he was marching toward Jack like a big furry tank. Her heart flopped. *Where was that damn security guard?*

She sprinted across the lobby of the world's largest pesticide company on a collision course with the guard stepping out of the men's room, pulling up his zipper. He demanded her ID—how would he recognize her with her hair a loose pile of straw and her slip ripped and dangling, looking as maniacal as the man with the mallet? Undaunted, she sidestepped the guard and rushed to the elevators, her chest heaving hard. All eight cars were somewhere else. The guard's shiny oxfords screeched to a halt behind her. *"Mrs. Henniger?"* he asked, incredulously. By now, Jack and the meat tenderizing activist were at floor six or higher, going up. She chose the stairs, two at a time.

"Planning to use that on me?" Jack asked the refrigerator-sized Greenie. The guy was brandishing the strangest weapon Jack had ever seen.

"Yes, sir. When my girlfriend ate your modified creamed corn, her facial hair went thick…and *curly.*" Their elevator was almost there. "Man, she used to be hot, but now she looks like Sasquatch."

Jack chortled ahead of his joke. "Hey—do you mind if I call you Harry? Please heed my advice, don't have kids," he warned the man. "Their feet will be huge. Their shoes, alone, will cost a fortune."

The man wistfully lowered his head and mallet. "That ship has sailed…"

"Look," Jack offered, pointing to the Pornhub site on his BlackBerry, "this will solve *some* of your problems."

Harry took a long peek and grinned large. "Thanks."

The door opened.

"Take my card," said Jack, his cigar flapping. "Better living through chemicals."

2
BORED ROOM

Fading away in a golf cart was not on J. R. Henniger's to-do list. He was happy staying just where he was in his teak-paneled, sound-wired kingdom on the fifteenth floor of his beautiful bronze skyscraper, the gem of the Soulard Historic Neighborhood District. He slid stiffly into his big leather chair at the head of the fully occupied table and picked up his BlackBerry. The other chairs had been set six inches lower than his, and locked. He'd made sure of that. The young yuppies sitting in them were intent on getting rid of him.

They didn't have to try to kill him, though. An alien parachuted from the top of his tiny game screen. He obliterated it. Somebody was, and he would be ready.

He'd heard their whines through his hidden microphones—how every time he opened his media flytrap with its tobacco brown teeth, they had to rescue the company. They could only dream of a severance package their so-called geriatric chairman would take. They'd have to up their game if they wanted him gone. Two more aliens blamoed.

An impertinent new smartass from Wharton stage-whispered to the table's amusement, "Somebody's past his best buy date." *As if he were deaf.* Jack looked over his reading glasses. All nods, no abstentions. Breaking news: he was a long way from the used CEO shelf.

He didn't need to see faces. His eyes were on his Black-Berry, and he had reached a critical point, level twenty-eight. *BrickBreaker* champion stuff. He shifted in his conference chair hoping to block out the intense itch— yes, *that* place again. he shifted in his conference chair hoping to block the distraction and reminded himself to take a breath now and then so he wouldn't pass out like he had at the last meeting. His body lurched in micro-spasms synced with his flying thumb action. Just four more levels, this round. He wished the corporate idiots would move the boring budget discussion along. He had heard it all before.

If they didn't see his timeless wisdom as priceless, at least the rest of the world did. The boys believed his success came from luck. *Fire them!* The Henniger Chemical pesticide empire meant an awful lot to him. Why not, after devoting forty years to feeding the world and single-handedly creating unbelievable shareholder value? They had zero complaints. *Level twenty-nine!* He looked up and relit the cigar clamped between his teeth. *Damn,* his reflexes were quick for his age—and his instincts, keen! He and his lawyer, Simon Steinhart, had cunningly tweaked his contract with the old board when he hit sixty-five. Remembering this, he relaxed....

"Jack...?" The disembodied voice was not a boardroom type. He didn't open his eyes.

"*Jack!*" A woman's voice—annoying, and not very smart. Familiar.

"Give him a little poke before he burns the building down, will you, Catherine?"

"He's sleeping," said another voice. "Can you *believe* it?" He opened his eyelids to see Ed Schmed, the new chief operating officer. Now there, was a jerk.

Catherine The Third was gazing down on him, smiling one of her plastic smiles and waving his lunch. Her hair looked as wild as Phyllis Diller's.

"I brought your liverwurst sandwich and strawberry gummy bears, honey," she said as she swapped his paper lunch sack on the table for something else.

"I'm awake!" he said, sitting upright. He wiped a tickly drool from his mouth with the back of his hand. "Just resting my eyeballs." He blinked hard. The crazy itch in his crotch needed a serious scratch.

After subsequent super-secret meetings with Zorox Industries, both sides claimed victory. A priceless deal for Henniger Chemical and a platinum parachute for him, Jack told Catherine, and laughed. She was not. "CEOs willing to settle for less are second-rate."

The deal clincher meant a short-term assignment for Jack. Zorox, a first-tier supplier, would take him for one year, not a day longer. The two companies would forget the past. To demonstrate renewed faith in the relationship, Henniger Chemical signed a purchase order to Zorox in the millions.

"This will tide me over till the next great thing. My own talk show or maybe a run for Governor." Catherine nodded. He loved an audience. "There have been rumors, you know. For now, let's say I'm booting up for a real-life ball breaker. My first order of business is to empty the swamp in Sales and Purchasing. I don't hand-hold halfwits."

"Wow," she said in a tone that echoed his thoughts. Only the world's best executive could save Zorox from its death march toward shutdown.

"I always come through, don't I?"

"You do seem to, Jack."

The chemical trade was ablaze with speculation on why the legendary wizard would bother with a loser like Zorox when he could be playing golf in the nineties in Naples? Why would Zorox want him? The answer was a no-brainer; he was too valuable to retire.

He caught his reflection in his shiny faux-leather shoes, musing at they would make ideal plungers. Of course, he planned to live forever. Because his play time was becoming more important, he would speed up the purge. There would be mixed admiration at Zorox, just like everywhere. One couldn't ignore that his intellect and exemplary people skills made others look bad. Naturally, they feared him. But as long as he fixed their mess, who cared? It wasn't like he would invite them home for martinis and dinner.

His favorite perk was Zorox's one remaining jet, a sweet

leather-upholstered G-4 with a fully stocked bar and an ample-breasted flight attendant. Her two small kids had a dad behind in his child support. There would be plenty of hours onboard with the redhead, the tenacious female reps, and flirtatious Pussi, the COO's administrative assistant. He would take them all for a ride.

Some things a wife didn't need to know.

3
GREENIES NEEDED

Simon Steinhart, Esq. was cold stone hard. That, and his tough negotiating skills endeared him to Jack, who, thanks to Simon, had seen his demanding ex-wives buckle at settlement time; There weren't many attorneys Jack respected, but this guy was different.

Jack sat in Simon's richly paneled law office shooting for level thirty on his BlackBerry, one eye on Simon, giving him a speedy critique. Simon looked agreeably smart today in his custom-tailored suit, Hermès tie, and gleaming diamond cufflinks on his starched French cuffs. His hair was slicked back, Thirties-style, and graying at the temples. Next to Simon's high IQ, Jack respected his total lack of empathy—except when he refused to discount his inflated fees, like now. He eyed the half-inch thick estate planning bill on Simon's massive desk.

"I'd like to kill her, Simon."

"Sure, keep your legal costs down." Simon pushed his tortoise shell glasses back up his nose and slowly circled his balance on the invoice twice with his Montblanc pen.

"Still, most people do it the conventional way. They don't murder each other."

"I've put your kids through college with my last two divorces," he said, lifting the statement with a slightly trembling hand.

"You want me to get her rubbed out? I've told you since the beginning, you can save on my bill if you throw her some premarital crumbs—excluding stock options, of course—and split the post marital gain when you die. Maybe you and Catherine would get along better if you did."

"Split them, and die?"

"Both."

"No way. What has *she* done?" Catherine had reminded him of sweet Mumsy when he married her, in retrospect, a mistake.

"Nothing, apparently," Simon poured Jack a bit of gin, which he accepted and stirred with his finger. Simon opened a bottle of S. Pellegrino for himself.

"She can't even cook. Besides—I'm the one who rakes the money in."

"But you'll be dead anyway. She'll be your widow and you're not leaving a cent to Gracie's daughters. What's the difference?" Jack hadn't heard from the step-twins or his ex-wife since Simon had settled their bogus lawsuit.

"Principle, principal. Besides, why does a widow need much money, anyway? They don't *do* anything… *go* anywhere good." He snuffled up some postnasal drip and continued. "Good thing, too, they're a menace on the road. Catherine would waste it on the ladies' flower club."

"And the Humane Society."

He steadied his hand, shaking slightly on the tabletop. "Yes, Simon, and frankly," he brightened up, "I'd like to see my name carved on the new Duke library. See, if I pledge today, I can enjoy the glory while I'm still around…fill another two garages from Christie's. I have my eye on a red '63 Ferrari GTO."

"Didn't they throw you out of Duke?"

"My point." Jack paused, thinking. "You know, I made a great deal of money off those midterm test copies. A *great* deal of money. Anything wrong with that?"

"Just the school."

"Ha-ha," Jack laughed. But there was nothing funny about his underwear again today, dammit. He itched. Gerte Schmaltz was using far too much expensive laundry soap. Catherine wouldn't slow the housekeeper's wastefulness down. He gave himself a long, thoughtful scratch. *Why not kill them both?* Jack adjusted his trousers. "Sometimes I think about doing it myself."

Steinhart cleared his throat. "Do I look like a sex therapist, Jack?"

"You look like a smug Harvard thug getting rich off the estate planning you peddle at my expense. Sometimes, I do want to get rid of her."

Steinhart looked out the window. "If you're serious, there are people out there willing to do whatever. Nobody we know personally, of course. Just say the word."

Jack couldn't tell if he was joking. "For God's sake, Simon, she undresses in the *closet*."

"Got it," Steinhart said, and made a few quick notes.

4
OILY SALAD DRESSING

Catherine stood at the butcher block dicing a long zucchini and wondering how to bring up the postnup. She looked past the smoldering fire to Jack who was seated in the comfy new chair with his favorite cat on his lap. Fluffy's tail twitched to the movement of Jack's thumbs on his ancient BlackBerry which dinged like an arcade game. The ergonomics of the new Cutco chefs' knife pleased her. This one was sharp enough to slice through a fire hose. It would be her murder weapon of choice, that was, if she were to go any crazier from loss of hormones (which she needed), or maybe something else. Feeling flushed, she wiped her brow with her bare forearm and took a sip of Pinot Noir. She had just redone the spacious country kitchen, adding the antique French cook stove and the plaid wingback chair. Jack had griped about the extra expense but had finally realized that having a refrigerator in the same room with the stove and sink was a plus. Finished with the zucchini, she chose an onion and minced it without mercy. She and Jack used to talk while she prepared dinner, before his cell phone obsession.

1999

Catherine was struck by Cupid's bow at the '99 Medi Spa Expo. She had come to the convention center to drop off her divorce complaint, knowing that her husband, Marvin Quackenbush, would be away from the stand for his weekly recovery meeting. At the moment, his twin twenty-year-old technicians were keeping a handsome visitor amused. Giggling, they held a shiny Dr. Marvin shopping bag open for the well-dressed man to shovel in *Eye Excellence*. Other heavy bags hung from his elbows.

Being single again might not be so bad, she thought, adjusting her pinching underwire bra before charging into the tent. "Mr. Clooney—I've seen every one of your films!" George, noticing her immediately, smiled, revealing his perfect teeth, and she swooned like a rock band groupie.

He was broad-shouldered and tall with a square jaw and Hollywood brown eyes, his head sodded with thick, white—executive—hair. As her own eyes adjusted in the Zen-like tent, she realized, the glowing Zeus before her was not George Clooney, the ghost of Cary Grant, or even Jon Hamm. *What a dummy.* He was the notorious Jack Henniger of Henniger Chemical—the richest, most talked about man in town. His patrician face and risky business tales were often in the news. She looked him up and down. Not everyone liked him, but she certainly did.

"An honest mistake I hear all the time," said the charming older man while nodding to the jolly young girls with their beautiful skin and pouty lips. One offered a silver tray filled with *Quick Repair* samples. "My ladies at the office love your products."

Apparently, they had already met the considerate Mr. Henniger. Her compliments to Dr. Quackenbush. Marvin's young assistants, trained to say they were forty, tittered like the three shared a big secret or wanted to. The boss' wife cleared her throat to interrupt.

She tried not to gaze at him like a baked fish with its head still on, but she felt excited like she never had with Marvin. Dislodging an awkward piece of parsley between two teeth, she blabbered, "I had Middle Eastern for lunch. Tabouli." Spotting the cases of product samples, she asked the twins, "What else can we give this nice gentleman?"

"Oh, hello, Mrs. Quackenbush," the twins chimed, causing a painful gas bubble.

"*Mrs?*" Mr. Henniger asked, with a flattering hint of disappointment. His gaze caressed her figure like she was the last truffle in an expensive box of chocolates. He tossed a tube of crème without looking, missing the bag.

"*Miss,*" she blurted recklessly, embarrassing herself. The girls would tell Marvin.

"I meant to say, you *missed*," she back peddled as she reached down to retrieve the stray sample. She winced. "I'm still married, of course… to Dr. Quackenbush."

"Shame," he said and shook his head. It was hard for her to tell if he meant the word as a noun or verb.

He offered her a manicured hand, which she squeezed perhaps a moment too long.

She accepted his offered business card, appreciating its heavy weight and thermo-raised letters.

"Jack?" She smiled, handing him one of her new Bible sales cards.

He responded in a gravely smoker's voice with smiling brown Hollywood eyes, his hand now touching her arm, "Call me anything, as long as it isn't late for dinner." But his beautiful eyes had said "bed," not dinner. For him, she could be on time and learn to cook.

Feeling on the wild side, she whispered over the convention hall din, "You know—you look a lot like my second husband."

He arched a bushy black eyebrow. "How many have you had?"

"One," she answered with a nervous giggle. His kind laugh emboldened her. She read the backside of his card. It read 'Call me' in precise block-letters which said a lot about leadership, a trait that made her feel tingly. Perhaps the most desirable bachelor in St. Louis was interested in her? And here, she had only been hoping for protection, since Marvin had threatened her reputation. It had been hard to land her position in door-to-door sales as shy as she was, and as a single woman she was going to need the income.

Marvin stored his Peptide Recovery Complex samples under the registration table. They retailed at a hundred a tube. Thinking fast, she handed Jack the entire case, which he had accepted, grinning.

BACK IN THE KITCHEN

"Tell me again about your Chateau Margaux, Jack." It was his favorite story from Paris, when J.R. Henniger launched Agent Brown, their all-time best defoliant. The dusty bottle of Bordeaux, autographed by the French Ambassador, was still in his wine cellar. Jack cleared his throat and tapped his cigar ash, bobbing his head slightly.

"When I finish my email," he said, his thumbs re-engaging. "Roll the log a quarter turn, will you, sweetie?" Gerte had started the hardwood all-nighter before leaving for the day. Seeing that the poker wouldn't budge the enormous log, Catherine used the oven mitts. The log was very heavy, but she managed to turn it so it would burn steadily till morning—especially with… all the scrambling black… She gasped.

"Jack—look! The log is loaded with carpenter ants!"

"What?" Jack yelled, cupping his hand to his ear, half-rising from his chair and back. "Something happen to the car?" His thumbs relaunched on his cell phone keys at reckless speed. She crunched a fleeing ant with her house clog.

Fluffy sprang off Jake's lap, waking the terrier who scratched at a flea and rolled over in his dog bed, reminding to stir her soup. She swirled her wooden spoon, thinking of how to bring up her desired trust changes without ticking off Jack, who planned to live forever.

Jack shuffled over to the new kitchen counter. He plopped some fresh ice in his glass, refilled it with gin and battered the cubes. Drink number two; she was counting. He cleared his throat; he was always doing that from his cigars.

"So, if you remember, the CIA had me set up a sting with a camera and mike in my room at the Ritz—the Presidential Suite," he began.

"And your briefcase contained the fake formula."

"Right, for Agent Brown, we were selling a ton of it to Defense."

"Someone in France was stealing our country's corporate secrets."

"Their spies were hitting hard. Washington wanted proof. Thanks to me, the ladies were caught on tape."

"You made the perfect leading man," said Mrs. James Bond. They both laughed and he coughed. *The cigars.*

"Let me tell you, it was quite the romp on the Louis XIV bed with the five naked call girls," he chortled. She last remembered the naked call girl count to be three. "Then I pretended to fall asleep, but I didn't miss a move. They photographed my file, threw their clothes back on, and left, tout de suite.

"Then they took your wallet, and Madame Ambassador got stuck paying for the evening in the Hemingway Bar." He nodded.

"I invited her to my room to review the tapes. Great body, you know—that's how she made it to the top. She paid for the suite, too, and as a special thank you, gave me the bottle of '52 Chateau Margaux inscribed with my ballpoint."

You were impressive, Jack. With gratitude—Pamela H.

"Nice," Catherine said, thinking how now was the perfect time to bring up the postnup.

"I plan to pop that cork the day I retire."

"And then you'll take me on the cruise?"

"Catherine, please—no wine before its time. Remember my contract with Zorox."

She slumped while he pried open the peanut can, counting out the usual twenty-two. He plopped them in a Pyrex custard cup and placed it by her wine. She could never be skinny enough to please him anymore. Jack was a label reader and when it came to her waistline, he liked to stick to recommended portions. He was studying her thickening midriff when his BlackBerry dinged. He focused on it, intensely.

"Something at Zorox upsetting you?" she asked, noticing that he was scratching *there* again.

"Nothing the great Pussi Galore can't handle," he said. Catherine stiffened. She was weary of hearing about Mrs. Puziari's brilliant achievements. "Quite the office gal." Her lip began to quiver. "Jealous?" Jack teased. She turned away. "The girl is a very fast typist—but she's so homely, her mother slapped her in the delivery room. He shook his head, exhaling a plume. Don't forget, she came with my job. Certainly not my type."

She reached for a peanut. "Not your type."

"Too MOR," he said in his drunk English manor voice. Mr. Elder Tech's hip new texting lingo and his long-nailed administrative assistant didn't add up.

"Let me guess," she asked in her frozen butter voice. "Male order raunch."

"For cripes sake, Catherine, middle of the road. Walmart—Chou Mein Street. Beijing, China." He blotted his runny nose with an index finger and stuck it in his mouth. She handed him a tissue from her pocket and looked toward the dark kitchen windows. His thumbs resumed their clicking.

She stiffened. Something was moving around outside the window in the dark. There was no denying that they were being watched.

"Jack," she spoke in a heated whisper, pointing her Cutco knife at the deck door and stepping back. "It's something hairy."

The dogs whined and scuttled in a frenzy toward the door. Jack, in his chair, leaned lazily away from her to turn the knob, opening it. The dogs flew outside and off the deck like a fire station full of first responders.

"It's only Rocky waiting in his geranium box for a scrap," Jack said matter-of-factly and sauntered to the island. "Maybe you do need a vacation." They were both overdue for that cruise.

"I've begged you not to feed racoons at the kitchen window." His love of animals had always impressed her. *But.* He plopped his crystal glass on his coaster and reached for her fresh salad dressing, sticking his same finger in for a taste. "*Ach!* Too much oil." He leaned across the kitchen island to grab the vinegar, toppling over her wine glass. Teetering like a park toy, he latched onto the new soap-stone counter.

He resumed the subject of his assistant with a giddy laugh, "Pussi's fingernails are as long as her feet." Cather-

ine buried her nibbled fingers under her thighs. His gran-
diose belch made her cringe. "Yeah," he said, "her spikey
high heels look like ocean freighters with masts."

"You've told me about her Jungle Jane jewelry and
zebra print handbags."

"Sheena Queen of the Jungle," he slurred, quite drunk
now. "Here's a thought—*you* can coach her on class."

Catherine nearly choked on her peanut.

"I'll mention it." *Jack's* taste that was off, and not just
from smoking Robustos. He dropped a hot cigar ash and
extinguished it with his slipper, glancing up in time to
notice her clenching fist. "There's really no need to be
hostile, dear."

She didn't buy this snake oil pitch. A speed typist with
long fingernails?

She had once heard a journalist ask him his secret to
marital harmony. "It's easy," Jack guffawed, "if you make
the little woman think your girlfriend is a dog's dinner—
you'll have it made." The journalist had laughed self-consciously as he scribbled notes for his cover story.

Jack studied his buzzing BlackBerry, drawing slowly on
a freshly lit Grande. There was trouble on his face.

5
CARL THE
NAUGHTY DRIVER

"What's up?" Catherine asked, edging closer to Jack, who had precariously propped himself up against the counter. His thumbs whirred on the tiny keyboard, nothing but a blur. She rested her hand lightly on his fragile shoulder, only to have his waving elbows dismiss her like a chicken in flight. Her hand recoiled faster than a dropping tape-measure. She wiped her favorite knife dry and placed it with the other ones in the drawer.

"When I finish," he said, blowing her off. He was aglow with perspiration. She wished she knew what drove him to overwork at this latter stage of life. Maybe someday he would call it quits. She was only half sure he ever would. She wanted him to take care of her, like in the beginning, when he had made everything broken in her life whole again. She would always love him for that. But sometimes, like now, it seemed like his BlackBerry had replaced her. She reminded herself that she was looking at a man with a mind ravaged by time, who couldn't mean it. At his age, she would expect him to act like a jerk now and then.

A few minutes passed. He plopped his phone on the counter and ratcheted himself upright, one vertebra at a time. With his martini in hand, he shuffled across the kitchen to the bar for another. The third one.

"Jack, I asked you what."

"*Hah?*" he answered without looking up. He was focused on getting all the gin in the nice crystal glass. His hand tremor was more pronounced than usual. She grasped his forearm to stop the ice cubes from shaking.

"What's bugging you?"

"*Well,*" he said, clearing his throat while adding fresh cubes to his glass. "Bentley sent Carl home for a few days." George Bentley was number two in the failing company. "In military terms, Old Carl was court-martialed." He swirled his gin in a circle and downed an ounce.

Confused, she stared at Jack. She'd come to admire the retired police officer, his driver and bodyguard. Carl Farrison was a loyal employee, a dedicated family man. She had always felt safe with him, even after he had accidentally shot himself answering the cell phone in his pocket.

Finished with shopping, she had called from the Plaza Frontenac Neiman Marcus package pick up. The poor man could not drive for a month without sitting on the pool toy she had given him.

But he had not complained once.

She thought of the delicious pears and tomatoes that Carl's garden-loving wife had canned, and how Carl had often talked about their grandkids and the church softball league.

"You won't fire him, will you?" Jack grew silent. He and Bentley had been sharing Pussi since they'd let Jack's first admin go. There had been an 'honest to God catfight' between the women in the ladies' room, and Carl, trained in NASCAR crowd control, had leaped in like Sir Valiant to break it up.

Jack flicked an ash in an empty Pyrex dish. "Come to find out, after he drops me off, the old boy drives the company car back to the office instead of going home to Milly's piping hot dinners."

"Is that so wrong?"

Jack gazed in her eyes without blinking, "Perhaps using the ladies' computers to 'get off' on porn sites, is." She shifted uncomfortably in place, saying nothing. He continued, "Well, Bentley thinks so. Your buddy Farrison is *finito.*"

She took in a Yoga breath, exhaling her dismay. People had been disappointing her lately.

"So, early this morning, Bentley rolls in to find the monitor festooned with—"

Catherine blocked her ears, cringing at the sound of the word. Even more, she hated the image of Jack's nice driver surfing for *it*. A smart, decorated street cop like Carl would know how to cover up his trail. "Imagine how that Quaker rubbernecked those high-definition shots."

"On whose monitor?" she asked, her antenna rising.

"Pussi's. Farrison is a moron—an authentic DOM." *Carl, a dirty old man?*

"Why blame poor Carl?"

"Couldn't have been Pussi. She was with me." Catherine flinched. "The entire evening at the Merrill Lynch dinner."

"Geeze," she said, slapping down the salad bowl, launching artichoke hearts. "What an embarrassment for poor Mrs. Farrison." She shook her head and reached for a sponge.

"And from now on," Jack began while he doddered in his leather moccasins toward the dinner table and stumbled on the cat, smacking his hip on the corner of the island. "Ow! *Dammit!*" Fluffy shrieked and scrambled off. Catherine wiped up the artichokes while Jack rubbed his site of impact, frowning. "From now on," he said, "Farrison can buy sex toys on his own PC."

6
SNATCH.COM

JACK: F.U.B.A.R.

STEINHART: What??

JACK: For cripe's sake, Pussi, updating our site, left her computer on for Bentley's viewing pleasure. He's "apoplectic"

STEINHART: WTF?!!

JACK: Yeah, Bentley came in early. Crotches, everywhere

STEINHART: Nothing left for her at Zorox anyway. Company's going under

JACK: She framed Farrison. He's "toast"

STEINHART: Smart girl—Butmann will write him a check and he'll go away happy

STEINHART: BTW, she's hounding me for her next honey-do payment early. Will tell Butmann, ok?

JACK: I give up!!! So, she's spending her rehab money on booze again

JACK: Now to business. How's my <u>Snatch.com</u> patent coming?

STEINHART: Patience—legal questions take time

JACK: Patience, my ass. I have a phone-sex gold mine here—Pornhub on steroids!!

STEINHART: Another great idea, Jack

JACK: Right. Snatch Prime will deliver free to your door—the ultimate convenience. Sound good? Pussi, working on the distribution part. The sexting medium is ON FIRE since I invented it

STEINHART: Right, Jack. Who guessed that picture of your jockey shorts would go viral?

JACK: LOL—Anthony Weiner took the heat. But listen...great new development with Pussi!!! I'm bringing her home. More efficient. She'll run the website from our basement office

STEINHART: I'm still recommending divorce

JACK: No need! Catherine clueless, sex with her was like doing it to an unbaked pie crust. She was a bore

STEINHART: Reminder, Mrs. Puziari is married to the mob. We can't buy you out of much more excitement. Very lovely girl, but risky. Get me?

JACK: Trust me, Simon, nobody knows "edgy" like Pussi.

7
THE TROJAN PONY

Jack leaned over the expansive bed to whisper a steamy greeting in Catherine's ear. "Happy Birthday, timeless beauty." She opened a sleepy eye and yawned as his skinny grin docked on her lips like something warm and wet from outer space. His breath smelled of cigars—he'd had his wake-up Robusto already. She waved him back.

Surely, he wasn't asking for sex. "Hmm?" she mumbled, sliding her tongue over her sticky bite splint, ejecting it just in case. She gave his fragile hand a gentle squeeze, aware that its volume was waning, as were his other body parts. But getting older was part of the deal and birthdays were for thinking about that. A day of promise and surprises lay ahead. Stretching top to bottom, she unwound her sixty-seven inches and swished her arms between the slippery percale sheets. When her hand touched Jack's warm thigh, his leg jerked out of her reach—his pesky restless leg syndrome again. "Thanks, Captain," she said, her smiling eyes overlooking his disabilities, "for making me feel special." Maybe something good would happen in bed later, although he had complained lately how getting it on at his age was like playing pool with a rubber cue stick. He sprang from the bed, hopped into yesterday's tightie-whities, and headed toward his closet for a favorite hotel bathrobe. Groaning, she pulled herself to the edge of the bed.

The six dogs rose from their beds and followed him as he hobbled toward the hall door, shouting like a television evangelist. "*Girl,*" he declared, his skinny lips grinning impishly, "your life is about to change! Gerte prepared a special breakfast in your honor." he rubbed his tummy. "Blood sausage...my favorite."

She wiggled her nose and plopped her bite splint into the drinking cup. "I'm so happy for you."

"With Cream of Wheat. Gerte's culinary *piece de resistance.* I didn't know you'd learned to like it. She insists that you have."

Silence.

"Hurry and get dressed or you'll have to eat it cold. Wait until I tell you all about your wonderful surprise." She watched him lope off, happy as a raped ape, dragging his bum foot the length of the second-floor hall.

She rifled through her clothes hangers with anticipation. Yesterday, her greatest wish had come true. Jack had cleverly retired from Zorox a step ahead of the bankruptcy sheriff.

Her maturing midriff in the closet mirror caught her eye. *Another birthday, another inch.* She pulled out a pair of jeans. Men had once stopped mid-sentence to watch her pass by in them. She put them back and slipped into a bigger pair, sucking in her gut to fasten the waistband. A surprise trip would mean manic aerobics.

Maybe New Zealand, but a romantic Greek cruise would not be shabby. She buttoned her blouse imagining the two of them leaning over the *Seabourn's* rail as it pulled into Santorini. The color of the water there was a beautiful aquamarine. She selected a cashmere sweater of that color to wear.

The best gift would be his time, something that would make them feel closer, like a new tandem bike, or a two-person kayak. It was going to be so different with him home with time on his hands. He could finally finish the postnup, so that she wouldn't have to worry about money when he died.

The sweet stench of cream and blood sausage twitched her nose hairs on the way downstairs. It was early for a heavy meal, but she could be a good sport, she decided as she stepped into the spacious new kitchen.

Jack stood grinning next their housekeeper, Gerte Schmaltz, a plumpish older woman with a large space between her teeth. She was holding a bouquet of dyed carnations and a flaccid helium balloon, reading, *"Over the Hill!"*

"Thank you, Jack," Catherine said, smiling weakly.

"Happy birthday!" he said, and laughed, pointing at the carnations. "Sorry about the cheapo arrangement. Twinkies blew my order. My retirement party was too much business for a discount florist. My party was where your beautiful long stem roses went. My new driver forgot to grab them."

His feckless explanation triggered an unpleasant memory of her twelfth birthday, when after a particularly bad gym class, she had come home to find an incontinent old woman living in her bedroom, Daddy's rich Aunt Mable, looking like a diapered Wu-shu wrestler.

Needing a book under her bed, Cathy had tried to enter her room, but the hysterical half-naked stranger had shoved her out and locked the door. Sobbing, she had run for help. But Daddy, outraged at her disrespect for the elderly, had made himself clear that her bedroom, and everything crammed under her bed, were in 'his' house, the one that he had paid for by working long, hard years stuffing blood sausages and kielbasa. She had talked back, and he had removed his belt and threatened to give her something to cry about on her birthday. Daddy, as the guardian of Mable's estate, had decided that, until a government bed freed up at the nursing home, Mable and her dwarf-like pug, Sugar Boy, would stay. Cathy had been relegated to the sofabed with its hard steel frame and wafer-thin mattress, while the jowly Aunt Mable wheezed around naked with Sugar Boy sniffing at her puffy blue ankles when he wasn't humping her legs or stuffed ponies. She couldn't have a girlfriend play over for a year.

Otis brushed against her leg, bringing her back to the present. She reached down to pat him, trying not to think of how the Basset Hound's long, flat ears reminded her of the old woman's breasts which had draped like flapjacks over her flabby marbled belly.

The smell of the hearty birthday breakfast generated goobers from Otis's jowls. "Good morning," Cathy said to

Gerte, who volleyed back a dour expression as she untied her crispy starched apron and smugly eyeballed the Mylar balloon.

Jack glanced at the balloon. "Looks like Twinkie messed up more than the roses."

Catherine smoothed her hair and smiled politely. Special occasion planning was Jack's admin's job. Mrs. Puziari had been busy planning for his office retirement party.

"Have a cup of coffee, Frau Henniger," Gerte offered. Her coffee looked more like creosote today than usual.

"Thank you," Catherine said reaching for the mug, bumping off the cigar Jack had left burning a black ring on the edge of the butcher block. A dead ash wafted to the floor. Gerte, frowning, swiped the floor with her dish-towel.

Jack did a dramatic drum roll on the butcher block and waved his hands. "Ladies, get ready for a real surprise!" Gerte froze in breathless suspense, no doubt wondering how much Jack had spent on her this year. "Some of your friends have personal assistants," he said, smiling broadly. "Why shouldn't my sweetie?" Gerte, within earshot, tossed her head with a haughty air and busied herself wiping the counter with the same towel.

"The lovely Jill Knox has one," Jack sparkled and did the Elvis Presley thing with his hips, nearly losing his balance. "So does your fat friend Pat, who needs to get her trailer licensed." He made a large gesture with his hands and batted his eyelashes, looking more dumb than cute.

Jack's BlackBerry dinged, interrupting. He turned his

back to spend a few moments with it alone while the two women waited in suspense. Catherine felt her jaw clench. Her dentist had warned her to be conscious of the habit when she wasn't wearing the new bite splint.

Suddenly, he gleamed with the pleasure of giving, or perhaps, something else. "With Pussi here, we'll live like we have always dreamed," he announced.

With Pussi? Catherine felt like she had been cracked in the head by a golf ball.

Whenever Jack grinned like a hyena, a shiver came next. "You'll have more time for well-earned fun." So, her birthday surprise was Pussi, not a romantic trip, or Jack's promised trust revision either. "Think of it," he continued. "You'll be a woman of leisure. Ride horses with your girlfriends—visit friends in far places—take your relatives back to Poland. *Please.*"

Jack laughed with merry glee, while she sank in her chair, feeling older than the rotten smell in the room which had not come from Denmark.

"And Catherine," Jack advanced, "the *best* part of all is that the world's most efficient assistant will be working here, at the house! Yes! Isn't this *wonderful* news? Anything you need—five full days a week—and only a dumbwaiter away from your little desk upstairs." Her blood rushed to her feet. *Sheena Queen of the Jungle, working here?*

Catherine felt like a field mouse under a red-tailed hawk. She squeezed the painful hangnail that she had almost winkled off. "What would she do all day besides paint her nails?"

Jack persisted cheerfully. "Don't worry, sweetie, Pussi

will stay quite busy just handling me alone." He placed his hands on her shoulders. "My gift to you is for financial details to never burden you again. Pussi has already procured everything she needs: files, computers, printer/fax machines." Catherine felt her blood pressure stoke. "Consider the old basement family room our new home office," he said with glee.

She frowned. "It might have been better if you'd talked to me about this before hiring her." Gerte conked a dish as she stacked them in the cupboard.

"Look, sweetie," Jack countered, pinching his eyebrows together. "She's a simple girl—a *bean-counter*, for cripes sake. She goes home each night to fry up hamburger helper for her husband Vinny, a racetrack man between jobs again. They have money problems," he said with uncharacteristic concern. "She would have been out of work at Zorox by next week," he lowered his voice and swung head swung solemnly, "and headed for a homeless shelter."

Catherine felt another hot hormonal rush and slumped. Jack tapped between her shoulders to help her stand up straight. She shirked away. "We wouldn't want *that* to happen, now, would we?"

He had an earnest face. His hand rubbed her shoulder, softening her up a bit.

Another memorable birthday. She gnawed on her throbbing hangnail, a tough habit to break. She braved a mouthful of Gerte's triple strength coffee, forcing herself to swallow while the housekeeper watched. "I know you're thinking of my best interest," she said to Jack half-heartedly. Gerte stood by the sink fanning her own hot flash with a folded grocery bag. Jack took a celebratory draw on his pungent Cubana, exhaling blue smoke in a perfect round ring. "Good girl. You hate balancing books," he said with youthful exuberance. "Sweetie has written her last nasty check."

She smiled a tepid smile and patted Jack's hand, reminding herself that Jack was an official geezer, and that change was hard on the geriatric. Pussi may have become part of his accustomed routine, but her antenna was up. The birthday pony could be a Trojan Horse that she would be mucking up after soon. Gerte untied her apron and slammed the knife drawer shut.

8
THE ROYAL ARRIVAL

At precisely 8:25 Monday morning, thumping waves of "Achy Breaky Heart" drew Catherine to her bedroom window. Hoping to catch a glimpse of her new assistant, she looked out. A shiny mauve Jeep with gold-toned wheels squealed slowly around the tight turn on the Henniger's rear driveway where its contents could be unloaded under the big deck at the back of the chalet-style mansion in the woods.

This was the kind of splendid Spring Day she loved; the week's warm weather had encouraged her poolside hydrangeas to explode into jumbo pompoms. The fragrance pleased her as much as it did the buzzing yellow honeybees. Gerte and Virgil, the caretaker, were buzzing around, too.

Jack had been prepping them earlier. "Want to see you two roll up your sleeves today," he had fired off. "Show the new girl how hard we work here. Don't want to find out later that Pussi had to carry any heavy stuff while you were on a snack break—or off smoking cigarettes." He had kicked something with his shoe. "Is that your butt?" Catherine didn't like the nasty filters scattered around any more than he did. She had tried to persuade Virgil to quit, but nicotine addictions were tough.

"Sorry, sir. Having a hard time cutting back." He coughed. "I'll get it."

"Today, everybody picks up their butts like French cadets," her husband's voice rose, making the dogs bark, and then he left.

The pulsing car disappeared under the deck and came to a stop at the basement door. Its deafening radio blared until the engine stopped cold. Cuddles the Doberman was fixated on the noise. Leave it to a guard dog to get aroused over country music. The Jeep door opened, with its penetrating dinging replacing the other racket. Cuddles clicked his nails along the redwood deck, barking himself unglued. Catherine's face prickled.

She decided she would remain upstairs pulling dog hairs off her sweater instead of standing in the downstairs doorway delivering the meet and greet. It was kinder to give Pussi time to settle in, anyway. Virgil and Gerte had the welcome party covered.

The six dogs, frantic to go out after eating, had been clawing at the screens, earlier. Knowing how Gerte resented cleaning up dog piles, Catherine had let them out. And now, Gerte's voice sounded panicked as she struggled to lure them back from the woods surrounding the house. Except for Cuddles with his anal retention issues, the other dogs, feeling lighter, had decided on a possum hunt. Visitors to the Henniger estate arrived and departed all the time. The dogs usually grew bored after sniffing new visitors. Gerte clapped and hooted, but the big one, Cuddles, kept barking. Like Catherine, he must have sensed that something wasn't "right" about the Jeep's driver, too.

A woman under the deck shrieked, "Control your killer dog, or I'll call 911. Whose job is it to keep them in their crates?"

Safely hidden from view at the window, Catherine frowned at the housekeeper as she ratted on her with ease. "The *Frau* wanted them out."

"I'm not budging from this car until you do something with that animal. That's your first order of business. Mine is working on Mr. Henniger's new calendar, and he won't be happy if he don't get it by five. Therefore, you will move my boxes in."

A sharp yap preceded a guttural growl. Virgil must have yanked Cuddle's choke collar. A moment later, Pussi Puziari's feet hit the asphalt with a slap. Her new Personal Assistant had arrived.

9
BELLY BUTTON BLING

Despite his creaky joints, Virgil could still mobilize when he had to. He snagged the ring on Cuddle's choke collar with a finger and yanked, difficult with the desperate dog lunging left and right, barking the short black hairs stiff on his hackles. Cuddle's thick saliva glistened like liquid rubber cement. He jerked the chain, suspending the yelping dog with his paws paddling circles like Wile E. Coyote.

"Sorry, Miss," Virgil murmured, diverting his eyes from the gangly brunette. He lowered the furious dog and extended a grimy hand.

"*Mrs.* Puziari," she corrected, rejecting his hand as if he never bathed. "You're Virgil Hester and Gerte Schmaltz, I presume." He didn't like the tone of her voice. It was nasal and high-pitched, and made him think of middle school shop class. "It's a pleasure," she said.

Cuddles howled.

Sweeping past them, Pussi headed for the basement door like she knew the way. Virgil found her tall for a woman, maybe five-ten in flats. She was Olive Oyl skinny; not movie star beautiful like Mrs. Henniger; the way country boys liked their women. Pussi's skinny peg-pants made him think of spray painted four by fours. Under her peekaboo blouse, she wore a tube top tiny enough to show off something sparkly in her belly button.

"Don't never let them dogs near me, okay?" she warned. "I'm sure Mr. Henniger told you how bad their hair is for my medical condition." Virgil gripped the wriggling dog's chain.

"Psychosomatic Respiratory Asthma," she said, pronouncing her disease smooth as a drug rep. She took an inhaler from a pocket and snorting it said, "In the future, have some respect for me and my life-threatening sickness."

Stuck-up bitch. His finger relaxed its hold on Cuddle's choke collar.

Gerte stood by Virgil's side, fanning her perspiring face. Scouring the newcomer, her eyes seemed to fix on Pussi's feet, which were the same length as his. The battle axe would not put up long with her guff. With the voice of a stopped-up SS border guard, Gerte said, "You! Take off your shoes when you enter this house." She closed the heavy door hard, leaving him outside with Cuddles.

Mrs. Puziari swished through the entryway and tossed Gerte a Starbucks cup and large box of manicure items. "I was up the whole night packing for this move," she said. Gerte fumed as the new girl flipped off her super-sized flats, one hitting the pine-paneled wall, the other landing somewhere down the hall. It was not the first time this girl had stayed up all night.

Gerte pointed to the perfect row of shoes, boots, and slippers that she had lined like a piano keyboard against the knotty pine wall. *"They go there!"* This female was anything but a lady. Gerte retrieved Pussi's dirty flats and placed them next to the others. "You will wear your house shoes for *Herr* Henniger," she informed with precision. Her shoe rule made the floors so much easier to keep clean.

The gemstones on Pussi's painted toenails were as grotesque as her massive bunions. "I would buy myself some slippers in a bigger size, if I were you," Gerte said.

"So, like where is... the *Mrs.?*" Pussi asked in a quieter voice.

"Ach," Gerte answered, shaking her head to show disapproval. "Where else, but back to bed?"

10
DRESSING FOR SUCCESS

Catherine, dressing in her closet, slipped a hand in the pocket of her navy blazer, pricking her finger on a forgotten plastic sword wedged between a five-dollar bill and valet slip from the Women's Club Spring Fling. She had meant to add it to Jack's used toothpick collection.

She had grabbed her keys from the valet board and hurried to the parking lot to beat the crowd of society ladies accumulating under the portico. Jack usually self-parked when he didn't have a driver. Small talk made her uncomfortable.

Catherine was going to be Pussi's boss, and first impressions mattered. With that in mind, she chose a khaki-colored pencil skirt to go with the blazer and skipped the chunky gold earrings. She was only going as far as the basement. She kept the earrings in the deepest drawer of her leather jewelry box so that they wouldn't get scratched. Instead, she selected the matching necklace, a favorite from Jack, which she liked and wore often. She applied only lipstick.

What she needed was a smile to hide her humiliation. She wiped a blob of coral lipstick off a tooth and wiggled her feet. The worn house clogs ruined the whole look, she hated wearing them in the house. She could buy new ones if she wanted, but one old pair was quite enough.

11
TRAILER PARK QUEEN

At ten a.m., Catherine tiptoed into the former family room to be greeted by the scent of burning watermelon candles. Her busy new assistant made a gangly silhouette against the luminous new computer monitor, in the otherwise dark room. Catherine cleared her throat as she flipped on the light.

The screen flashed to a desert scene as Pussi sprang to attention, her long bare feet dropping off the paper shredder. Catherine breathed in, and out. Pussi, thank God, was not his type.

Jack had sworn that Pussi's colorful tattoos and piercings had helped her to clinch the trailer park beauty queen title. Maybe so. Catherine surveyed the new basement office. Her leather sofas and big screen TV remained, but her exercise equipment had been exchanged for a wall of beige file cabinets. Her favorite gold-framed bird engravings had been changed to a row of homey village scenes with little windows all aglow.

"Welcome to our happy home, Pussi," Catherine said

while studying her up and down. If Jack was going to cheat, it would not be with this one, she thought, smiling. Her imagination about Jack being unfaithful had been playing unfair tricks. With the ceiling light on, she could see that Pussi had dressed casually for work. Her bare midriff gave Catherine a chill. "You're everything my husband promised."

"Need some hot coffee?" Pussi asked, frowning.

"Gerte's pitch tar? No—thanks." At least they would agree on that.

"Nice to meet you, sweetie. I'm looking forward to taking over."

Catherine said, "Mr. Henniger says you do an excellent job of handling him."

"He's an old softy, Mrs. Henniger," Pussi said with conviction.

"Please, call me Catherine," she insisted, fidgeting with the toothpick, admitting, "it's hard to know what to ask you to do, I'm used to doing it all."

"Okay, figured that, so I already done some stuff for ya'," Pussie said, her jaw dropping slowly as she focused on her neck. "OMG…that is a beautiful necklace. The mister buy it for you?"

Catherine touched the expensive treasure. "It was his wedding gift to me." She pointed to some cardboard bank boxes in the corner of the room. "Holiday cards," she said. "We can put the new return addresses on our master list, if you sort through them."

"Okaaye," Pussi said agreeably, "I already got the 'personal' and 'important people' cards marked. Heads up, the boss thought it would be cool to have Congressman Wright and his wife for a dinner party." Mrs. Wright was on the Opera House board. The Wrights were difficult to please. "Here's what I done," Pussi continued. "Them two was free Saturday. Got 'em booked."

"*But—*"

"Right—you had plans, so I changed them, honey. For dinner, the best catering people's Moveable Munchies, owned by my cousin Wanda, who was only available for larger parties, so I've got eight or nine other yeses so far. Wanna see her menu? It's very popular."

"Ah—*sure,*" she said with a smile that sank lips. A house full of people. She took the menu from Pussi. The Wright's choices would be cheeseburgers, pizza and quesadillas. "And the beverages?"

"Wanda serves only the best hard liquor: Carnaby, Gilbey's—and Whaler." Catherine was unfamiliar with the brands. "and the people are bringing their own beer."

"I see," she said, wincing, "BYOB?"

Pussi nodded. "BTW, I signed you up for the fancy cooking class Mr. H said you were dying to take. He'll be *so* happy." Catherine's jaw ratcheted a notch tighter.

"Cooking" was one word that Jack might have used. She sighed.

"Class meets every Saturday for two months." Pussi grinned like Chucky the killer doll. "I'd plan on a whole day including travel to the Jefferson County Community College. *Credits* for it, honey. Course, you don't really need more cred—"

"But they would require my old grades."

"Done, sent 'em by email."

Catherine felt suddenly warm. "Tell me, how did you get my transcripts?"

"Said I was *you*." Pussi was so cheerful. "All's I needed was yer social security number. It was easy."

Catherine searched for something a nice lady might say, anything, although she really wanted to slap her.

Something glittery caught her eye. "You have a huge diamond in your navel. Is it new?"

12
LIQUOR CABINET MATH

"Gerte! Have you seen my gold necklace?" The *Frau's* voice was inaudible over the racket of her closet drawers... opening...slamming. *Mishuga, again.* Gerte's eyes were glued to her horoscope. "It's driving me crazy!" shrieked the maniac in the closet.

Gerte hmphed to get her point across. This was her coffee break. "*Frau* Henniger, crazy is a short drive around the block for you," she said, refocusing with difficulty on the tiny type. "How would "I" have seen it?"

"I think I put it in my jewelry box, like always!" The short panting breaths that sometimes sent her back to bed for the day were back. "But maybe I left it on the bathroom counter when I washed my face."

"*Frau* Henniger. If I owned nice piece of jewelry, I would treat it better." Gerte thought of the new bag from South Side Pawn and Jewelry in the *Herr's* humidor and wondered what he had bought this time, and for whom. She placed her finger on Sagittarius and looked up. *Frau* Henniger was rocking her head in her hands, looking pale.

"Maybe I put it in my purse," the *Frau* said, turning blue. Gerte thought about reminding her to "breathe" more slowly but didn't.

"*Ja,* look in there," she said, "unless you've lost that again, too."

"I did look but found nothing. Please keep an eye out for it. Do you think Borislava could have sucked it up with the vacuum?"

Gerte shrugged. It wouldn't be the first time she'd had to remove that bag. Too many electronic controls for this Yugoslav maid. She was unprofessional with the Miele—especially when she scrubbed the Berber wool carpet to the beat of her grapevine songs. "I will personally empty the bag and go through the trash bin," Gerte said. The *Frau's* forgetfulness had been causing her extra work. "If your valuable jewelry is in this house, I will find it." She plopped her horoscope down and stood up, feeling every pound of her weight in her knees. "Maybe your dirty little Basset Hound stole it, like he takes everything. *Frau* Henniger, you must have set it down for the dog to eat."

"Then look for something shiny under the bushes," said his third wife, her eye was twitching again. "And please tell the others."

Gerte was proud that nothing ever escaped her. "Every inch of the property will be combed."

Anyone could see that the *Frau* was not intact these days. Neither was the liquor supply in her husband's "adult beverage" cabinet. She had noticed the drop while adjusting the levels herself. *Herr* Henniger had never missed the tiny amount of schnapps she drank on days when her bad knee *kvetched*.

But whole bottles were a different story. Somebody in the house had a liking for vodka and Bailey's Irish Cream. She cringed at the thought.

Perhaps the fancy third *Frau* had been lapping his liquor on the sly. It was no surprise that she could not keep track of her valuables.

Gerte's feelings still stung from what had happened earlier. The *Herr,* ambushing her during her daily liquor level check, had forced her to swallow his schnapps so blazingly fast it had burned on the way going down. Clearing her throat, she had cleverly slid her small drinking glass between the wall and the ice bucket.

"*Herr* Henniger! I was about to make a shopping list for the liquor store."

"Let's go through the cabinet together...shall we?" he had responded in an unfriendly tone. His anger had been exciting as they stood side-by-side, examining the bottles in the cabinet. They were the perfect couple, she, and *Herr* Henniger, inventorying his liquor supply, together. Never had she felt as close. The manly fragrance of Androgel had permeated his no-iron shirt, titillating her senses, making her glad that she had not laundered it. He had read each label and handed them back to her to wipe with a clean, damp, rag, all during which, he had fussed with his private parts.

Everything was going fine until he spotted the vodka bottle filled with water. "And *this?*" he had questioned in a subdued tone. "Did you drink this, Gerte?"

"*Nein, Herr* Henniger!" she had cried, pinching her

nose with her fingers to show how offended she was. "Only *Ruskies* drink vodka!" She could have told him then about the real problem drinker in the house; his wife, the one whose strange habits had lately been on the rise. But she had held her tongue.

The cure for the *Herr's* unhappiness awaited him directly under her sweat suit—not in a bottle. She ran her fingers up her torso to unfasten her brassiere. It would feel good to press her cushy nakedness against his. She was pleasantly *zaftig*—although it was "firm" love that he craved. What he needed was the calming effect of a dominant woman like herself. She knew tough. Soon, he would know how ideal they were for each other. She had known for years.

He had been an arm's length away, and she was just about to lift her sweatshirt, when the expression on his face turned intense. He had set his violated vodka bottle down, slowly.

Would he brush her cheek and gently feather her lips with acceptance, or thrust himself hungrily upon her ruthlessly pinning her down in an inescapable lower body lock? Or, ashamed, would he hand her *Frau* Henniger's riding crop and ask for lashings?

The schnapps broke the spell.

"Why in the *hell* does my "pear" look so low?" She pivoted away so he couldn't see her guilt from having drunk his home-stilled batch.

"*Ja*," she humphed and jammed the swollen cork into its bottle. "See, one must push these in more tightly, *Herr* Henniger. Alcohol evaporates."

There was silence until his eyes popped open. "Gerte! What the *hell* do you know about my Chateau Margaux?" His tone was harsh. He held an empty red wine bottle up to the light and pointed to the date.

"*Nineteen eighty-nine.* Can't you see?" Her reading glasses were in her sweatpants' pocket. Her eyes darted from his beautiful browns to the empty bottle in his hand, and back again. She didn't need glasses, yet. "You?"

"*Nein!*" she fired back defending herself, adjusting her sweatpants, backing away. "Why not ask your *missus?*" It was time to put more itching powder in her underpants.

13
REGURGITATING BULLIES

Catherine, feeling queasy, slid down her dressing closet wall until her bottom hit the floor, where she sat, thinking, as her stretchy Armani gown turned into a circus tent from her knees. Jack was in the closet fussing with his safe again. He had been feeling his gin while they were strolling at the benefit tonight, he had refused to keep his opinions about the women to himself. The Humpty Dumplings, Elmer Fudds, and Knicker Bockers had caught his imagination. But he had not noticed her pretty, new red dress. She changed into a robe to hide her love handles as she advanced to the relative safety of the shower. Letting the steamy double spray soothe her, she stared across the spacious marble bathroom until her eyes froze on that toothbrush. Unless she was crazy—someone had cleaned the bathroom with it, and she had thrown it out. But someone since had returned it to the toothbrush stand. She let herself throw up… nerves, of course, her suspicions were playing tricks on her; no one of sane mind would do such an evil thing.

14
SQUISHY SEATS

"*Dammit.*"

Catherine quivered at Jack's voice blasting through the heavy furnace room door. It opened, he entered and stomped his wet feet on the runner. "Which one of you geniuses left my windows down in the monsoon?" Catherine gulped. Pussi and Gerte sauntered out of the basement office to see. Jack held her dripping purse in his hand—the one she had just been scouring the house to find. He dropped it at her feet. "Is this your expensive Neiman Marcus handbag filled with rain? It was weather-vaning on my Beemer, scratching the hell out of it."

Desperately late for her hair appointment, she had, in fact, taken Jack's car without asking. But he had parked his non-air-conditioned classic in her designated parking spot. With respect for her fresh hairdo, she had suffered all the way home with its windows rolled up, and it had been hot. Jack was in one of his increasingly frequent bad moods. She braced for the rest of the rotten fruit to hit.

"Thank its Gucci buckle for the gouge in my paint."

Her Cadillac—well, Jack's, according to the registration papers—was still in the bump shop with a disfigured front axle, the mechanic had explained. Virgil insisted on washing it for her. On his way to the car wash, a front wheel had flown off. There had not been enough lug nuts to hold the tire onto the axle, the steel had smelted on its way to the ditch. It was a miracle that Virgil hadn't flipped it, he might have been badly hurt. She would not have been as lucky.

Gerte loved a good domestic drama. She wiped her perspiring brow. *"Ach, Herr* Henniger," she ratted with deliberate slowness. "The one driving it was *Frau* Henniger."

Delighted with her bloodless entry blow, she laughed like an evil clown and turned, facing Catherine. *"There* is your missing handbag." Jack's eyes were glued on Pussi, upstaging the housekeeper's scene by blowing on her wet Zebra striped nail polish. "Naturally," Gerte continued, "I set my silver polishing aside to assist in the search—I looked everywhere, even under the pile of her expensive new clothes on the closet floor." She gazed at the ceiling looking like the Saint of all Purses. "Frau Henniger, you must have left your bag on top of Herr Henniger's car. You should be more careful. Just look at your *costly* bag from Neiman Marcus—"

"Destroyed, Gerte," Jack fumed, "like the soggy leather seats in my beautiful German car." She had been perplexed. Jack had drilled her against putting anything on an automobile. She wouldn't think of doing it or slamming a car door. Even when you weren't getting sleep, certain things were hard to forget.

Jack was drenched and cold. "I'm so sorry," Catherine said.

Gerte and Pussi smiled like they had swallowed a bowl of buffet table shrimp.

As Catherine remembered, with the thunder clapping and her bladder about to let go, she had been in a rush. The cold canine noses had tried to probe up her skirt as she had reached for her purse behind the seat of the classic car. With the bag on her shoulder, she patted the dogs and made a run for it before the downpour, entering the house under the deck into the furnace room. Hurrying past the office, she stopped to quickly check in.

Pussi was relaxing in her swivel chair with her tattooed feet crossed at the ankles on the shredder. Gerte was folding Coffee-Mate into her coffee with a Bavarian commemorative spoon. Catherine cleared her throat, and Gerte rocked to attention, madly wiping a dollop of silver crème from Grandma Kowalski's teapot. It flew from her hand and crashed. Catherine could only stare at the ugly, large dent.

"Looks broke," Pussi said, cracking her gum.

Catherine, bursting in tears, had dropped everything, and rushed upstairs with Gerte complaining of the incompetence of Polish silversmiths as she hobbled behind.

Carpe diem. Stealing other people's belongings had always intrigued Pussi. It was a bad habit, but it felt so good. It would be a pleasure to explore the rich bitch's purse. The little raised numbers on the credit cards made her heart race as she caressed them. She peeled off some bigger bills. They were nice to touch and take. A few missing ones would never be noticed. Besides, it would all be hers before long.

She smiled. Today was payday. Jack always stuck something extra in her pocket while he smothered her with smelly French kisses. He'd be home soon, which was good. She was completely out of liquor. In the meantime, she would amuse herself by emptying pills from a bottle marked Myrbetric. Whatever it was, if the bitch was taking it, it would be interesting.

Shaking the bottle, she popped in five or six pills, then dug back in, for some expensive lipstick. Not her color; she wore pink. She whistled a long breath through the spaces in her teeth, thinking. Too bad the coral *had to break*. She squeezed the two halves together to make the stick look whole, getting some under her nails, then re-stuffed it in the tube, dialed it down, and replaced the top for the next user.

Smiling, she tossed the tube in the bitch's purse and wiped her fingers off on the lining. Next, she pulled a few blonde strands from the missus's hairbrush and placed them inside her desk drawer for a future Miss Clairol Day. Her new life as a rich blonde would be more fun. Vinny, he liked brunettes. She didn't give a fuck what the floppy Wop thought. Both Vinny and the old "horn dog" had a big surprise coming. For now, she planned to have fun with the purse before the storm.

15
VINNY THROWS
THE JOCKEY

"Listen good, or I'll kill you," said the leathery man with a reason to his finish the eight–year-old off. He had spotted the worthless punk blowing off his chores and grabbed a stick and chased him until he had a good hold.

Vincent, Vinny they called him, was bored. He had cut out early to hurl potatoes at the barn cats. That was for after chores. He swooped the boy up by the neck of his dirty T-shirt and swung him above the parched potato field at eye-level.

Vinny wriggled threw down his burlap sack, the few little potatoes he had half-heartedly dug up, rolling out. Showing his fists and the whites of his devil black eyes, the little bastard cursed, "Lemme me go, you dumb shit!"

The sweat fell off him in sheets. "I'll keep it simple for your puny brain," he sneered, tossing his kid like a fresh-twined bale with a thud to the ground. "Do you think you can remember now? Work is what people like you and me do to eat, you loser."

He felt whipped from another day of picking potatoes in the punishing Arkansas heat. It hadn't rained in days. His chest squeaked from smoking too many cigarettes. His exhaustion, however, could not stop him from caning the boy like his own *Babbo* had done to him.

The old man snarled, "Change your ways, or your wise guy uncles will feed you with the rest of the slop to the hogs. Waste not, want not."

Vinny yelled, "Let me go, you *prick!*"

As he recalled, Babbo had yanked him to his feet by a handful of uncombed hair and hit him over and over with a stick—and it had hurt, the son of a bitch, the jerk. He had waited until later to burn down the barn.

Vinny's first legitimate job had been in agriculture, too—doping racehorses for his uncles, who always called him Small Potatoes. Like they did with all the new guys, the bosses made sure that Vinny's roots would be deep. The company motto, "*Waste often—want not,*" was a funny twist on his old man's motto.

Even back then, he had had a quick fuse. Richie Zabaglione had called him out to discuss his starting drunken fights in the stall row and warned him that his unfriendly actions would come to a halt, or else.

They were just waiting for their chance to screw him, and he wasn't going to let them. Then, like now, he would take no crap from dummies. His job was fixing races, he wasn't afraid to beat up a wise guy who refused to play follow rules.

He had enjoyed fucking up Johnny Tyrone, the jockey, in Little Rock. He had throwed him on his skinny little ass in Rosie Flight's stall and smacked the water bucket over his head. The water had splashed on his custom-made suit—and he had gotten horse shit on his nice Gucci shoes. Worse, he'd sprained his shooting wrist punching the douche bag. Tyrone was out so long from the impact to his jaw, that even Vinny had his concerns— although the asshole wouldn't be the first jerk he killed. Nobody changed plans before the race on Vinny. Rosie Flight was going down.

Tyrone and his scumbag trainer wanted her to win. They had a deal on the side—just the two of them. Vinny, with his thousand bucks on True Tribute, couldn't let that happen: not with those odds. A little injection from the vet, and Rosie would stumble. Meanwhile, Dr. Jones had growed tired of waiting and left.

Son-of-a-bitch Tyrone must have liked the stupid horse. Maybe he'd had something romantic going on with his four-hoofed girlfriend and didn't want her to die. Vinny was left with no choice but to make sure that Rosie's jockey-shit would not feel like riding.

After all that, Zabaglione put a different rider on Rosie, and she *still* come in first. Vinny's horse, True Tribute, come in third. Zabaglione had him roughed up for stealing the petty cash for his bet. Vinny, stunk and needed to learn what they did to *ladros* who caused grief in the family, Zabaglione said. He could excuse a small fart now and then, but Vinny stunk.

Remembering that day, Vinny headed home and cracked open a fifth.

He still hated him.

16
GERTE LANDS
A WHOPPER

Gerte sat in her kitchenette glumly peeling potatoes for *Herr* Henniger's hash browns and eavesdropping on his and Pussi's conversation. Like a good *Schutzstaffel*, she took her reconnaissance job seriously. So far, the sound bites filtering through the cold air return seemed boring compared to yesterday's shocking discovery that Frau Henniger was pregnant. She shook her head, reached for another potato, and sighed, reflecting on how, over time, she had uncovered some excellent secrets from this exact listening post, "doozies" from the household wastebaskets, too, treasure troves of intelligence essential to her work.

Under the usual financial reports and junk mail in his wastebasket, she had discovered something of extreme personal interest. Her eyebrows stitched together as she ruminated. A baby would mess up her plan and mean extra work. Although the previous pregnancies hadn't kept him from kicking a woman out, now he might stay with the *Frau* for endless years. After more than a decade between himself and the twins, not even friction remained. The settlement must have been huge. She comforted herself believing that her future would still be with him—she would just have to wait longer before she became the one who got the spa mani-pedis and twelve-minute foot massages. Someday, somebody else would still change her toilet paper rolls with their ends on the bottom.

She drew a quiet breath. She hated children with their messes and complete disrespect, especially in the United States, and Italy. She despised their whining and lack of order.

The voices grew louder through the heating ducts. Her ears pricked up at a word.

"Money? You want to give me money. I'm afraid not, Jack. I ain't killing this one. He's your heir—our flesh and blood." As Gerte's heartbeat whirred, the paring knife she had borrowed from the *Frau's* Cutco set, slipped cleanly down her left index finger, taking a long slice of skin with it to the floor. She winced and listened harder.

"I see, you're throwing me and our baby under the bus, after all that I have sacrificed. I ain't givin' this kid up for nothing! Raw emotion resonated through the galvanized ductwork. "I don't believe in abortion no more."

She was overcome by waves of relief, the test strip in the wastebasket belonged to the lovely Signora Puziari, not the Queen of Ice. She, who washed the bed linens, had been slow—and stupid. She felt a pang of empathy for poor *Herr* Henniger, a desperately lonely man, forced into relations so far below him! For weeks, the tramp had been hiding her weight gain under her roomy work-man's overalls, a sight with her jumbo pink slippers. Pussi lowered her voice. Gerte strained to hear. "Jack," she said, "if you don't stand by me on this, Vinny's gonna use me and our baby for target practice and it'll be yer fault, and yer not gonna get away with dumping me, honey."

"Sorry, Pussi, this one is yours." His voice was gravelly from his cigars, yet brave. "I refuse to get trapped in something I'm not willing to do. You forgot to take your pills."

Gerte remained stone-still on the pinewood dinette chair. She set her bowl on the table and propped her arm on the chairback to slow the bleeding. Pussi's revelation helped blocked the pain. A small puddle of blood melted into the nice wool carpet below. Pussi cranked up the volume. "*My* memory? Did you forget how often you said you loved *me*? You said I would make a perfect next wife!" Gerte sucked on her bleeding finger and cringed. An outrage. "Expect a paternity test!"

"Wait, Puss—I could be willing to make it even more financially acceptable," he said. "You could get a bonus at Christmas, besides enough money to cover the abortion. May I remind you; this isn't your first?"

17
PUSSI THE
PUNCHING BAG

Vinny had been suffering in silence for months over his inoperative pecker—his faithful friend, temporarily disabled with a textbook case of Low T. Lately, "Mr. Whacko," as Pussi called it, couldn't do nada. He knew the commercials. Four hours sounded about right, but some things you don't talk about with the boys, so he planned to ask the doctor, maybe keep an activity log. Pussi needed it often, and hot. Nobody could satisfy a broad as good as he could, just not "now." He wanted to help her out, but there would be no fun in the fart-sack until the old woody got fixed.

Every day after the last race he and his associates frequented the Tender Bottoms Roadhouse to enjoy the live artistic culture with a few rounds of poker and some shots of Cutter's. The boys talked about their work— waste management, horses, human trafficking, but they also bragged how smart their kids were and how good their *comares* cooked. Lately, they had been ribbing him like he and Pussi didn't *do* it. "What's with your photos of tomatoes and zucchinis, Vinny?" He hated their snickering. "With all the great sex you brag on, how come there ain't no *bambinos?*" One day, he'd have a son and he would teach him to shoot at squirrels and neighborhood cats with his trusty AR-15, or the Ruger semiautomatic that he used for contract jobs.

Pussi contorted herself over the back seat of her new company Jeep that she had parked in the garage of their semi-rural ranch. Straining for the last grocery bag, she grunted loudly. Vinny stopped cleaning his rifle at the workbench to make a "sheeze" sound. She placed her hand on her swelling belly, a twinge that foretold of her future. She was twisted over how to tell him about the baby. This would be tough to pull off. She should have tried harder in the sack, because while he was a *mortadella*, he was not quite a moron. She handed him the shopping bag with her marinated herring and touched her tummy again, feeling its firmness through her overalls. It was her zillion-dollar meal-ticket, and she was keeping it. No matter how Vinny reacted, she was going full term with this one, five more months. In the long run, this would be good for them both. Nothing, or nobody, could keep her out of Neiman Marcus now. Especially Vinny, who could rot in Hell if he didn't smell the opportunity of a lifetime.

"Pussi, my pasta eating little mama, what's happening to your shape, baby?" he asked, goosing her bountiful butt through her Carhartt denim overalls. "What are you stuffing in your pie-hole on your Jack Henniger lunch breaks?" She whisked his hand away, but he patted her stomach, anyway.

"So you think I'm getting fat, do you?" she accused.

"Yes, I do, *puttana*," he countered, using the mob word for whore.

"I'm over thirty. she shrieked. "What d'you expect? I slave all week at a desk to pay off your gambling debts and buy booze." She tossed off his hand, indignantly.

"Watch how ya' talk to me, stinkin' *bitch!*" He grabbed her by her hair and pulled her close, his hand patting her swelling shape. "You're growing like a *pig.*" She pulled away. As if his low wattage brain bulb suddenly lit up, he raised an eyebrow and said, "Like you was expecting a *baby.*" He lowered his chin, daring her.

"What if I *was?*" she countered and gave him a shove.

"I've taken all I'm taking from you, *pucciacha!*" When Vincent Puziari was pissed, he swore in Italian.

He dropped the bag with the herring, shattering the jar. He had figured out the baby couldn't be his. Forming a fist, he punched the air, lightning fast, like he would finish her off and whack the baby, too.

"Let's see if you are, or not," he threatened, swinging his knuckles at her jaw.

"Don't you fucking *dare!*" she shouted, rubbing her chin while guarding her belly, her eyes opening wide, "Vinny, *no!*" she screamed. "Leave us alone!"

18
SOMETHING YA JUST GOTTA DO

Unaware that she was dreaming, Catherine rushed in and out of the French Provincial, portrait-lined bedrooms, desperately in need of a powder room. She wore the same beautiful lavender evening gown that she had lost in the melee at the Last Chance Black Monday Sale. She clutched the white gloves from her first wedding and a new silver evening bag. Her mismatched shoes were still under the dinner table. After the salad course, she had slipped away amidst plenty of red wine, live chamber music, and laughing at Jack's CIA story, but would have to hurry now because Jack and the entire table of important people would be furious from waiting. A spot of lipstick would make her look better, oh, yes—but the only color in her silver purse was pink. A phone rang behind a door down the heavily carpeted hall. Madame Ambassador's bedroom. She would have a phone in her bathroom. Catherine followed the ringing. It was probably Jack, angry about the ruined lobster bisque. Thank goodness there was a toilet behind the door...a pleasant convenience.

She could go, and talk, at the same time. She picked up the receiver and situated herself. But the ringing curiously continued. She looked with suspicion at the phone, then at the Ambassador's silk settee that she sat on, Second Empire. Old Aunt Mable sat on the bidet. *Jack would be mad.*

As the horror of her nightmare woke her, Catherine realized that she was holding own phone. Hoping the call would be quick, she said a groggy "hello" into it.

"Who is this?" said a gruff voice on the other end.

"Catherine Henniger. But I'm sorry, can't talk—"

"The famous Missus, eh?" said the man, insensitively. "This is Vincent Puziari, baby. Pussi's husband. *Vinny.*" He paused. "Hear you keep yourself in nice shape." He hacked a few smokers' coughs. "Pussi, yeah. She ain't goin' nowhere today. She feels... ill."

Pussi had seemed ok the day before, except for her unusually fast weight gain. Bloated from some bug going around, perhaps. "Oh," she said.

"She took a little fall off the step ladder," Vinny explained. "I found her moaning on the garage floor this morning. Guess her phone just slid out of reach. Drove her to Urgent Care; a few bruises, nothing serious, just a broken nose, a few ribs. She'll be back to work in a week."

"How awful! I'll let Mr. Henniger know. Please, tell her not to worry—we'll get along fine without her." Catherine smiled thinking of just *how* well they would manage. "We do wish her a speedy recovery," she said.

19
PLEDGE OF ALLEGIANCE

Catherine set her Women's Decorating Committee report down, wishing she had a door to her work area. She would bolt it. A week without the accident victim had been a pleasure. Pussi, who had dropped a few pounds, was awkwardly mounting the steep steps to the open loft, about to violate her space. "Too bad about your fall," Catherine said, watching her teeter from the heavy kitchen garbage bag stuffed with third-class mail.

Her floppy slippers made her think of rabbits and workers' comp. Instead of her roomy Carhartt overalls, Pussi wore patent leather booty-shorts and an extra-large fuchsia T-tshirt, too small to accommodate the mind-boggling increase in her bust size. Her spindly legs were blotched by green and purple bruises, and her chin and head, bound by triple-wrapped gauze like she had walked off a mummy movie set. The tip of her nose peeked between two narrow eye slits. Vinny, who had blamed an innocent step ladder, had no doubt pounded the crap out of the Puss. She wondered who had paid to minimize her nose and supersize to Elmer Fudds.

Catherine tried not to gawk at Pussi's puffy eyes and cheeks. "Wow, that's a mountain of third-class mail. Allow me to help," she offered, reaching for the weighty swinging bag, missing. "You shouldn't carry such heavy loads after your...fall."

"Ugh," Pussi said and dropped the sack with a thud on the loft floor.

"You should work for the Postal Service." Catherine sipped her steeped iced tea and smiled. "I feel for our letter carriers, especially during holidays, which makes me think of bills." She tapped a pencil on her glass while giving Pussi the evil eye. "I've been meaning to ask you where they have been going lately. Is Mr. Henniger opening them?" Pulling back her shoulders, she swiveled her desk chair to face her straight on. "I always have paid them on time, you know."

"Him and me, we've been doing it." Pussi placed her hand on her heart as if to recite the Pledge of Allegiance. "Paying bills, I mean. He wants to unburden you." She pulled a pen from her hip pocket to scratch under her facial bandage. Catherine's gold Cartier. "He says you can't handle pressure." She blinked her discolored eyes.

Jack should keep his opinions to himself. Catherine raked her fingers through her hair as she searched for just the right words. "This bill paying arrangement makes me uncomfortable."

Pussi, chomping on gum, nodded like her head had a broken spring. "Okaaaye," she responded in her grating voice.

Catherine pursed her lips. "I feel like a third wheel."

"Okaaaye," Pussi repeated, snapping the gum and smiling. Catherine wrinkled her nose and ground her front teeth, back and forth. The dismissiveness of that favorite word, and gum chewing with an open mouth, annoyed her.

With retirement time on his hands, Jack had worrisomely decided to tackle the payroll and finances. He was sometimes impulsive; he had recently received a royal email from Prince Abdul XXXIV and had wired him one hundred grand. The deposed Nairobi prince's cutlass-wielding second cousins on his mother's side, activists from the Riyadh branch, had pulled off a coup, leaving him with nothing but his unnumbered account in Lichtenstein, in urgent need of infusion with francs. Many lives would be saved by supplying emergency first-aid kits with protein bars, premium coffee, Amazon gift cards and flavored condoms. Would Jack help his loyal subjects, mostly sick orphaned children? Or, let innocents suffer? He would get his hundred back, plus a forty-percent share in the Prince's diamond company, *and* the honorary rank of General in the Royal Army. He would receive a free dress uniform and medals to wear to formal events. Pussi checked every day for His Highness's package. So far, what you could expect from a third world country, Jack explained.

Catherine could no longer see where the money went. Jack, frugal with certain things, was also the consummate collector of cars, watches, military memorabilia, and other expensive items. "Like high-end jellybeans," he'd say with a twinkle, "you can never have just one."

And after all the years and promises, he had not enhanced his trust in her favor by a micromillimeter. "One more John Hancock from Steinhart and your old age will be carved in stone."

Pussi leaned across her desk, causing the stitches in her microscopic, short shorts to scream for mercy. Catherine looked at her with a sinking feeling. Pussi knew too much. What had she meant by "him and *me*?" Jack had rarely opened a check ledger, before. He was hiding something.

"Got time for your schedule?" Pussi whined. Catherine winced at the smell of her gum. Watermelon was worse than grape.

"I suppose…"

"Okaaye…a teensy change. The box office mixed-up your dress-rehearsal seats, and you're going Thursday, not Wednesday. Mr. H needs his new driver Thursday. It'll be a long drive for ya' back and forth, so you should leave early. You get your roots done with a haircut from four to six. You can make it if you go straight from the Opera House." Pussi laid an envelope down on her desk. "Here you are, I almost forgot your allowance."

Catherine, frowning, picked it up and looked at the twenty-dollar bills inside. "Thank you," she said as she shuffled through them. "What else?"

"Thursday's Gerte's birthday. Mr. H gave her the day off. I ordered pink carnations and arranged for a cake. Wanna sign?" Pussi asked, placing a card on Catherine's keyboard, offering her missing Cartier pen. "Your hubby and me already did."

She took the pen. "Ah, sure. Cute." A cartoon squirrel held a modesty balloon that popped out on a spring. "Go, NUTS!" Pussi, truly taken with the card, hee-hawed. Catherine found a spot under "Jack and Pussi" and signed.

Pussi dabbed the tears of laughter from her black and blue eyes. "Yer hubby has a meeting downtown today. I'll be leaving early, too." Catherine kept the pen. "See ya," she said, and snapping her gum, she disappeared.

It was a cool, sunny day. Catherine hoped to stretch her legs with the dogs outside, but the dog walk could wait. She was on her own to answer phones…which could turn out to be good; something about those bills smelled like a rat in a wall. With the house to herself for a while, a rare chance, she would take a trip downstairs to hunt for a live one.

She made a quick assessment. Virgil was at the landscaping place getting a load of mulch; Vinny's nephew, Billy Redd, the newest helper, was somewhere making use of the dry weather to pull prickly thistles. He wouldn't dare come inside, Gerte didn't allow it—he was always filthy. Billy had that ex-con look with his pointed goatee and sunken cheeks as bony as a drug addict's. He ate with his fingers like a famished raccoon. She didn't like the way he leered at her like he had something untoward on his mind. Jack insisted she imagined her concerns. His boy was a wicked-good auto detailer.

The old rec room had assumed a certain homey office

charm. Pussi had festooned her desk with so many vintage rubber Smurfs, there was hardly enough room for the Thomas Kinkade prints.

Catherine was drawn to the wall of beige file cabinets, a logical place to start. She rested her hand on the closest mid-level drawer, her breathing picking up fast. She did not want to get caught.

She gave the first drawer a yank. Locked. The other drawers were, too, but she was not one to give up. She sank into Pussi's leather desk chair trying to think like a criminal. Pussi would hide the key in a convenient place. Catherine searched the underside of Pussi's desk drawer but felt nothing but concrete hard gum wads. Frustrated, she pinched a blue Smurf, surprised to feel something hard in his bottom. *The cabinet key!* She perked with excitement, tugging on it till it budged. One more squeeze and the key was free. She smiled.

The middle drawer took the key and opened smoothly. Inside, was a treasure trove: a petty cash box, postal meter and a cache of checks and statements. She grabbed a handful of canceled checks in various sequences, some signed in her own scrawly hand, and some Jack's. The other ones made her stop for a breath. Why would Pussi keep a batch of blank checks, perfectly and identically stamped with Jack's signature. Digging deeper in the drawer, beneath an issue of *People* and a six pack of grape gum, was a J. E. Henniger signature stamp and ink pad. Did Jack know about this? There were playing games being played. Now, to discover where the stamped ones went.

20
PLEDGING FOR
CHURCH CAMP

The court had awarded the four kids to Virgil's ex, Janice. The twelve-year old girl still lived with her. The sister had tragically drowned in the tub when the babysitter checked on her pizza. Their two boys had since grown up and moved on. Janice, morbidly obese, a genetic thing on her dad's side, did not work for money. Virgil and his ex had never got along, but he was proud he never missed a support payment.

He lived alone in his mother's manufactured home, fifteen miles from his job as Henniger's caretaker. He had supported Ma in her final years, paid her doctors' bills and for other necessities and covered whatever she needed until the end. She'd left him her ancient double-wide on a quarter-acre of hilly rural land, a meaningful and useful gift, as was her 19" color TV. He had pitched out her stacks of dog-eared *Star* magazines but couldn't bring himself to part with the miniature porcelain figures or hand-crocheted afghans that filled the space under her bed. Everything else, including Ma's clothes, had went to the neighbor. Her last year was a tough one for Virgil, dealing with his younger brother, Joey—with his serious brain injury from toppling off the trailer roof. He had gone to a state facility. Virgil had hoped to use Ma's liability insurance. But she had let her extra policy lapse, just like her term life. She had blamed herself. Virgil had been disappointed, but Joey had never knowed the difference.

Virgil poured the fuel mixture into his scrappy-looking orange and white chainsaw, shook it a bit, and fiddled with the choke before pulling on the short, frayed rope. You could do damage with a chainsaw; he'd learned that from experience. You didn't know pain, till you slipped while you carried one and it chewed through half your leg. He always kept his duct tape handy in case.

With his magic touch, he twiddled the finicky machine to a satisfying roar, happy that he wouldn't have to go back to the barn to fetch the other saw. Today was the first day of church camp. They would be unloading a busload of kids by eleven this morning. He felt tired. He wished he slept more like normal folks; he wouldn't have to go through so many cigarettes.

Mrs. H had asked him to clear brush in the back woods and make a flat area large enough for nine or ten pup tents and a circle of picnic blankets. "Any place, as long as it can't be seen from the back of the house or the pool." He cut some bramble and set a pile aside for their campfire, then trimmed a few branches and straightened up, admiring his work, happy with the clearing he had made for the kids at the First Southern Baptist Church's Annual Children's Bible Camp.

A buttery engine fired up, Mrs. H's Cadillac. She pulled out slowly along the twisting back driveway. He wanted everything to be perfect for her. He was her age, mid-forties—but the outdoor work had taken a toll on his body, which made him look much older. Gerte thought he looked sixty-five.

Wheezing from the pollen, he felt ancient this morning. His lungs didn't work like in his younger days. Before Joey's accident, when they were removing the rotten part of the trailer roof, they had found a warehouse of mold. It was still there, and so was he, but sometimes his lungs squeaked so hard that he could barely speak. But he could only put his trust in the Lord and take it day by day.

He liked his job, but wished he made more money, he hated falling behind. Pussi had promised to discuss a pay bump with Mr. H, but after several months, still no word. He'd like to pay down his credit cards—the cost of gas for going back and forth to work and picking up his daughter was killing him. Mrs. H had surprised him the other day with a grocery store gift card. "Just because," she'd said.

As her car approached, he rested the old Stihl chainsaw on a stump and tapped the Marlboro pack in his pocket. She would never know how much her gift card had helped out.

"Morning, Virgil," Mrs. H called out from her open car window, waving. He grinned and waved back, his heartbeat doubling. He skipped across the poison ivy patches to reach her car where she waited with a foot on the brake, smiling. "You look spiffy this morning in your new Bobcat hat." He tipped it like a ballplayer.

"Mrs. H," he said, breathless when he reached her car. He held a hand on his sore back and rested the other on her car door. She was Grace Kelly in his mom's movie magazines. Her blonde hair was done in a bun, Ma had called them, like Grace had worn in her pictures. He wanted to reach through her open window and pluck out a hairpin—let her hair tumble where it may. He wished he could grab her and hold her close to his chest and show her what a man in love could do. Mrs. H was above his class, but he could fantasize about killing the old dirtbag and marrying her. Something was bugging her today. If she only knew about the women Mr. H dragged in—how many, and how bad they looked. He wouldn't never tell her—couldn't, he needed his job. She was so trusting. He was ashamed that he had bought the cigarettes.

"Hey, Missus?" he said, growing teary-eyed. "Thanks for your kindness, lady." He shook his head, gaze down, clearing his throat. "Your gift card, it come in handy, ma'am. Long time since I ate good fruit, better than you what get at the Gas and Go." He smiled big. "I'll be making you an apple pie soon." She swore that his pies were outstanding. He was proud of that.

Her gaze fell on the pack of cigarettes stuck in his shirt pocket. He knew he should have slipped them into his pants. She was about to say something but didn't. He hated to let her down.

"You're *very* welcome," she said, her smile sweeter than his pie filling. "Apple is my favorite, you know. I'm heading to an event downtown and I have an appointment later today. I'll be back early evening. I'm sorry to miss all the church camp fun." She laughed lightly and said, "Keep the wild partying down to a roar!" He laughed back, nodding, feeling ashamed for wanting to party in her pants.

Catherine tucked down her chin, avoiding Virgil's eyes, noticing her leg. Her skin had popped through a hole in her control-top hose, a mushroom cloud with a run wider than a two-lane road, shooting south to her high-heel pump. Lately, every pair in her drawer had a run, but she tried to be so careful. It seemed she couldn't pull herself together anymore. But this morning, there were more important things on her mind. Like calling her lawyer and laying it out for Jack about Pussi.

"Thanks for preparing the site for the campers," she said, flashing a warm smile. "I forgot to tell Mr. H about the church camp, but a little prayer on the property can't hurt!"

"Hallelujah," he said. "Twenty-two campers counting your pastor, the teens and their chaperones."

"Mr. H will be gone most of the day, and he won't care, really. They might even want his autograph. He would love that." She pointed to the woodsy glen roughly seventy-five yards away. "Is that where you're setting up the kids—out there, behind the house?"

"Yes, ma'am, ground's higher. Less chance of mosquitoes and snakes. Close to the house, but still unseen." He stopped talking for a rattling cough. *The cigarettes.*

"Virgil, I know you will make everything great," she said, and restarted her car. "Be careful with that chainsaw."

21
USED PASTA WATER

Catherine drove in moderate traffic wondering why Jack had been so mean to her lately.

With clear roads and good weather, so she would make it to the rehearsal, late as usual, but would only miss a few minutes. It seemed she could not be on time or do anything right in Jack's eyes. Her exit ramp was coming up soon. It was hard to tell when with the hog carrier in front.

Steinhart, that two-faced weasel, had run a thorough background check on her before their wedding, and to prove what trust meant, she had signed his "temporary" prenup, so much for trust. She wished she could have interrupted Jack's breakfast tirade to tell him what she had found, because Pussi, so perfect in his eyes that she wouldn't steal a paperclip, was cheating them. It could wait until tonight.

The rant over his recycled pasta water had swallowed up time. It was one of his so-called inventions, an "all-purpose aphrodisiac." He kept the long-lived swill on hand to slip into her various recipes. She complained about what the starch did to her meals, but Jack was set in his ways. This morning, he had had a meltdown while she was giving the garbage disposal a whirl. Despite refrigeration, his goopy mixture had developed a sex life of its own. "Boiling kills everything, but stupidity," he had said, unkindly.

Catherine glanced in the rearview mirror, ready to make the lane change, her little finger fiddling with the hole in her hose. Certain things in life could not be fixed. Closing in behind the semi, she noticed a few tails and snouts poking through its gate holes above a dirt-sprayed bumper sticker, *How's my driving? Call 1-800 Eat Pork!* The word pork had been replaced with an expletive.

Day Two of the dress rehearsals attracted the more enthusiastic dance aficionadas, but not her usual opera friends. If Pussi hadn't messed with her calendar, she could have gone on Wednesday, found a safe acquaintance, and enjoyed white wine and amiable conversation in the lounge during intermission.

She called the ticket booth wondering where to park. Ruth, a kindly ticket lady she had known longer than Jack, answered.

Ruth whispered loudly, "There's something you'll want to know about your seat change." Catherine didn't understand, she hadn't asked for a change. "Your ex-husband, the doctor, and his new boyfriend have free seats next to yours." She gasped. "I'm sorry," Ruth added, "I'll do my best to move you during intermission."

She felt her throat go taut. Dr. Quackenbush would

liven up the performance. She was unprepared for a public brawl.

"Good to know, Ruth, thanks," she said, her innards twisting like an overstretched phone cord.

Marvin Quackenbush of Dr. Marvin's Mighty MediSpa, the go-to guy for Botox and fillers in St. Louis, was how she had picked up her facial tic. Their short-term marriage was her dirty little secret, and she wanted to keep it that way. At their wedding, he had taped three by five cards to the bottom of his shoes that read, *"HELP ME!!"* The guests in the temple had laughed so hard, they had ignored the fancy lace on her designer wedding gown. She should have tossed her bouquet to his inconsolable mother and sprinted for the door but hadn't. During their tedious six-month marriage, she had grown familiar with the doctor's odd proclivities. At first, she had enjoyed the best laughs of her life, but before long, Marvin had begun to act strange, especially on weekends with his buddies in front of his forty-two-inch TV, his altar to the throwing, catching, hitting, whacking, rolling, kicking, and bouncing of round objects. She would buy and serve their ice-chilled brewskis. Afterwards, the guys would stagger home, and Marvelous Marvin would plug his thumb in his mouth and nap in a fetal position while she bagged the empty cans and pizza boxes, cleaned out the ashtrays and rewrapped the dips. Marvin had not been the straightest arrow in the quiver, her therapist believed. He had been desperate to crawl back in the womb; his mother's, not hers. What he liked to get into best, was the medicine cabinet, filled with prescriptions for any mood that he would write for himself.

Her most indelible memory was the miserable after-noon during hockey when she left him for good. Backing her twenty-six-foot rental truck down their boulder-lined driveway had been tough in pouring rain with its hard-to-reach pedals; the clutch had screamed and smoked. She had dodged the trees and rocks without denting the sides, as the naked doctor had swung from the door like a circus monkey, waving his goodbye banana.

"Don't leave," he had shouted, "the plants will die!" She had lain on the truck horn in hopes a neighbor would call 911 and split as fast as she could without breaking the Waterford over the speed bumps.

Marvin had been a mistake, but if it had not been for his filler display, she might never have ever met Jack.

The St. Louis Dispatch was the first to call them the "Golden Couple." When news of the wedding hit the press, Manic Marvin's drawers spun into an uproar. Powered by premium *chutzpah*, he worked through multiple layers of assistants, giving away free Botox treatments until he could forewarn the old billionaire of doom.

"Jacky," Marvin had spoken with a tell-tale sniffle, "You're a guy who likes to save, so spare yourself some misery and put your money in your face." Marvin contin-ued, "Why let your gorgeous looks go? Come in for free filler. And heed my warning…this bitch is *crazy*. Don't make the same mistake I made."

While Jack swore that he had brushed him off "like a chigger," a letter on Jack's mail pile proved Jack had taken Marvin up on his offer. Steinhart's letter had threatened a suit over the migrating labial filler that had erupted in boils on Jack's face. The wedding portraits had required extra retouching. Marvin had settled.

22
PLASTIC DINOSAURS

The stickers on the eighteen-wheeler reminded her that if she could not see the driver, he could not see her. The rehearsal was waiting. Slamming the pedal to the metal, she cranked the wheel ninety degrees, making her move. A horn blasted, shocking her, knocking her nearly breathless and frazzling her facial nerves. She spun the steering wheel hard to the right to avoid a collision. Nearly striking a van in her blind spot, three teenage girls, the backseat passengers, tumbled back and forth. As fast as the driver could pull away, the windows went down, and out came middle fingers and four heads shouting, "Rich bitch!"

Catherine veered off, her heart flapping like a fresh-hooked pike. She skidded to a stop on the can littered median, where she sat in a daze noting numerous empty Budweisers. She managed to catch her breath before her face turned blue and she would need a winch to unclench her teeth. Feeling reckless, she watched the van disappear up an exit.

Several moments later, she rolled the Cadillac back on the freeway, bringing it back to the highway speed limit, and noticed that a car, flashing its lights, was moving up fast in the far-right lane. The van ahead had disappeared. She turned off the radio with a shaking hand as she watched for the City Center exit. Appearing in her side mirror on her right, she could see that the lone car was a beat up, Japanese type, a Honda perhaps, she couldn't tell for sure as its every inch was painted Planet Earth Green and weirdly decorated with plastic baby dolls and dinosaurs. She had seen the crazy car before, but where? It had darkly tinted windows and a weird plate number, SPF-80, the same as the sunscreen in her foundation. The car was so close she could almost feel the impact. Her gut tightened in time for the deafening jolt which wrenched her head to give her a view of the flying green toys.

The alien machine took another wild swerve into the Cadillac's right rear quarter panel, making it shoot like a pool ball on an angle. Her wheels squiggling, she regained control by sheer luck alone. She had seen the technique used in crime films when bad guys bumped off the good ones. A metallic taste seeped into her mouth as she forced herself to think. Only a crazy person would deliberately try to kill her.

But then, the menacing green machine pulled alongside the Cadillac, matching her speed. Where had she seen it, plastered with its "Save the Planet" bumper stickers, on Soulard Street? Stepping on the gas, she wished that she could see the driver—get a description for their insurance agent. His tinted glass was too dark, but the aggressor lowered his window, giving her a glimpse as she tried to keep away from his car, now crossing the lane and siding closer.

The driver wore a gray ponytail and sunglasses. Rear wheels wobbling, he pulled ahead, then slowed enough to hurl something at her—a 12-ounce Modelo beer can. Then he peeled off on the exit and vanished. He was nothing but a texting drunk with class envy, she decided. Yet, she had every reason to head home and did.

23
LORD HAVE MERCY

Virgil bouncing the Bobcat toward the campsite, was surprised to hear rock music blasting through the trees—not what a person would expect at a Baptist children's retreat. He checked his watch. Noon. After the short, busy morning, he was looking forward to eating the sticky bun that he had saved from breakfast. As he drew closer, he realized that the pool speakers, belching in irritating pops, were the source of the noise.

"Girls, Girls, Girls!"

Ricocheting through the thicket of oaks, Mötley Crüe crackled at full blast in jarring bursts. Mr. Henniger was supposed to be gone, but Virgil guessed he was home. Who else would be messing with the pool speakers? He hoped the boss would remember to flip off the main switch before he messed with wires.

He lined up his tires by a sunny fern patch and turned off the ignition to survey the otherwise peaceful scene through the plastic windshield. He smiled. The church campers looked comfortably settled in.

Fifteen or so well-scrubbed preteen boys and girls sat cross-legged on stadium seat cushions in a circle with their parent chaperones and pastor. A few had their eyes fixed on each other. They were all holding hands. The pastor turned his face to the sky, then spotted him and smiled broadly before nodding his head to his flock.

"Just checking, most revered... uh, your highness, sir," Virgil said, feeling awkward, hesitating as he approached the group. "Do you need anything?" He felt underdressed in his work clothes and embarrassed to interrupt. Back at the house, the loud music started up again. What the *hell*, he thought, looking in its direction, scratching his head.

"Brother, you look like a faithful follower of the word," the Baptist pastor said in a penetrating voice. He gestured to the group. "Please join us in our special conversation." He paused to take a breath and waved him in. "We are all his children. He loves you, too, brother. When we want, He gives, and asks so little in return. Problem is, most of us don't know how to ask." He put his hand on his heart. "Friends, are you ready to give your wish list to the Lord?" The group made room for Virgil, who joined their circle on the ground. Sitting cross-legged with old legs was easier in the past. Cleaner hands than his own, were offered from the left and right.

Mr. Henniger's voice suddenly boomed above Mötley Crüe. "*Hah?*" An equally loud, but high-pitched woman's voice responded in a few garbled words, followed by a peal of familiar laughter. Virgil cringed. *Pussi*. Why the hell she was back at work? It was her day off.

"Everything," continued the pastor, raising his voice

a notch above the screeching sound, "comes to us in ways that we do not understand. Thank you, Jesus! Let us bow our heads and talk with Him in silence, sinners." The pastor pointed at Virgil. "Hear *us* Lord. Forgive our wanton desires that please the Devil. Give us what we truly need!" The pastor paused to let his words sink in on both sides of the pearly gates. "Are you ready, boys and girls? He's listening. Go for it." All heads dipped as the campers spoke in their own private ways to the Lord. Virgil asked, too.

24
TINY BUBBLES

Pussi balanced on the edge of the big stone hot tub, submerging half of her twelve-inch foot. The temperature was ideal. She wore nothing beneath her new pink satin robe except a thong for modesty's sake. A houseguest had left them hooked on the sauna door. They were hers now.

She was pleased to see that Jack was ready and waiting. He was in up to his shoulders, boiling like a crab in a big pot with a cigar between his teeth. She ran her fingers ever so slowly along the edge of her robe—showing only a tease of her new, fuller breasts. She paused and fixed her eyes provocatively on his, enjoying his lascivious face while she slid her fingers down to the belt and gave one end a tug. The slippery pink robe fell off her shoulders and puddled at her feet. The thong went next. She stood motionless on the edge, a rare Picasso portrait, unveiled for his examination. Jack took an approvingly long draw from his stogie and blew a blue smoke ring that rose with the steam.

There was truly no fool like an old one, she thought, popping a smile. In a way, she did kind of like Gramps, and even the smell of his cigars, the scent of rich men's money. Something that, right now, she needed badly. Today's plan was to improve her financial health and have a little fun while at it. He wasn't the only one who liked sex. She'd gone to a lot of trouble so they could be alone for the day and "party hardy." Fortunately, Mrs. Wimpy had fallen for her trick. She would be enjoying those cute men in tights on stage about now.

Today was all Pussi business. The apartment Jack had rented for her was going to work great. It was close to the U-Pawn, with a small second-floor balcony. Having her own place, she could keep Vinny out, and enjoy more privacy with Gramps. Or not, depending on the sexual whim of the moment. For now, though, except for the beverage fridge and a flannel-lined sleeping bag, the new apartment was empty. She would need some furniture and a mattress, where Jack, she snickered, could unwittingly knock her up again. Her eye was on a "sleep by number" model, and they were pricey. Her account would need plumping.

Jack placed a delightful bottle of champagne next to two fluted glasses on the ledge. She was drooling already. "Champy" of any brand—was her favorite. Her new place was super low on booze, but she could buy some on her way to the mattress store.

She had the type of body again that Jack liked—real skinny. She tried her best to stay like a stick to accommodate. She had shaved down her weight after losing the baby, without cutting out eating. She did love her food. Her secret to a good figure was to not hold onto it long.

She admired how Gramps could still get it up, unlike Vincent the Flaccid, the stupid bastard who could rot in Hell after killing her security baby. She would have fun making another one, though. The old guy could still spring a stiff one when the conditions were right. Her lockable mailbag of sex tricks certainly helped. Gerte innocently delivered it to him from her basement office several times a day…their private joke. He had his own bag, too, for the occasional new mail-order item. She had learned on her past job, hookers made more by encouraging an old guy's fantasies, no matter how odd. Jack's spontaneity kept her guessing. To his credit, he was thirty-one flavors. Most old guys were plain vanilla.

From the look on Jack's face, he was ready to party. She liked the music when he cranked it up loud enough to feel in her bones, like now. She swayed her hips in a smooth figure eight.

"Hey-hey-*hey, baby!*" Jack hooted with a dirty grin. "Oh, yeah—you are looking *good* without that baby in your belly! Shake the new tits Daddy bought you!" He nodded to the beat of the music. "Love your new nose minus the hook. Could have hung a hat on it before. Climb in, water's a hundred and four—come here, say thank you to your sexy old man," he shouted loud enough to wake the dead, brandishing the bottle and opener. "Look what I found in the cellar for my sweet, huge-breasted, Pussi!" She stepped into the cauldron, bobbing a floating dildo aside. "I thought you'd enjoy sharing something extra special to celebrate our first anniversary with style—one whole year of knowing each other. A dangerous, exciting twelve months!" He pulled her near with his free hand. It felt good on her waist.

"Ooh, champagne, how *yummy! I* hope it's from Michigan."

"*Hah?*" he shouted above the deafening music, cupping his hand behind his ear. "You're the best thing that ever happened to this eighty-year-old dick. Come 'ere!"

"Ooh, Popeye!" she cried, "You're my sex god!" He said her Olive Oyl voice sounded helpless and cute. Jack was sometimes Poopdeck Pappy, but she kept her opinion to herself. She tickled her floating breasts against his hairless chest and brushed her leg over his. He puffed his cigar, obviously enjoying the feel of her naked body on his.

The popped cork flew down the redwood steps to the patio. "How 'bout some bubbles to go with our bubbly?" he asked. She could feel his excitement. "*Mais oui, ma cherie*. Give me a kiss with zee pouty big lips of yours! Push zee button on zee left—at zee top," he directed. She obliged and the Jacuzzi bubbles roared. They would have fun the whole afternoon.

"You are *such* a clever girl," Jack said to his agile personal secretary. She was adept at all kinds of logistics. He only wished he'd known her while he had been married to the other two.

Jack, who was a master at creating the correct mood, felt the striptease music was perfect. He had carefully selected it from his private collection kept in a cigar box on his mezzanine. A piece of yellowed tape across its top was marked, *Jack Off,* an endearment the boys at his boarding school had used for him. He set the song on continuous loop, pleased that it was finally playing smooth.

"Girls, girls, girls...Red painted lips and fingertips."

The dogs in the house began to howl. Jack was in the mood for an anniversary treat: a pole dance, performed by a pro at his very own hot tub. The pool pole on the ledge with the brush on its end would be perfect. But first, a drink of champagne. The bottle, a *Dom Perignon,* 2010, was a good year, quite drinkable. No point wasting a second or third peak since she would drink anything with alcohol. He wiped off the dust with a wet hand. Personally, he preferred gin.

"Welcome to Henniger's Hot Tub Hottie Show!" he announced in his best Ed Sullivan voice, the wordplay clearly over her head. "Ready for a *really big glass,* are we?" he teased, slowly half filling her flute. She nodded. "Bottoms up!"

"To *us!*" she gulped.

The champagne was okay. But it would taste better licked off her freshly plumped up lips, but first, the live entertainment.

25
JACUZZI FLOOZY

Jack was in the mood for some old-fashioned pole dancing, traditional bump and grind would be nice, but any routine would do. An expandable pole with a brush on the end leaned against the corner of the super big hot tub. The pole would be perfect.

Pussi held the bottle against a backdrop of sunshine to gauge how much champagne was left. Half down, the rest in the bottle. She laughed, tipping the heavy bottom up. She took in a gulpful letting some run down her leg to her tattooed toes. *This is what money can buy.*

Jack grinned like a tall dog stealing a steak from a grill. Through the vaporous steam, he watched his naked goddess twirl a slippery spin around the skimmer pole to offer her footsie. "Cinderella?" Prince Charming snatched her foot and held on while plucking each toe and theatrically licking his lips. "Eeenie, meenie, miney, mo," he said to her peals of laughter. The speakers blared.

"Girls! Girls! Girls! Trick or treat, so sweet to eat… at their best when they're off their feet!"

"Oh, *yeah!*" he exclaimed, giving her foot a solid yank toward himself in the middle of the cauldron. She crashed backwards, splashing on her butt, her chest becoming an inflatable dingy. *Kerplunk!* She screamed, they both laughed, water splashing everywhere. "Ship a *ho!*" he laughed with delirium, grabbing the dingy.

"You know the house rules, Pops, no touching the entertainers!" she yelled. "Show me the money!"

Catherine rolled the Cadillac across the bridge. She would tell Jack about the lunatic hippy and his car of doom the moment he returned. She had calmed herself down by taking slow, deep breaths and repeating, another day, another "crazy" the entire drive home.

Today was a beautiful one. Except for the bible campers, she was going to enjoy having the place to herself. Comfortable shorts, a T-shirt and her running shoes would feel better than the ripped pantyhose and her hot high heels. A soothing walk with the dogs through the gardens was in order. The flowers looked amazing, thanks to Virgil who had repaired the break in the sprinkler system after the with the wholesale petunias delivery truck had crushed the water line. The light was perfect for shooting flowers. Her phone was fully charged with plenty of memory on the card for extra pictures.

Windows down, she embraced the fragrant early summer, feeling calm again as the soft air stroked her face.

Suddenly, a surprise. Loud music, playing out back. Apparently, the bible campers liked rock, she thought with a shrug. As she rounded the bend to where she parked behind the house, she was surprised to hear that her peaceful Walden Pond sounded much like a biker bar, apparently, the bible campers liked rock. The dogs, trapped in the garden room, were howling themselves unglued. She could not make out the lyrics.

"Girls, Girls, Girls…long legs and burgundy lips—dancing down the Sunset Strip!"

She recognized the raucous song, and Jack's voice—and his laughing. But what was he doing home? What about the campers?

"Up the old flagpole!" Jack roared as two sets of hands clapped to the beat. She parked and reached for her purse and phone, switching it to its camera mode. She swung her legs smoothly out of the open car door and closed it softly behind her.

Back at the campsite, Virgil hoped the pastor was nearing the end of his long-winded prayer. He felt guilty about praying for himself—and worse, for sitting when there was work to do.

"One more time around the pole. Kick your leg up for Daddy like at the old job!" squealed the racket from the main house.

The boys' and girls' laughter was clearly interrupting the cleric's train of thought. He pushed on, "A vision came to him in a dream, an angel, but he was not afraid—"

"Yeah, baby," Mr. Henniger's voice again, sounding like Austin Powers. *"Flop your knockers! Whooeee! Jiggle 'em like Jello!"*

Virgil's face seemed hot. He glanced sheepishly around

at the amused faces of the boys and the raised eyebrows of the adults.

"Fair's fair!" Pussi's loud voice insisted. She was drunk, again. *"Sugah stick, baby!"*

"Hah?" Mr. Henniger shouted. He couldn't hear worth a shit.

Trying his best to focus, the holy man fought on, "Then an angel spoke to him—"

"SUGAH STICK!"

Catherine watched the spectacle, mouth agape. Knees wobbling, she approached the jacuzzi, silently snapping photos of Jack's retirement fun. Now it was clear why Pussi had switched her days at the Opera House. The naked assistant twirled around and around the pole, drunkenly oblivious to her presence. *Click, click.*

Jack roared with laughter. *"Ooh, yeah...shakin' it! Heh, heh. Now I've got it!"*

Glaring, she yelled at Jack, "And I have you—by the balls!"

Pussi stopped mid-pole and shrieked, "Shit!"

By now satanically possessed, Catherine rocketed up the redwood deck steps to wallop Jack in the back of the head with her shoulder bag and rip out a handful of Pussi's wet hair. With superwoman strength, she dragged the flailing assistant and her champagne bottle off the deck and down the steps to the flagstone and smacked the Jacuzzi-floozy's butt with her high-heel, sending her streaking through the woods on a naked course toward the campsite.

Catherine bellowed at the shoeless assistant bounding through the poison ivy. "Set your bunions in my house again, I'll f-ing finish you both!"

Stunned into rare speechlessness, Jack tossed the bobbing dildo at a bush and sank in his pot, stewing over how things had gone so wrong so fast. Pussi the Perfect had royally goofed.

Back at the campsite, what would be considered a miracle was eminent.

"And so, boys and girls, moms and dads—I say to you," said the pastor in a determined voice, "As in the days before fig leaves, if you believe, it will come. In His holy name," he said, bowing his head, "let us pray together for a sign—"

Everyone heard the bloodcurdling screams, especially the frustrated pastor. Church camp wasn't as easy as he had hoped. His flock raised their heads in the direction of the crashing brush closing in from the direction of the house. Was *this* the sign from above?

Galloping toward their camp circle as fast as a bullet train, a naked woman clutched a green champagne bottle, her breasts swinging like heavy feed sacks. The grinning boys pointed, while the girls started crying. The parent-chaperones blinked in disbelief as the nudist hurdled over their circle of campers, landing in the middle before clearing the other side to vanish in the cornfield.

26
PULLING THE PLUG

Catherine stood on the jacuzzi deck, her eyes laser blasting Jack, who was sweating sheets and not from the heat. It was a rare moment when he was caught off guard. He drew on his cigar, avoiding eye contact. He was buying time blowing smoke rings until the perfect words reached his lips. He sometimes complained that the maniac in her was lying dormant, waiting to strike. She counted to ten.

"Sweetie came back early from the opera," she yelled even louder the speakers.

Not a sound other than bubbles and music.

"Similarities between you and a cogitating human being are coincidental," she said, fantasizing pure violence. "Tell me, you're not as stupid as you look. *Nobody* is." She swallowed, dry, wishing that he would break the awkward silence. He knew better. "Turn that goddamn music off!" she yelled, channeling her Great Aunt Mable.

Jack snatched his dinging BlackBerry and thumbed a rapid text—to Steinhart, she guessed, a no-brainer. Jack had good instincts. This was a war zone, with name, rank, and serial number only.

Judging by the expression on Jack's pale, pruny, face, he was in a state of red alert with one minute to disassemble the bomb and save the empire. She wondered how long he could boil in a hot tub before having a heart attack. She assessed the scene of the crime. Next to the two neatly folded pool towels, were two of her own crystal Champagne flutes, wedding gifts from Marvin's sister. The empty one was rimmed with pink lipstick. A matching satin robe with a large pair of rhinestone sandals lay next to the other glass. And a thong.

"*Smile!*" Catherine ordered. She could almost hear the pounding in her head as she crouched for a close-up, tilting the phone to make Jack's head look more pea sized. "It's for the cover of '*Who's Who in Hot Tubs!*'" Jack's wrinkly thumbs ground to a stop. He extracted the cigar from his mouth and looked at her. "*Girls, Girls, Girls*" continued to blare from the speakers. Smoothly, he reached for the remote and clicked it off, his eyes on the Cadillac.

Jack asked nonchalantly, choosing a minimalist approach. "What in Hell have you done to the car this time?" She ignored his diversionary tactic—the crunched rear quarter panel could wait. "What are you doing home early?"

"Jack, what were you thinking?" she replied, pumping her hands, palms up. He said nothing. She gave the empty champagne bottle a shove with her foot. "Were you and Coco Channel celebrating our divorce?" she asked with contempt.

"Come *on*, sweetie. It wasn't what it looked like."

My name is Catherine, dammit, you *liar!* I should have known not to allow that bitch in my home." Her shrill shriek strained her throat. "Hey, Pussi," she yelled in the direction that the naked admin had bolted, "you forgot the rubber-stamped checks!"

"Oh, Catherine, don't be so ridiculous*!* Men and women are different. There's plenty of food to eat for everybody—I might even be able to work *more* into the trust for you now. You'll see. We'll talk!"

Two could play the quiet game; she went mute.

He wiped the sweat from his brow, expecting the usual what am I—chopped *liver sob*. The look she gave him was so cold, she gave herself chills.

"Might as well get it while I can," he said, breaking the silence. "They say that sex when you're ninety is like driving with a rubber golf club."

She snapped another one for her lawyer. "*You* are completely *pathetic!*" she huffed, imagining what another ten years of marriage would be like.

27
TEXTING AND BOILING

HENNIGER: Tell Buttman to get out the check-book again

STEINHART: *Now,* what?

HENNIGER: Catherine is going to file! Pussi and I were in the hot tub. No big deal, a little champagne, that's all. She was supposed to be at an opera

STEINHART: This one will cost you, one way or the other. Word of this gets out and they'll all crawl out from under their rocks, tearing up their non-disclosure agreements

HENNIGER: There goes my Henniger stock

STEINHART: Promise her a chunk to tone her down. She'll never divorce you with that stupid prenupt still dangling out there

28
BIG BEN

Catherine, frothing at the mouth for divorce, threw her shoulders back and stomped toward the reception desk. The wall clock in the well-appointed law firm lobby gonged fifteen minutes past the hour. She should have accounted for the unexpected traffic. Ben might be unable to see her. She deserved at least a mea culpa from Jack, some tiny acknowledgement. Anything, other than business as usual with "forget what you think you saw, since you just might be crazy." She was crazy all right—crazy mad, and scared that he would beat her to divorce court. She should "trust him," he had said. That was a laugh. She brushed a dog hair from her sweater.

She announced herself to a pleasant receptionist, who would certainly let her know, and settled into a leather club chair, reaching for a copy of *Town and Style* Magazine. She flipped to the charity event photos out of habit. There were four new pictures, with Jack looking perfect, as usual. Her eyes were closed in every shot because he was the story, not she, part of the deal when you were married to a celebrity. At least she wouldn't have to look stupid in magazines much longer. She wouldn't be in any. "Morning, glory," said a jazz announcer's voice. She glanced up to see Ben Williams, ready to personally escort her to his office. He had recently lost his wife—a horrible accident, she had heard. He looked like something Fluffy might have dragged in with his fingerprint coated tortoise shell reading glasses. His necktie had little boats on it and egg. It was wrinkled. "Shall we retire to my chambers?" he asked, his tepid smile offering slim hope.

"You look good, Ben," she lied, grabbed her purse, and followed.

Although his office didn't have a corner, it had several nice windows and a sofa and chairs. If it wasn't for the dog at home, he told her, he would live in it.

He ushered Catherine to a chair and poured her a glass of water, dribbling some on his gleaming mahogany desk. He wiped it with his hanky and took a chair for himself.

"I'm sorry about your wife," Catherine said softly as she settled in. She was beautifully dressed except for a run in her stocking. "May I ask how she died?"

"A rattlesnake bite, Catherine." Whenever he spoke of Jeannie, he relived the guilt. Her agonizing death had been entirely his fault. "We were cycling," Ben said, sharing a bit of the story. "Not easy." Her eyes were an amazing shade of blue.

"Are you managing, okay?" she asked.

"Been better." He cleared his throat before dropping

the bomb. The firm's partners were sending him away for a long rest. Today was his last day in the office. "I'll be taking some time off to get some rest. Doctor's orders." Catherine grew pale. What he hadn't said was that his partners were making him leave, therefore, doing Catherine a favor. The hole in his chest was so big that there was nothing left to give. He couldn't remember shit on the anti-anxiety drugs. He wanted to finish her postnup, but the timing couldn't work. Henniger had good a thing going with Steinhart's light and airy prenup and for him, stalling merely meant paying higher legal bills, something a billionaire could easily afford. Ben touched her hand. "Catherine, you look upset—I feel rotten for abandoning you. I promise that somebody here will take care of you." He turned his head to stare out the window. The day was gray.

"I don't know what to say, Ben. I can't do it without you," she broke down. "I can't handle that jackass anymore." She told him about the hot tub and the checks and the crazy things that had been happening to her. "Some days, I feel like I'm losing my mind." Her breathing was like a small, trapped bird's. She rubbed her forehead and rocked, about to faint. Thinking fast, he pulled a paper lunch bag from a drawer, took out his sandwich and Moon Pie, and handed her the bag.

"Here," he said, "place this firmly over your nose and mouth and breathe in and out. You're having an anxiety attack. I know all about them."

He slipped his arm around her shoulders coaching her on using the bag. "I'm telling you, I'm done with him," Catherine said.

"But a divorce for you at this time is out of the question."

"What?" She stood up. "I don't *care*."

"Yes, you do. The terms of the prenup are not in your favor."

"Do I look like a murderer?"

"No," he laughed, "and killing Jack off wouldn't work for you, because you would be bad at it."

"Don't be so sure," she said with a little smile.

"I repeat, Catherine," he said, noticing her lovely mouth, "Until the postnup is complete, there is *nothing* in the trust for you, and well, Jack has no incentive to change it."

"He'll self-destruct at this rate."

"I recommend a super-secret, jumbo, term life policy." He lightly squeezed her bare forearm. "It will protect you until we can get what we need. If he should die before then, you'll walk away smiling. Before I leave for Arizona tomorrow, I will pull one together that you will get Jack to sign."

"It's not going to happen, Ben. He'll never sign."

Ben smiled, "Well, I'll be back before a year. I don't believe for a minute that you, with all your feminine charms, won't think of a way."

PART TWO

TWELVE MONTHS LATER

29
BOBO DOC AND THE BMW

County Road 167 was empty in the predawn darkness. It was early for most, but not the Rastafarian garbage guy riding high on the back of the roaring Waste Management truck. It seemed more like midday to Bobo Doc Daley as he bobbed in syncopation with the truck's darting head lamps. A lively Bob Marley tune streamed from the two tiny speakers duct-taped inside his colorful wool cap.

Bobo Doc shivered and prepared to hop down. He was a warm-weather man. He gulped in a chest full of hope with the icy fog. Someday he would return to what was left of his exotic balmy paradise, the beautiful island of Montserrat. He and his little brother, Alphonsis "Digger" Daley—driving the rig, down there—had been among the large group evacuated following the first fatal volcanic eruption. They were just kids then, and orphans.

His index finger, poking through a hole in his worn-out leather work glove, stung from the cold of the ladder's steel grab handle; a momentary distraction from his broken back tooth which throbbed more than usual on this frigid Spring morning. He could feel Digger's downshifts through the tooth. Digger had agreed to yank it after work with a pair of pliers. Bobo Doc winced at the thought and exhaled a big breath that formed a frosty cloud suspended in the air, now behind them. Like his bad tooth, his twenty-five-year-old bones felt the big truck lurching through the raggedy downshifts, too.

The brakes screeched to a halt in front of the large brown gate. In the headlights' bright beam, he saw the kind of thing a hot-blooded Rastafarian man wouldn't forget. Parked by the bins was a fancy old black and white car; its windows, mostly steamed up. Bobo Doc paused to take in the scene. Two figures moved slowly about inside. The man wore a red shirt. His shoulder had cleared a peephole in the glass on the passenger's side, big enough for a view of the action. A white man. His hand kneaded a set of black, billowy breasts as if they were made of pumpernickel bread dough. They were attached to a very young girl, her dark hair braided with colorful beads.

Feeling a hot flush on his face, he fought his lopsided grin as he hustled, eyes down behind the busy pair to tackle the Henniger's cans.

"Black and white, white and black," flashed through his head. An aspiring songwriter, he allowed himself to admire the cadence of his words. He made a mental note to work them into his next rapper song. Trying his best not to look, he emptied the heavy containers and put them back in place while whistling Arrow's *"Hot, Hot, Hot!"* Then he leaped on the truck's platform, holding on tight, and pounded the side of their truck with his boot. Digger, down below, re-spooled the rusty rig and jerked it back down the road.

30
EARLY RISER

Catherine's eyes, dry since Jack had turned up the radiant floor heat, opened with the sunrise. She picked off a bead of crusty sleep and stretched her foot across the sensuous silky sheet, hoping to touch his leg. It wasn't there. Nor was the rest of him. She stretched again and yawned, waking up. With Ben Williams away, and an apology and offer of stock from Jack, the heat of the jacuzzi party had cooled. Jack had demanded her immutable faith, and she had promised to trust him in a "blindfolded" sort of way. They'd been trying to make their marriage better, but lately, Jack had seemed preoccupied again with something. Maybe just growing old and trying to keep up with himself.

She sighed from yet another night without deep sleep. She put on her white terry robe and coaxed her new Peninsula Hotel slippers from under the bed with a toe. The slippers had been a stocking stuffer from Jack. She slid them on and shuffled her way to the toilet across the bedroom to the spacious marble-floored bathroom, glancing at her old Seth Thomas clock to note the time. Six a.m. Why would he be out of bed this early on a Saturday? Before the hot-tub fiasco, his routine had been early get-ups like this, but since, he'd slept in a little longer most days. She might have missed an appointment on his calendar and slept through his chauffeur pulling in under the deck. Craving coffee, she decided to skip her usual grooming ritual and took a direct route to the kitchen.

She wove through a pack of wagging dogs on her way to the Nespresso machine, and said "good morning" to each with a pat. Placing her cup under the nozzle, she hit the brew button then gathered her usual breakfast items: a grapefruit, the milk, her secret Quaker's Oat Squares. She nearly overfilled her bowl out of habit, but instead, stopped and put a sensible handful back. Even her best jeans were getting snug. Fluffy rubbed a persistent figure eight around her legs. It was the milk, not love.

A familiar car door clunked in the distance, the BMW. She glanced out the window, surprised to see it park in front of the guest house garage and then Jack walking toward the house. With her heart spinning, she stashed the Oat Squares box behind the pots and pans and raced to the laundry room half-bath where she kept her emergency mouthwash and extra hairbrush hidden under the sink. She was surprised by what she saw behind them, a bag of green pellets that looked like miniature Irish Spring soaps. For rats. They belonged in the garage, or the garden shed. Someone could make a mistake. She smoothed her root-free blonde hair and swished a swig of minty liquid in her mouth. The warm water felt good on her face which she dabbed dry before quickly blowing her nose. Jack's heavy steps were coming upstairs from the basement to the kitchen. She squeezed a blackhead on her chin and pinched her cheeks to a rosy glow, hoping to pass inspection.

The door burst open and banged against the windowsill, unhinging her. A noisy, rumpled version of Jack from the night before entered, dragging his gimpy foot the way he had since he had begun playing *BrickBreaker* for hours without budging. His geriatric specialist swore that he had never seen a case as severe. His sheepskin moccasins complied with his mandatory house shoe rule. He called them his standby batteries because of the static electricity they made when he shuffled on the carpeting, especially when the floor heat was on, like this morning. Jack planted a painful, cigar-flavored kiss on her mouth, and as usual, she recoiled from the spark like a dog zapped by a malfunctioning shock collar. She rubbed her stinging lips, managing a brave half smile.

Instead of an English-cut business suit, he wore the same clothes as he had last night; his baggy corduroys, cinched by the weathered leather belt that he had had since the Sixties, and his favorite red western shirt with the mother-of-pearl snaps. He liked its fit so much he had bought two, but their slim-fit cut was beginning to call attention to his midriff. While some wives would make their husband's socially marginal clothing "disappear," Jack disapproved of women tampering. She didn't like to touch his personal stuff. That wasn't to say, that she never did.

"I thought you might have gone to a meeting," she said. "You were up so early."

"What are you doing out of bed? You never get up at this hour." Jack glanced at his BlackBerry and holstered it. His hand was trembling almost imperceptibly. "The Beemer had to be warmed up before the mechanic showed up. Its paperwork was in the garage."

She took in a breath, examining her fingernail ridges as she thought. Since when did a car mechanic show before noon? "I didn't see one on the schedule," she said. "What time is he coming?"

"You have a problem with the mechanic?" he said, his eyes narrowing.

"I'm not *upset*, Jack—I'm just wondering."

"If your Pussi replacement could please stop making personal calls and spend a day learning secretarial skills, you would be better informed," he said sharply. "She was *your* idea."

Catherine set her hot cup on a beer coaster. "It's just, I didn't know where you had gone, and I was starting to worry—especially so soon after sunrise," she said, closely watching his face. She cracked the refrigerator open and reached for his special orange juice, Tropicana with "some" pulp, never the pulp free. "Let me pull something out for you to eat," she said softly, working on the other half-smile.

"No thanks," he answered, yawning broadly. "I'm heading back to bed." He swooped Fluffy up, kissed him squarely on the mouth and carried him up the back staircase, hobbling as he did after doing too much sitting.

31
MOMMY DEAREST

Saturdays were for errands. Gerte, laden with groceries and drycleaning, arrived at work her usual half hour late. Whenever she heard Thirties' music on the kitchen radio, the Hennigers were eating a breakfast that they had fixed without her. They expected her to work until noon, and why she often finished her chores early and dreamed up some item she had missed buying at the store. From work, whe would make a direct track for home. They always forgot by Monday.

Her cozy rental flat was small but orderly. She called it her own, which she could without a man or any debt. It was more than her Mutter had ever had. Her mother—if one could call her that—had been an exotic performer. Gerte preferred not to think about her postwar Germany childhood. Four years at the Berchtesgaden Orphanage had been a long time for a little girl to wait for an unwed parent who promised to return but didn't.

Her best efforts to please Mutter had been unappreciated.

The fire had been an accident. Gerte, eight, had been expected to launder and press Mutter's tiny sequined costumes while the professional dancer slept during the day. Gerte had set the hand iron face down on the board and left to eat some cookies. "You are stupid, sneaky...and fat!" Mutter had railed, smacking her hard on the face as the firemen hosed down the flat.

Fifty-five years later, Gerte could still feel the shame. She had stood on the orphanage steps crying as the blonde dancer's cab had driven away. "When I find another place, *Pummelige*, I'll be back," Mutter had shouted. She had never returned.

The Frau, like Mutter, was an expert at discovering the overlooked task at five o'clock. Pussi Puziari had been worse—Gerte did not miss her. But there was still one too many women in the house.

Gerte carefully listened for their footsteps. She knew better than to get nabbed in the kitchen by the *Frau*. The weekend was too short as it was. She would hang out downstairs and when the coast was clear, head upstairs, do a quick kitchen cleanup, feed the dogs, and slip quietly away. She would drive directly home to tend to her African violets and heat up her own meal of pig hocks and sauerkraut, then prop up her feet up and dig in, watching her 12:30 Lifetime Network love story.

She had just carried in an armful of dry cleaning and groceries through the lower-level entry to her headquarters, the small basement kitchen. After plopping the bags on her tiny eating table, she had taken out a Tupperware container for her "to go" box, all the while listening through the ductwork to the Henniger's breakfast conversation. Her morning's "kill," consisted of small amounts of whatever wasn't in a can or sealed package. A little warm bakery bread, some fresh fruit, a meticulously sliced chunk of imported cheese, and choice deli-counter lunch meat, buried in the extra refrigerator behind the milk and German beer. She had treated herself to a slim-cut piece of delightful Italian salami, folded into quarters, and delicately placed on her tongue where it had exploded with garlicky flavor. Unlike some housekeepers, she would never take more than an indiscernible amount, considering her faithful years of service. They could never eat it all and *Herr* Henniger did not appreciate waste. Hearing the kitchen chairs moving, she picked a tooth, and went upstairs to say, *"Guten Morgen."*

32
HAWK'S EYE VIEW

Catherine spent the rest of the morning doing mail at her desk while Jack fiddled with something in the garage. When her stomach rumbled, she set her work aside and took the front staircase down to the kitchen. Jack was already seated at his usual place at the long pine table, facing the window, from where he could forecast the day's weather and watch small woodland creatures cavort on the deck behind the house. The fat black squirrels that lived low in the sugar maples were flicking their tails. They had stirred the six Henniger dogs into a fervor of indignant barking.

The deep grove of virgin oaks that reached a quarter mile up the woodsy hill to the back drive were beautiful. Her own seat faced into the kitchen, which she preferred as she was alone a lot. She liked to see who was using the basement steps or entering the house from the garden room off the deck.

At the moment, Jack's nose hovered over a fading head of frothy Warsteiner he had poured into a frosty mug. It was melting flat, which was hardly "Jack-like." He seemed as detached from his beer as he was from her, and on his BlackBerry, again.

She was careful not to startle the elderly man as she stood behind him. "How's your day gone so far?" she gently asked. No response. He had ignored the Beltone appointment that she had made. More than his hearing loss, it was his inattention due to the damn BlackBerry. No one was using them anymore. Jack grunted and jerked a little bit. What could the attraction be? She rubbed his tense shoulder muscles, lightly, ground control, attempting to contact the pilot." How would you like to wash down a liverwurst sandwich with my homemade tomato soup?" He grumbled. The BlackBerry dinged, sparking his thumbs to fly like bees on its tiny keyboard. He was in another one of his trancelike states, completely unplugged—oblivious to her presence.

Meanwhile, looking, she found she had a million-dollar view of Jack's handheld device, which, at the moment, featured a woman's crotch in excellent definition. Gasping, she took a half step back on her rubberized legs. Stiff in the joint, his index finger failed to whisk him back to his previous screen fast enough… to his email box with the unopened attachment at the bottom.

"In *God's* name," she shouted loud enough to make him levitate, her hands assuming a death clutch on his trapeziums. "What are you looking at?" She caught a fleeting glimpse of the sender's email address—a man, that, was a relief. It was an easy one to remember, dick.blower@gmail.com

"Look, Catherine," Jack assured her, nonchalantly setting his electronic wonder down. "That was just a girlie shot that the guys in the group sent. Guys will be *guys*—heh, heh—it's *completely* harmless. I hate to be the only prude in the bunch—but I'll tell them to clean up their act since you insist."

Her eyes trained on the phone as Jack flicked to his home screen.

He set the BlackBerry, screen side down on the top of the waxed pine table, then removed his week-old cloth napkin from its monogrammed silver ring. "What else do you have to go with the sandwich?" he asked, unfurling his stained napkin. He placed it on his lap and took a long swig of flat beer.

As she mixed up the salad, she added more vinegar.

33
YOU, AGAIN?

Thanks to his nutritious pasta water, the spilled tomato soup that he did not strain through his cowboy shirt had tasted full-bodied and tasty. However, changing into a clean shirt had slurped up precious time. Minutes mattered on a first date. He wore his Navitimer watch when making a good first impression mattered. It showed one o'clock. Catherine the Third had engraved it with *Yours through Eternity* for their tenth anniversary. He figured it would be bad luck to run into her on his way out to meet Brenda, but he would have to go through the kitchen on his way to the basement stairs to get his shoes. Entering the kitchen, his briefcase swung from the sudden stop he made when he saw her. He grimaced. Catherine was blocking the door like she was an attendant looking for a tip—how about Sea Biscuit in the fourth, Catherine? The clock was ticking, but he could make up lost time in his Porsche, something that most men his age couldn't do.

Catherine was wearing her "I'm the last to know" expression. It was best not to give a woman the chance to say no.

"They want to tape another interview," he said, firing off a tiny lie, while tapping his foot. Her chin shifted downward; a sure sign that she wanted to talk.

"I was hoping we could spend a little time going over the trust," she said without making eye contact. That was the dead last thing he wanted to do before Steinhart had his next strategy. He shrugged, knowing how silence was golden.

She fidgeted and looked at him directly. "Then— when?"

How about "never," Catherine. Does "never" work for you?

Like the other wives, this one griped about not having enough security. *How much stuff does an old woman need?* Catherine would be fine.

What the hell was she worrying about? That Ben Williams twerp, her incompetent attorney, had obviously put her up to this.

"But I mentioned it to you at lunch, Jack," she reminded him with an edge.

"If you didn't mumble, I would hear you." She had to learn to project. Sometimes she didn't even open her mouth when she talked. He motioned toward the basement door to hint that he had to go.

"Did you erase them?" She was still on the rag.

"No, Catherine, because I was busy changing my shirt…but like I said, I'll tell the boys to leave me out of the loop in the future, if that makes you happy. This new network request just popped up. They want my comments on the Brussels' GMO protests." The former great executive, Consultant Jack, granddaddy of genetically modified food, was busy in retirement spinning little white lies—because she made him. "Now, may I go?"

"Yes, sure, thank you," she sighed like a loser and squeezed his elbow. "I'll record it for for later."

Jack shifted his briefcase to his other hand and pushed on the door handle. He was ready to make his lower entry getaway. The Porsche would be outside the door, he thought when it dawned on him. ...*damn it!* It was Saturday. Gerte's car would be parked as close as she could get for her big grocery unload. He'd have to take the old Beemer. Why not? It was a pleasant day to go topless.

He pointed a finger at Catherine. "I have no idea when, or if, it will air. You *know* as well as I do how it is with the Media. You're the story until another body bag comes in. Then, you're *nobody's* news. It's a crap shoot." Her bad posture didn't escape him. "You should watch that slumping—hey, I have to go."

"Of course," was all she said, stepping back to let him pass so that he could go earn a living.

"Another day, sweetie, another ten grand," he said, quickly moving past her to the basement stairs door. "I'll be back for dinner by five."

34
WIE GEHT ES IHNEN?

Jack sprang from the bottom step to the furnace room, colliding with Gerte, who had rushed toward him with her mountain of dry cleaning. Her slippery plastic bags and awkward metal hangers went this way and that, causing a wreck. The wily housekeeper had been lurking in her little kitchenette waiting for the upstairs door to open so that she could launch her ambush.

She "humphed" a weak apology as they both stooped for the shirts. On her way up, she squeezed his tensing bicep, her eyes latching onto his with a deer-in-the-headlight look; it was something he did to women.

"Gerte, *wie geht es Ihnen?*" he asked, looking at the furnace room door. He had chosen the wrong words—a mistake. A guy should never ask a German woman how things were going.

"*Ja, Herr* Henniger. *Gut, danke!*" Her eyes bounced girlishly; her laughter jaunty as she blocked his way to the door. What was it with the women in this house?

"Schnucks grocery was crowded," she complained.

"The lines—they were long. I had to park so far out, a shame—all those handicapped spots and not a car in one of them. I am the one who deserves the parking permit, what with my bad knee and all." She put her hand on her upper thigh and pressed out, grimacing. "It hurts when I move it like this."

"Hmm, yes," he said. "Better get a special permit. How is that knee, now?" Another mistake.

"Painful when I stand or walk…"

"Way too damn many crip spots," he interjected, hoping Brenda would not lose her patience from waiting and leave. She would look as good in person as in the nude shots with Pussi.

"You cannot see a doctor in this country without waiting a month," Gerte continued, "They want their tests; then you fill out paperwork, they take your money. They expect their payment, or they don't unlock the door." She paused for air, winding up for the pitch. "Everything is free in Germany."

He shook his briefcase and said, "Yes, well, all right, then—"

"I bought you your favorite cheese," she said with a coquettish smile, her eyelashes fluttering like butterflies. "I had to teach their stupid counter girl what an Appenzeller was." Her eyes narrowed as her boring monologue rolled on. "They shouldn't hire people in the deli section that don't know—"

"Couldn't tell a Gruyere from Velveeta, eh? Listen, I'm late. Let me help you with these shirts." He rushed armful to her piney kitchenette, laying them on top of her chair.

"Then the fruit—*ach! Frau* Henniger loves those giant greenhouse strawberries, and most people don't know the difference, like you and me." She smiled, getting high from his deep brown eyes now darting between his watch and the door. "We older people remember real fruit. Here, they grow it big and colorful with no taste. *Ach!*" His leg jittered to get away. "Expensive, too. I do my best with the grocery dollars you entrust to me."

Gerte, glued to his tail, continued talking while he slipped into his Naugahyde loafers. "*Ja,* and then the woman with her two dirty children and welfare card was in front of me, holding me up, like I had all day."

He had one hand on the door. "They ought to have a separate line."

"Her handbag was filled with coupons for the cookies and gigantic Coca-Cola! It's no wonder that American children are fat and do not learn in schools. Between the schools and their terrible diets, what does this country expect?"

"I get you, Gerte. Too many unhealthy people. That's how they get that way. Well, look, I really—"

The housekeeper waved a red shirt on a hanger. "I have your other favorite cowboy shirt. I made sure the underarm stains were out this time." She pointed to the collar. "I mended the little cigar burn for you."

"Excellent job, Gerte. *Schoenes Wochenende!*"

35

DUST MITES AND CENTIPEDES

THE TEMPTATION

By the time Catherine heard the furnace room door slam, she was already in his quarters. She squinted at the sunlight that streamed through his balcony window, but nothing could brighten her mood. Her gut wanted to twist like a garden hose.

The sunlight cast a glow on Fluffy, snoozing like a warm cinnamon bun on Jack's cracked leather desk chair. Except for the occasional ear quiver, the yellow tabby lay motionless, snoring softly. The shadows from the massive oaks waltzed across the paintings on the walls of Jack and his classic cars.

The horizontal surfaces in Jack's room were deeply coated with dust. She fought the temptation to write a note in it. He, like Gerte, would not notice.

His antique writing desk was piled with untouched investment statements, board reports, magazines; smothered by a second layer of sticky notes, business cards, dry pens, and catalogues. She shuffled through the clutter, launching a few cat hairs as she peeked. Gerte refused to straighten the cluttered gentleman's room, and forbid Borislava, who was fine with that.

Jack would be appalled to discover that his wife went snooping in his space, something she started after she had thrown out Pussi. Her eyelid twitched a bit. It was her shameful, secret habit, but she hoped to find the answer to Jack's complex mind, hidden somewhere in his room. While she felt closer to him when she touched his silky ties and Egyptian cotton shirts, his photos and heirlooms, the little items on his dresser top, but the phone numbers and women's business cards stuffed behind his mirror frame caused concern. After her recent brush with death, she would sometimes feel crazy with loneliness. The train had kept going, leaving little of her good Tumi suitcases, and the car. It had been a miracle that she had survived the failed brakes.

Sometimes, like now, when nagged by suspicion, she would look in his shirt pockets and open his drawers, hoping not to find *new* stuff. Her therapist felt that her compulsive "need to know" was an addiction, driven by fear. Jack might still use that CIA camera—she had warned, but she had only laughed; she would have been busted by now.

Dust mites always made her sniffle. She felt a sneeze beginning to percolate.

She could not forget the hot tub and the rubber stamp, all his lies from just a year ago. She dabbed at her dribbling nose. Jack had given her his word. But he was at it again.

She blew her nose on a tissue. The picture on his phone today had made her feel self-conscious.

She needed to face the truth; he wasn't interested in her anymore. She pinched an inch on her waistline, another on her hips.

She looked all right for her age in clothes, she supposed, but the thought of being a single in a two-piece world was scary. Most men were married or interested in prettier women. There weren't enough well-meaning acquaintances or low carb recipes to help her find another man.

She was about to sweep the cat aside and reach for his desk drawer when the sneeze came. A rogue ash on Jack's tower of work folders broke in two pieces and fell on a *Guns and Ammo* mag, scattering everywhere. Eyes tearing, she opened the doors of Jack's smoking balcony for some fresh air. She blinked at the view of the circular drive and formal gardens by the bronze fountain which graced the front of the house. It was springtime. Cupid and his accompanying water nymphs would be operating soon, as would the pool and spa. The manicured lawns swept from the house down the hill to a greening glen and five-acre lake and dock.

There had been a time when he would smoke on the balcony, at the small wrought iron table, but since he had lost his sense of smell, he would envelope himself in his cloud of cloying smoke, anywhere. "Go outside?" he would ask, admiring a long one. "Whatever for?"

THE LOFT

Catherine's nose twitched again, and not from the cigars. This smell was stronger than the goulash of stogies, dust, and prescription testosterone gel. The draft from the open balcony door was drawing a pungent odor from the loft above. There was no doubt of its source. She shot an exasperated look at Fluffy, who was still zonked out on Jack's desk chair soundly snoring, thanks to his freshly emptied bladder.

Catherine followed the smell up the narrow steps to Jack's abandoned side of the loft, a space which was open to the room below. Jack's side, identical to hers, was connected by a smaller balcony with matching doors. Dividing the two spaces was a plaster wall with a cubby-sized window. Her side was her daily workspace, but Jack's had become a storage room of rare collectables like his boyhood toy car and lead soldier collection. A bookcase housed and his hardbound schoolbooks behind glass. A comfortable leather love seat and marble-topped coffee table were opposite a large analog TV and a jumbo video cam that no one watched or dusted. Entire shelves were filled with blank or copied VHS tapes. Along the loft's maple railing, were multiple stacks of them piled on the floor. Cats loved clutter. The accidents were also difficult to remove without expensive, professional help. Crawling on her hands and knees, she pressed her nose to the floor and sniffed like a hound on a trail until the scent lead her to some items between the sofa and wall.

THE MOTHER LODE

Several coffee table books were stacked on the floor with the framed photos of Jack's stepdaughters. Behind them was a soggy canvas beach bag, its St. John's Club logo barely legible through the bag's bleeding colors. It had been a lovely honeymoon resort with beautiful white sand. Fluffy liked sand. She held the souvenir between her thumb and forefinger, careful to not let anything drip on the rug.

Some well-aged newspapers lay on the marble coffee table. Wrinkling her nose, she set the bag down on an article about Jack and pulled the sides of the bag apart to look. Inside, a white hotel towel was wrapped like a turkey roll around something firm that must have meant something to him. Why else, would he have hidden it behind an abandoned sofa with dust mites and centipedes?

Just as she was about to dismantle the item, a clatter interrupted her. Downstairs, the dogs were piling into what Jack called the family dog spa off the kitchen, the garden room. It was a seasonal rainforest to the tropical plants that Virgil hauled onto the deck each Spring. Gerte was down there, doling out their second course of kibble. She fed them too much. One day, Jack's complaints had almost driven Gerte to quit. "If their bellies hung any lower, Borislava could use them as floor mops."

A cacophony of whines and clanging metal ensued as the dogs nosed their aluminum food bowls like hockey pucks across the Saltillo tile floor. Gerte, exasperated, shouted to the Basset Hound in German, *"Ach! Nein, Otis... Phooey!"*

Cuddles and Tiny were *Schutzhund* trained Dobermans, predictably protective and smart. Joey, the yellow lab, who was wet half the time, liked to cool off the guests with his pool-water shakes. Her favorite dog was a feisty Jack Russell named Beanie, the "alpha" dog who brought in the biggest squirrels. None of the dogs came when on the hunt.

Gerte was yelling again at the most independent and poorly trained one in the pack, a fat, toy-hoarding, Basset Hound named Otis; the canine version of a human "foodie." His favorite meal was the cats' pate, but then, the dog would eat anything. He would distract the others with a howl and clean their bowls. Catherine could hear his wolf-like growl, an intimidation tactic he used when the others complained.

She turned her attention to what was in her hands, something of obvious value, carefully wrapped.

36
DISROBING THE DILDO

Catherine's teeth tapped like they did when she was anxious. Dr. Payne had warned her to wear her bite splint so her facial muscles would not end up like a body builder's. She hadn't seen the splint in days. She poked her tongue between her teeth so she wouldn't clench.

It was time to solve the mystery. Maybe Jack, feeling romantic, had hidden her anniversary present in the dripping honeymoon bag, maybe the foot-long Rosenthal ladle that she had seen at Neiman Marcus, or a gift of special jewelry. Perhaps he had even shopped for the right thing himself, a hardship since the public was not shy. "You're Henniger, aren't you? My grandpa still talks about the day you visited the plant in eighty-five, said you was a regular guy. Mind if I take a photo? Wait till he sees it!"

Catherine carefully unrolled the towel. When her curious fingers felt rubber and a super-sized dildo flopped out, she grew faint.

37
MARRIAGE IS FOR DATING, STUPID

The attractive young brunette stood on Washington Avenue in front of Charles P. Stanley's Cigar Bar where they had agreed to meet. Jack sized her up and was pleased. Pussi's friend had a better body than he had expected from the picture. She held a shopping bag from the cigar shop in her hand. He inched the Beemer up to the curb and relocated his briefcase to the back. She climbed in.

"You," he said, grinning broadly, "are *gorgeous*." Her bulging breasts were perfect, although her legs were a bit fat. "What's a sophisticated girl like you doing in a small town like this?" She leaned across the console to hand him her purchase, extruding cleavage the way he liked, and smiled. Once she settled in the old bucket seat, she slammed the door, hard. He cringed, but said, "Thanks for getting them. How much do I owe you?"

"They're on the company," she answered breathily, adjusting her skirt, and looking directly in his eyes. Women sometimes compared him to George Clooney.

He smoothed his executive hair, which already perfect. She was thinking Clooney, he could tell. His right profile was his best. "I can't tell you what a thrill it is to meet you, Mr. Henniger. I've been trying to get into Purchasing since I started in Sales."

"How much time do you have?" he asked, wanting to devour her ahead of schedule.

"As much as you can spare. You're much younger looking than I expected."

He raised an eyebrow. "Good living through chemicals. I thought we'd take a little drive, go to a place where we could have a private conversation about personal chemistry."

"Anywhere," she said, crossing her leg, letting her skirt ride high on her large, creamy white thigh, like women did when they wanted it.

Jack balanced a cigar in his lips and steered with his knees. He wanted to feel the softness of her skin. He reached over, sliding his slightly shaking palm, high up the sales rep's skirt. She coyly moved down his hand and gave it an innocent squeeze. But Jack was having no part of the time-consuming game. He grabbed and placed her hand on the growing mound between his legs, unfortunately dropping an ash on her thigh. She shrieked.

"You shouldn't have said 'anywhere,'" he said, flashing a shit-eating grin. "I *might* take advantage of you." She yanked her hand away and sat up squarely, adjusting her hemline to cover more leg.

"How would your wife feel about us?" she asked, smirking.

"My *wife* and I have an 'arrangement.' She organizes our social life and takes care of the house…a life she loves, living off my wealth. A decent old girl," he said, tickling Brenda's thigh. "She's good at what she does, except for her cooking, or in bed—*forget* that. There's absolutely no passion." He sighed. "Once her aging female issues fell into play, she stopped caring about sex. Not that she ever did enjoy it like I do, in the same way." He brushed Brenda's breast with the back of his hand, eyes on her straight on, then back to the road. "Understand what I'm saying?"

She was feeling sorry for him, he could tell. "I can't imagine life without sex," she cooed. *The fix was in.*

"Yes, Catherine's a cold cod in that department," he continued, feeling the inside of Brenda's chubby leg between shifts. "As Henry Ford II once said, 'Never complain, *never* explain.' I've been divorced twice. Cost me a fortune." Like the hush money had that went to the twins, but Brenda did not need details. "I'm not looking for another one," he said, laying the boundary lines, "as long as Catherine doesn't care if I do *my* own thing!"

"Imagine, *me* meeting Jack Henniger! The man who has all the connections," Brenda said. After a few more miles to the Bear Skin Motor Inn, the rest of the afternoon was spent getting to know her.

38
THE PHONE CALL

The phone's ring restarted Catherine's heart. The super-long dong wasn't intended for her—or for a fishing trip to Loch Ness. It wasn't even Gerte's "secret" toilet plunger. Jack was at it again.

Gerte was refusing to answer again. Expecting Jack, Catherine flew down the loft steps, taking a shortcut through his closet to the bedroom phone, and catching it on the eighth ring after cracking her little toe on the dresser.

The pain was excruciating. She raised the receiver to her ear. Quivering, she steadied herself against the bedstead and managed a weak, "Hello?" Gerte, downstairs, would be smiling at the red light on the kitchen phone and slyly gathering her purse, preparing her early *vamoose*.

"Catherine, darling, it's *Linda!*" The voice was vivacious. "Linda Anderson. How have you been?" The caller wasn't Jack.

"Who...?"

"*Linda!* Linda *Anderson.*" Catherine felt a heaviness

in her stomach as the lady continued. "What in the world have *you* been you up to, Missy? No one sees you anymore." Catherine's lips moved silently. Somehow, she had to pull herself together, despite her wooziness. She ordered her shoulders to relax.

Linda continued in a subdued tone, "I saw you downtown in the BMW—which reminded me that I needed to call you. I *love* your new hairstyle; the dark color takes years off! I waved and beeped, but you must not have seen me."

"I'm so sorry—tell me again, when was that?"

"This *afternoon*, Catherine—right in town!"

She was vaguely aware of activity downstairs, Gerte was yelling again at Otis. The doors in the garden room opened and slammed, making her migraine eyeballs throb. She squeezed the lids together and reached over to pull down the shade.

"Oh, sure, *Linda*. I have a lot on my mind at the moment," she said, cutting to the chase, "What would you like to see happen?"

Linda was poised to strike. "The Historical Society Luncheon, of course. I was hoping that I could count on you, as an honoree, for some nice tables, again."

Five thousand for a Benefactor table.

"When?" Her fuzzy thoughts were focused on brunettes.

Linda cleared her throat, "Next Saturday, like our beautiful invitation says."

"Yes, sure," she answered, needing to brush the woman off. "I'll take three, feel free to fill them…we'll be out of town, I'm sorry. Will send a check."

Linda gasped as if she'd been pricked by a Botox needle. Outside, Gerte's car started up and motored off. "Such a shame that you and Jack cannot attend," Linda said. "The press will miss the most beautiful couple in St. Louis!"

"You're too nice," she said, her thoughts somewhere else. "Let's have lunch soon."

39
WHERE'S OTIS?

Catherine crawled across the bed like an accident victim, fretting over Jack's broken promises. After the jacuzzi fiasco, he had begged like a puppy, pledging to beef up her widow's pension with the sleeves off his vest. "You'll make out like a tall dog, sweetie—trust me. There's only one thing I ask. Please— don't tell her husband. Puziari will kill her. Me too." Recalling Puziari's oily voice and Pussi's bruises made the hairs on her neck spring.

Jack had left the other wives penniless. Divorced, she would be untouchable, and would have to get a job. Not an easy feat for an aging curiosity item. She could see it now: *Job Wanted for Golden Couple Reject.* The thought of pounding the pavement in sweaty high heels filled her heart with panic. Companies, as Jack had pointed out, liked younger people because they were cheaper. Besides, who would hire the big guy's ex-wife, and put an end to the internships for their kids, jobs for favorite sons-in-law, and sexy G-4 flights.

Jack had promised to make things whole again for them both. "Consider me reformed!" But a year later, they were still battling over the trust. Worse, Jack was at it again.

Thank God Ben Williams had talked her into taking out the giant life insurance policy. Knowing that Jack didn't believe in costly insurance, she had slipped the medical consent form into his signature pile—and damn, if he hadn't signed it after his third martini! She'd felt a bit ashamed...

She pulled a pillow over her head wondering how long he had been at it this time. Catching herself grinding, she stopped, knowing that her jaw could lock shut and she wouldn't be able to talk, eat, or drink without a straw.

If Jack only knew how exhausting it was to prep like a beauty queen every night, only to find him passed out in bed. After Pussi, things had changed with them. But now, she didn't give a rat's ass.

She wrapped her arms around knees and drew them to her chest, rocking herself to sleep crying hot, stinging, tears.

Barking woke her with a grippy feeling in her chest. Groggy, she glanced at the clock and was startled by the time, almost seven. It was Jack arriving, two hours behind schedule. He would be annoyed that she hadn't started dinner.

As thoughts of the day's developments flooded back, she sank back on the bed, thinking. She would pretend everything was normal and ask casual questions, start a log. Tomorrow, she would hear what Ben had to say. He would be leaving soon for the Lake of the Ozarks to catch some big fish with his friends.

Jack's jumbo-sized unspeakable would make a fine lure. It was still in the loft with the whole stinking mess of soggy newspapers. If he knew she had seen it, he might beat her to the finish with Steinhart whupping her rump with his prenup. The news of Jack's Godzilla-sized dildo would cover the Earth quicker than the internet if Gerte were to find it. Catherine frowned. The safest choice was to reassemble the tote and its contents, clean up the mess and get rid of the nasty cat smell. There was not much time before he entered the house downstairs. She raced back to Jack's room.

The towel she had left in the loft was now under Jack's desk chair. She scratched her head and stooped to retrieve it. Heart racing, she bounded up the steps to find AA batteries, miniature missile-shaped objects and small vibrators scattered haphazardly.

Holding her nose, she picked them up like living night crawlers, returning them all to the bag behind the sofa, except for the giant rubber dildo. Could it have leglessly vibrated away? Shrugging, she stuffed the damp newspaper clippings into a garbage bag, tied the handle and hurried downstairs to scrub her hands with soap and scalding water. Jack's cat wove in and out between her ankles at the sink. She poked him with her broken toe.

"Fluffy, where is Otis?"

40
GNAWING ON THE
NEW DOG TOY

Except for the garden lights, the estate was dark. Catherine washed and dried her hands at the kitchen sink. Outside, the Dobermans were busy heralding Jack's arrival, and bringing on one of her bee-sting headaches; this one would be a doozy. She usually had five minutes to pull herself together after the first bark.

Instead of a gourmet dinner, Jack Boy could have something fuzzy from the freezer drawer. Her eyes narrowed. "We'll give him something good, all right," she told Beanie with a wicked grin. They would not be dining together.

The small dog spun toward the basement door with her tail tucked, while the yellow lab, hearing the pots and pans banging, pressed his nose against the glass on the kitchen deck door and woofed.

She opened it, looking for Jack's car. "Go find Otis," she ordered the lab. "See if he's out there with Tiny and Cuddles." She flipped on the floodlight. Her headache felt nasty.

She selected a frozen block of Jack's vintage turkey-bean

soup from the Sub-Zero drawer. A smudged notation on the label read: *Thanksgiving, two thousand (something)*.

There was fuzz in the storage bag, not much, the soup would be okay. She dropped the block in a pot and added water, wondering what he would say when he limped in late this time without calling. He would have a story. Linda Anderson had, but then, people do make mistakes. The car in town could have been somebody else's custom-painted 1957 BMW. *Naw.* She thought again of Jack's BlackBerry shots and cranked up the Vulcan burner. She would play dumb and listen to the old boy talk.

Jack lurched his way around the back in darkness toward the basement door with the Dobermans nipping excitedly at his heels. He carried his briefcase and the new bag of cigars that he could barely wait to try.

Lacking respect for one's personal space, as usual, Otis padded across his path, tripping him. He soared through air like a sick baby bird, landing face down on the driveway with the Robusto between his lips.

He lay there, stunned, assessing the damage. *Superficial abrasions—yes, bones—fine, contusions—yes, clothes—wet.* His sexy new cigar boxes were scattered around the hydrangeas...and *damn it,* he hurt everywhere. He fumed. Catherine had no control over these dogs. The Dobermans, plodded over him with excitement, sure that he was playing dead. Just as the incorrigible Basset Hound approached, he shoved the big dogs off his chest. Otis seemed pleased with something large in his mouth.

Otis wagged his tail and dropped the object with a

thud on the ground by his hand.

Jack recognized the giant dildo. "Where in the *hell* did you find it, Otis?" Otis and growled at his impolite tone. Jack stretched to snatch it back from the dog. *This would not be for Catherine's eyes.* Even in the dark, he could see that Otis had chewed off an end. "Give it back." Jack inched his fingers closer to the object. The dog barred his teeth, he snapped back his hand.

Otis, wagging, picked it up and disappeared in the woods. Jack stood up, stiff as the Tin Man, and brushed himself off, then stooped to pick up the closest stogies. "Otis, you son of a bitch, you're one ahead of me," he said, breathing hard, patting his briefcase teasingly. "Fine, you keep it. I have more."

41
GONNA EAT THAT?

Catherine could feel the heavy furnace room door open and close. *Jack, returning.* She was feeling less brave than she had hoped. Her breaths were rapid and shallow, something that happened when she faced confrontation. She double-checked her phone. He must have been "busy" because he hadn't even tried. And after an enjoyable afternoon driving around with some brunette, he was about to make his "business as usual" entrance, two hours late, in his typical self-centered way. Yes, the Beemer—she remembered how much fun she and Jack had had when buying the relic on their honeymoon. He was determined to nab the rare 1950s car, like the one Elvis Presley had owned. It was a two-tone paint job, fully, if not correctly, restored. They'd flown it home from Germany in the cargo hold of a company plane, just the two of them, keeping each other warm, making out.

Catherine squeezed her shoulders together wanting to look as unyielding as she felt. This time, she would play it right. A vapid smile took shape on her lips and faded away just as fast. She had kept those hot tub photos on her phone for a reason.

That tiny voice was "pulling G's" in her skull again. *You're gonna decorate the walls with his turkey soup, right?* She shook off the fluttering feeling…she would outsmart it. The voice demanded, *Hey—you there? Show him what you do to a bully who lays your guts on a platter for the cats to eat.* She knew better. Getting emotional would only make him mad. The shadowy tales of Jack's ill-fated ex-wives had protected him like armored tanks. She would tread with caution. "Good thing the expensive crap you couldn't live without was made to last," he had told his previous wives. "*Please*…take it with you."

Tiny Voice had a point. *He keeps you down till it looks like up.* She started to cry, but stopped herself. It wasn't that she was *angry;* she knew how to handle rejection. She was afraid of not being good enough. Jack was on his way upstairs. The smell of his cigar wafted through the space at the bottom of the basement door, reminding her of how her life was about to go up in smoke. He was discarding her, like the other wives; like the ashes that he dropped all over the house. She would be careful. A single slip, and…

Her favorite Cutco lay on the pig-shaped cutting board next to the salad veggies. She liked the smoothness of its plastic handle and coolness of its blade. So sharp. What if—*what if,* she were to lose control? She cracked her neck, feeling the stiffness in her shoulders release. Her heart rate accelerated. *You can use my special Chef's knife to remove the smile from Daddy-o's philandering face.* She closed her eyes, straining to get a grip. Geeze, Louise, she thought. I have indeed lost it. She poured herself a glass of Chardonnay and took a gulp.

Remembering the sausage machine in the cellar by the marinara sauce, she set the Chef's knife down. Sooner or later, somebody would make a sausage out of him.

She couldn't be the only one to notice that Jack's brain wasn't as sharp these days. When powerful men retire, sometimes they, or their wives, do crazy things.

The melee was making its way up the stairs. Suddenly, she wasn't sure how the words would come out. She ran her damp hands through her hair, trying to stay calm. Tonight, she would just listen. Tomorrow, she would get a green light from Ben. Her sixth-grade safety-patrol training came to mind, with her memory reversing to the day that she was removed from the girls' safety squad without explanation. One of the mothers had filed a "nonspecific" complaint, sowing doubt on her character and heaping shame on her family. She hadn't understood; she had followed the rules and had been proud of her safety badge, the special sash, and the fine job that she had done helping little kids to cross the road. Her mother had assured her that the other girls, the popular ones, were jealous because she was prettier than they were.

Catherine was loaded for game. She tapped her fingers on the counter, aware of Jack's keen adaptive skill. "The secret to success is simple," he often said. "Learn how to fake sincerity and you'll have it made." Two could play.

Three of the dogs collided each other and the door, their tails whacking the white plaster walls. Jack managed to reach the top just as the door exploded from raw dog power, driving a pockmark in the new kitchen cabinet. The frenzied canines scrambled around him and his shiny bag of cigars, piling into the kitchen like an Italian family at a ski resort lift line. She struck a sour expression hoping to convey her sense of disapproval.

"Hi, sweetie," Jack said, reading her frown lines like tea leaves. He exhaled a stream of blue smoke around the cigar in his mouth as he collected himself. "What a day!"

42

VINNY AND PUSSI AT THE SUPER SEX

The cheap motel room looked like the inside of a dumpster, sheets and blankets strewn everywhere, empty whiskey bottles on the floor. Vinny was liquored up. Pussi's black tube dress, the size of a hand towel without a chick in it lay in a wad on the floor. He picked it up and in one seamless move, stretched it like Handi-Wrap across her face, pinning her head against the stained, half-dressed mattress, so close to her throat, that he could almost feel his hands slip to her skinny neck and squeeze. The glint of fear in her eyes pleased him. But he wasn't stupid. The only thing the old guy had that he didn't was money, and he wanted it.

Her nose poked through a hole in the dress, breathing moist breath that smelled like her cheap-ass whiskey.

"Struggling won't get you anywhere," said Vinny.

"Does controlling me make you feel good?" she snapped.

"My turn to talk," he said, slurring his words. "It's time for your rich old boyfriend to get relieved of a few extra bucks—and you and me are gonna help him out."Vinny's elbow buckled against the mattress and down he went, flattening her. She twisted, trying to squiggle out from underneath him and pull herself out. "Are you gonna get in the game?"

"Okay, *okay,* let me up! Leave me alone," she muffled her indignant words through the holes in her dress. He loosened his grip, letting her sit on the edge of the sagging bed. "How much do you owe 'em this time, Vinny?"

He brandished a full-knuckled fist. "Well, everything was fixed. We was waiting on our race. I was on top, betting good on the other nags." He released her so that he could scratch his head. "I was gonna buy my baby girl some high-class jewelry, soon as my win growed into something respectable. Constellation Comet was coming up in the seventh—he was our horse. Hundred to one, his turn to win, *our* turn, you know what I mean. We held him back all season when he wanted to run. He was *ready*, Pussi."

He watched her shift on the bed, waiting for the other horseshoe to drop.

"We was all gettin' a piece—we're talking *big* money, Puss. The horse was a runner, and nobody knew, we was *that* good." Vinny tossed the dress on the bed.

"Yeah, did ya' get it?" she asked, fiddling with her navel ring.

"*Shut up.* Just listen. First, Zabaglione gives me the bum's rush. 'Get lost, Vincent—not another dime!' he says. It's ten minutes before the race, so I says to him, 'I did the job perfect. Top down, like you wanted. This is the big one, Boss, we got the horse. We're up. We'll *all* be in the money—you, more than anybody. I'll pay you back for this, and the last loan, too, plus whatever interest you want.' Zabaglione liked that."

"So, he softens up—gives me a chance, and lets me use his hundred grand." He paused to see if she got what he was saying. "I knew I could pay him on the spot and still take a pile home myself." He looked at her soft, pouting lips and reached over, to wiggle the steel stud on the bottom one. "Some for you, too, honey. 'Last time,' Zabaglione says like he was serious." He paused to let the weight of it sink in. "He was." Vinny's hands were going clammy.

"You look like shit," Pussi said. She didn't look so hot, either.

"So, Comet's supposed to be a sure thing, baby, and everything's going great at first. Their rider is ahead on by mid-backstretch when Danny Marker gives her the reins. Off, he rockets on the homestretch, fuel injected, so far ahead of the field, I could almost taste the dough. But then, nobody could believe it. Marker fucking pulls him up! *Pulls him up!* And he comes in seventh—out of the money! 'What the hell?' we all say, and look at each other, 'What did that little bastard just do to our horse?'" He made a fist. Pussi winced. "Danny isn't riding these days with his broken leg."

"The sledgehammer?" she asked. He nodded.

"Here's the problem, Puss. Zabaglione's terms weren't his usual—my principal doubles every month. Zabaglione blames me for losing a pile. So now, I got this loan on top of the last one and I owe him seven hundred-grand—hell, maybe it's a *million* by now—and he wants it now, or they're takin' me for a ride. This time, he means it. He sent his goons here twice to rough me up." He scowled and flipped the bird to the door. "Juno and Viktor put me in Missouri Baptist. That's how I got my swollen lip. Does it look bad?"

"Try ice," Pussi said. "Works for me."

"I'm doing my best to come up with the money. Made a few bucks at Fairmount for Joe Benno and his boys the other day. They had a job for me to do on a couple of four-year-olds. I offered part of that fee to the Bobbsey Twins, but they turned it down—said the boss didn't want no trickles. That's when they did this," he said, touching his lip. "I'm not done with those pricks yet," he said, tightening his fist…

He looked at her. "Had anything to eat?" She craved sweets.

"Not much," she answered. "And I'm kind of hungry, baby."

"I still got some Twinkies left from the case that fell off the Hostess truck. Help yourself. He laughed and nudged a box out from under the bed with his foot. She stood up and bent over. She had a cute little ass. He pinched it hard, making her yelp. She took out four or five packs of yellow crème-filled fingers, ripped open the cellophane, and shoved them all in her mouth.

"I knew," she accused him, waving her finger with her mouth full, "that sooner or later Richie would get sick of being your fucking ATM machine. How long have I been tellin' you to stay away from the betting booths, Vinny?

When are you gonna learn?"

He drew his hand back to give her a good slap but dropped it in his drunkenness. She glared. He would save his energy.

"Okaay—fine way to impress your boss," Pussy said, sarcastically. "Just when you've worked your way up to the porn group! You brag on your knack for grooming young talent. I hope you stay alive long enough to enjoy the final edits."

"I can talk him into a payment plan, and you're gonna make it happen," he said. He watched her stumble to the bathroom and close herself in. "Listen, Pussi," he shouted through the delaminating door, "Your old pal can't keep it in his pants, I get that. I'm not telling you who to fuck, but if I had the money that SOB's got—" He raised his voice louder over the retching sounds. "You wouldn't be wasting your time with an eighty-year-old dick." He hoped she heard the last sentence while she chucked up the Twinkies and flushed.

43
SCENT OF A SKUNK

The clock pushed ten. While her talking points at dinner could have been brunettes in BMWs and cell phone photography, it was pointless to talk after Jack's drunken half-baked excuse for not calling. The atmosphere had been silent. "Phones," he finally said, "are not allowed during recording, Catherine." He stood at the sink loading dirties while she rinsed the soap from the soup pot. She had a strong urge to hose him with the sprayer, give him the cold shower he needed. What *does* a man do locked in a bathroom for twenty minutes, five times a day? *She believed she knew.* She had enjoyed watching the old boy eat his special turkey soup.

"They're clean," she said as she sized up the space on the countertop. Fluffy's nemesis, Jones the barn cat, was weaving in and out of the small window above the sink. He'd spent much of the day snoozing under a fern in the garden room, and was now nocturnally activated, ready for action. She shooed him off.

Jack shuffled around the kitchen in his cowhide moccasins, sipping after-dinner schnapps. He lifted his dog-licked dinner plate from the floor and chortled on the way up, bracing himself against the dishwasher to give Cuddles a pat. "They love to experience the essence of our cooking," he said. "I'm renaming Cuddles 'Coldwater' after the dog in my redneck jokebook. He waved the plate. "Not hygienic enough for you?'" he asked with joviality. "It's as clean as *Coldwater* kin git 'em!" Laughing, he pulled down the creaking dishwasher door about to add Cuddles's plate to the clean ones.

"*Stop!* Give me *that!*" she protested, taking the slippery plate from his hand, feeling like a first-grade teacher catching a seven-year-old smoking.

"There's plenty of room," he countered, missing her point, grabbing it back with a stumble before putting it back in, belching. He shook his head, looking surprised. "Oh, lovely...Gerte left the clean ones in again."

"That's what I've been trying to tell you, Jack," she hollered over the noise from the faucet. "You need a hearing aid!"

"Hah?" He bumped her with his hip and reached under the counter where Gerte kept the cleaning supplies. "I'll wash this one by hand," he insisted, taking a sponge from the bucket with the rags and scrub brushes.

"I'll finish up, *really!*" she said, reclaiming Gerte's floor sponge.

"There's absofucking nothing unclean about using good old soap and water to clean dishes with a sponge. Rinsing twice is the trick! People are dropping dead from superbugs thanks to over-sterilizing everything." While

Jack strolled himself straight to Sleepyville tonight, she and the dogs would take a post-meal walk to the gate.

His phone buzzed in his holster. "Ok," he said, with a dismissive wave, "sweetie, the dishes are *all yours*. I'm heading upstairs—to *poop.*" He was halfway to the staircase before she stopped cringing. Gripping the rail, he ascended the staircase. A few moments later, the bathroom door closed and locked behind him.

Jones did a figure eight around her legs. She never felt completely alone when the animals were close. Weary, she opened the screen door and let the dogs scramble out to whoop at their trolls. The cat coated her navy-blue slacks with his fur as he slid through her legs to follow the hunting pack. Gerte, who figured a few extra hairs in the margarine didn't matter, had given up trying to keep him off the counter. He was proud of the dead mice he brought in through the kitchen window and left on the sponges.

There was no telling how long she could stay in the house, Jack's house... *her home.* Would they split up the cats and dogs? Her heart sank at the thought, knowing that she would have mountains to scale.

For now, she would enjoy breathing the clean country air while she could. She threw on a light jacket and set off toward the gate.

Walking after sunset always helped to clear her head. The moon was rising full in the east, casting a shimmery glow on the nascent daffodils and Prairie Fire crabs. She had planted them on both sides of the half-mile long driveway for their brilliant color. There were a thousand flowering bulbs under the sixty trees that were now mature and in full, raspberry-pink bloom. She would never forget their scent, they smelled to her like Spring. The frogs in the boggy wetland were belting out their favorite love songs. She mused that the warmer temperature seemed to make them amorous. It had been too long since she had felt that way.

The long day's heat still rose from the asphalt. She tied her Cardinals jacket by its two empty sleeves and hanging it loose behind her back, closed her eyes to focus on her breathing. She opened them again and walked on. The numerous stars above reminded her of the countless women that Jack had pinched in front of her.

She stopped up the hill at a turn in the drive, where Jack liked to pause for a second wind. There was a sugar maple there with sappy past; a shrine to his ex-wife, who had found the tree as a scrappy, sapling hardwood and planted it. He had watched it grow tall and robust without her. Jack never mentioned the crabs. Feeling sad, she stooped to collect Jones, who was standing on his rear legs, begging to be picked up. She and her cat continued their walk with two of the dogs by their side. In the stillness of the country night, she gave the cat a squeeze.

Several minutes later, they reached the gate at the Baxter Road entrance, where she liked to practice her YouTube dog training skills by making them touch the gate with a paw. So far, her success rate was zero per cent. The Dobermans, disinterested as usual, had taken off to join the others who didn't give a cat's butt about higher education. Maybe, she was not the dog whisperer.

A vehicle on the other side of the heavy brown gate turned on its engine, startling her. Unhinged by the surprise, Jones rocketed off, punching a few claw holes in her arm. With the gate and bushes in her line of sight, she saw little of the dark-colored sedan on the other side of the gate that lurched into reverse and squealed crazily off to the west down Baxter.

Although harmless couples sometimes "parked" there, but after the pesticide mistakes at J.R. Henniger, serious threats had been made on Jack's life. A disgruntled employee with a pipe bomb once climbed over the gate and ended up suing them over his dog bites.

Jack wouldn't discuss the other episodes for national security reasons, but at times, they would have to secure the estate around the clock. There had been nothing threatening since leaving Zorox.

The Dobermans were yelping in the woods.

Suddenly, a skunk in that direction personalized the sweet night air.

"Go—dogs! Go!" she commanded, while running towards the house in a panic, hoping to round up the yet unsprayed. Her troops, only half-trained to mobilize, continued coming toward the skunk.

"Biscuit!" she shouted the magic word. Thrilled by the prospect of a treat, the dogs reversed course. Together they power-jogged the quarter mile back home in record time, forgetting about skunks, opossums, and other nocturnal things. She herded the joyful lot inside and rewarded them with a treat from the cookie jar. Tails wagging, they shot up the stairs and headed straight to their beds.

Left holding one biscuit, she realized that was one dog short, Otis. He was AWOL somewhere with the skunk—where he could stay.

She turned off the lights and climbed the back stairs. A glowing band of warm light spilled into the hall from under Jack's closed bathroom door. She stopped at the pine-paneled door to listen for signs of life. The sink water was running. She knocked. There was no response.

"Don't tell me you're still in there," she shouted through the door.

"Slow flow," Jack responded. "Be right out."

She continued to the cavernous bedroom, and sat at her family's precious Steinway, plunking out *One Enchanted Evening* by ear, a favorite tune of Jack's about love. She shook her head with rue; she might never have another.

Maybe he'd come sit beside her and say that he was a man in love. *Naw.*

The door down the hall opened. Clearing his throat, Jack treaded unevenly up the maple-planked hallway to his small pass-through dressing closet. He stood motionless at his dresser for quite a while. She could hear the pinging of his BlackBerry He wasn't coming. She decided to play another tune.

"Catherine, can you play *Far, Far Away?*"

She stopped and watched him separate their bed's percale sheets and climb in. Within a minute, Jack had plugged his BlackBerry to its charger cord and had turned off the light, passing out cold, still holding the phone. She resumed her playing with a pounding rendition of with tears stinging her eyes.

44
SHAKING THE BLACKBERRY BUSH

Jack lay spread-eagled on the center on their bed, snoring loudly. She closed her Wagner songbook and rose from the piano bench. He was still wearing his metal-framed trifocals.

Before today, she might have gone to sleep and dreamed of fixing their marriage. She rubbed her eyes from pure exhaustion, feeling more helpless than the night that she had lost her white rental car at Disney World.

The Dobermans circled and dropped with the thud of five tumbling kettle bells. A few brown eyes still peeked with waning interest at her. She thought about joining them with an old paperback she had bought for a friend, *"WIN WHEN THE OTHER SIDE IS CHEATING."* In it, U.R. Toste challenges his readers with thought-provoking chapters like *Snooping as a Hobby* and *Beyond the Lipstick on His Collar.*

When it's not your shade, your work begins. If he leaves his stuff out, he wants you to look. Is his cell phone locked? Laptop on? Don't forget his pockets, drawers, phone bills and credit card statements...

The brunette in the BMW had made her wonder whose marriage Pussi Puziari was rubber stamping now.

Ladies, once you're in, stay a while: Check those searches, texts, and calls.

Remember, a picture is worth a thousand boring words, so don't neglect those telling digital picture albums. Get the facts, ma'am.

It was an awkward stretch across Cuddle's bed to nightstand. She switched off the lamp and waited until her night vision kicked in. Except for the moonlight from the skylight, the bedroom was dark. She was alone with the sleeping dogs and tree branches tracing shadows on the maple floor. And Jack.

The BlackBerry in his hand pinged, glowing blue light, then pinged again. But Jack, sawing giant maple logs, did not stir.

"*Take a peek,*" said the voice of U.R. Toste, spurring her curiosity. She had would hate to see Jack's phone fall and break. Maybe as she moved it, a teaser text, a tiny morsel of the future, would pop up on its screen. She tiptoed around Cuddles, carefully trying not to creak the floorboards on her way to his nightstand, where she Jack's face and breathing, noticing his lips flutter as he exhaled. Counting the beers that he had gulped down at lunch; he had enough alcohol in his system to sink a boat load of livers. She extracted his prescription glasses before he could turn over and wake himself up and set them on the nightstand by his empty schnapps.

Watching his eyelids, she freed the phone from his

fingers, carefully. It buzzed, startling her. She almost let it drop. An evil feeling came over her, U.R. Toste. It was active and unlocked.

She stared at the strange phone in her hands. Jack could be asleep for a long time, but there were no guarantees and actions had consequences. He would go insane if he caught her.

Yet, anything she might learn, even if it hurt her, could help. She said a silent prayer. She was only looking for reassurance. Jack was lying there snoring, inviting her to help herself.

Her hands were as damp as the underarms of her baseball jacket, but she needed to know about the woman in the car. Knowing, would help her to sleep.

Toste's friendly voice goaded on. *How about that raunchy photo at lunch? Are there others?* And who were the guys in his group, having harmless fun? She stared at the snoring old man; his executive hair framed by the light of the moonlight and took the phone.

The BlackBerry pinged, snatching her heart from her chest. She pivoted in her stocking feet and slid across the marble bathroom floor as far away from him as she could get—her dressing room—and closed the door behind her with a click.

Breathing hard and hoping for a miracle, she hit his phone's small "BACK" button.

She could not believe her luck.

45
DRESSING ROOM,
NIGHT ONE

The little screen in Catherine's hand was the dressing room's only light. A teaser text appeared on the home page, she squinted without her reading glasses, able to decipher only the address.

Her heart dropped.

"Who? Captain, WHAT?" her lips mouthed the words. She rifled through her junk drawer taking the pair of broken readers with the missing right lens and temple that she had put there for emergencies.

```
From: CaptainThunderpants@me.com
Subject: Today in the BEEMER
Date: May 2, 6:50 PM EST
To: BrendaZabaglione@hotmail.com
Subject: Today in the BEEMER
Date: May 2, 6:50 PM EST
```

Today? The Beemer? Just what she needed, she realized as she went wobble-kneed, hoping that his phone would not go dead before she got to the bad part. She hung the crippled eyeglasses over one ear like a monocle. Tonight, she would learn the truth. *She had been a fool to forgive him!*

Now, or never, she sank to the carpet with her back against the wall and dug in.

From: CaptainThunderpants@me.com
Subject: Today in the BMW
 Date: May 2   6:50 PM EST
 To: BrendaZabaglione@hotmail.com

It isn't often I meet a woman as good looking as you with your level of intelligence—and class, frankly. It made me so happy when you got in touch with me (thanks to Pussi) Don't worry, we don't need to tell her! We wouldn't want her to get started on the booze again. What she doesn't know, won't hurt her. LOL. Goes for your husband, too. I'll be glad to advise you as to next steps that you may soon need to take, i.e., lawyers, etc... But for now, you deserve some fun in your life! Life, it's short——be happy!

I'm looking forward to enjoying our threesome next week. Can't wait to see you girls lying together naked. Four creamy legs. Meeting you today was just a tease—and harmless. We'll work it out with Pussi.

I would very much like something of you

to take to bed. SEND me a picture that shows your "stuff!" I promise to return the favor.

Business: Slim chance my wife will hack my phone and see my inbox, but to be safe, do create a male sounding User ID to make us appear less obvious.

Catherine is still my wife, but we have an understanding. She does her thing, manages our social life and the place. I bring in the money. It's workable, but soulless. Early on, she made it clear that sex meant nothing to her. What's a horny guy like me to do, baby?

Don't think I didn't notice *first thing* how nice your nipples looked under the pretty soft blouse you wore today. Can you take a picture for me?

Jack

46
DIRTY STUFF

Jack's BlackBerry was as cluttered as his dresser top with its used toothpicks and nose-blown paper towels. Most eighty-year-olds treasured pictures of their grandkids and garden club prizes. Not Jack, his album was an adults-only Library of Congress of people performing 'Ripley's Believe it or Not' acts.

Mortified, but unable to stop, Catherine scanned through files of uncomfortable contortions as fascinated as a gawker at a blood-splattered accident. Some of the subjects and even the pervert's wedding ring, were recognizable. He was playing roulette with his health and her future. But she was on to him.

Attachment: jpg
From:CaptainThunderpants@me.com
Subject: HEAT and EAT
Date: May 2, 10:17 PM EST

To: RichardBlower@gmail.com

HC wants WP to know that the sausage is back in the basement deep freeze marked, "Heat and Eat." Will tell C to defrost for dinner. He-he.

Successful sessions held today behind the locked door of my bathroom. Ha-ha. C knocked on the door, interrupting my important business. She wondered when I was coming. I sent her away!

Still on for our threesome Tuesday with your girlfriend Brenda? Oh,boy. XOX

From: RichardBlower@gmail.com
Subject: HEAT and Eat
Date: May 2
10:35 AM To:
CaptainThunderpants@me.com
Attachment: jpg

C is so stupid! Let her cook it. Hehehe! Here's a special close-up of my awesome new vibrators, in use while thinkin' of HC and toe-curling orgasms. You'll like!!

Countdown reminder for the F-fest, Tuesday, after AA. Don't be surprised by the camera. All in the works! WP loves her HC! Can't wait, baby Xoxoxo

47
RETURN OF
THE BLACKBERRY

O tis howled. Her eyes popped open.

I am sleeping on my dressing room floor?

Catherine's cheek was schmushed in a puddle of cold drool on the heavy wool carpet. Her prickly right hand was wrapped around something smooth and hard. She gave it a squeeze. *Jack's BlackBerry!* A sense of crushing dread returned.

The angle of the moonlight suggested that sunrise would come soon. Her pale reflection in the dressing room mirror made her heart jump. Who was the exhausted woman who looked so depressed and had aged so fast?

Part of her wanted to slip back to sleep to give her dream a better outcome. She had been in this house—and was confused. Jack was moving about, talking to a younger woman—not that attractive; his new wife and the house was hers now. She wanted to know if Catherine would share some decorating tips with her. Jack kissed his new wife, while mildly surprised to see Catherine. He seemed curious about her aging face and body. He pointed a craggy finger toward the door. "Pussi says it's time for you to leave," he said. Skinning and quartering her heart could not have killed her faster.

A wolf cry sounded from the deck below, followed by the sweet and sour smell of skunk wafting through the screens.

The first thing Jack checked upon waking was the time on the BlackBerry she held in her hand. He was an early riser. She gulped as she assessed her challenge. She had to return the phone to his nightstand and climb into bed, as if she had been sleeping there all night. She would have to reopen the dressing room door and creep across twenty feet of marble bathroom floor without waking the dogs, or him. If lucky enough to reach his nightstand, she would have to find and connect his charging cord to the odd shaped port and lay it face down on his nightstand before she could silently back up on her hands and knees, fast as she could.

If she messed up, she would be looking for a one-bedroom apartment in the morning. Otis, woofing again on the deck below Jack's window, was reading her mind.

"For *God's* sake, Otis," she whispered frantically under her breath, *"shut up."* He was hungry and bawling at the setting moon. And she was still in the dressing room and wishing for a brown paper bag. She popped open the door with the heel of her hand; it smacked against the plaster wall with chattering reverberation, putting her into a frozen state for a very long moment.

With her heart racing, she dropped to the floor and slid like a jungle lizard back across the bathroom to the bed, praying that Jack would not wake up and look down.

The dogs still peacefully snored.

Jack's nightstand, looming ahead, was bathed in the waning moonshine. She cringed as she advanced with each creak of a floorboard. Fluffy, standing by Jack's dangling foot on the bed, hovered while peering quizzically. The cat jumped with a thud to the floor, and like a furry troll under a bridge, began to snake under her armpit and zigzag her face, the scent of fresh-killed mice was on his breath. It was hard not to sneeze at the stray hairs tickling her nose. When the dreaded sneeze came, she failed to muffle it. Fluffy, only wanting to be stroked, flopped, and rolled seductively. The sheets above her rustled slightly. Jack turning. *Still safe.*

An arm's reach of the nightstand, Fluffy batted play-fully at the charger cord, as Jack, three feet above, gave an apnea gasp and lifted his head. Resettling, her resumed making "phewie" noises with his lips. Fluffy shot off in a wild skid across the slippery bathroom floor.

She plugged in the phone and placed it face down on the bedstand, not expecting it to brighten the room as it did. Her eyes darted to Jack's face, seeing no change. As soon as the phone went dark again, she reversed on all fours as far away from the phone as she could.

Finally climbing in, she jerked the bedding out from under the snoring sandbag's leg and pulled the covers over her shoulder, taking care not to touch him. The prospect of sharing a bed with a bucket of garden snakes had more appeal.

48
CHICAGO OR BUST

The world was abuzz over the wedding of Prince William and Kate Middleton at Westminster Abbey. In Chicago, the wedding of Tiffany Thompson, Catherine's goddaughter, would be grand, yet on a lesser scale at the First Fourth Presbyterian, or was it the First Third Episcopal on Michigan? It sounded like a bank to Catherine, who had put the date in her planner the moment Maggie had invited her to play a role in her only daughter's happiest day. Jack had opted out, but had encouraged her to go, and before she knew it, she was hosting a fancy bridesmaid's luncheon at the Peninsula.

Catherine was dead tired after her wild night of Black-Berry picking. Looking at divorce herself, it felt like she was packing for a funeral, not a wedding. The timing of the trip was unfortunate, but there was no way she could miss this wedding, Maggie would be crushed.

It was to be an elegant affair. The bride and groom and the wedding party would leave the church in a cavalcade of Rolls-Royce convertibles for a high-society reception at the Union Club. Three hundred strangers were sure to help nurse her post-traumatic stress syndrome. Maybe she would linger in Chicago a few extra days. She dug in her underwear drawer for her nice La Perla bra, the one that concealed her nipples under a light weight knit but came up with two or three other ones that no longer fit. Gerte had put it in the dryer.

Catherine's therapist thought she had a bad picker, her first marriage to a nut and this time, a serial cheater. She should have known when in the spirit of full disclosure on their wedding day, he had mentioned his mother's former bridge partner. "Sweetie," he had bragged, hoisting a colorful flag, "she was hot for my bod—beautiful jugs for her age."

Getting ahold of Ben Williams was a must. He was in court for the morning. She needed her smart lawyer to help her shape the escape plan. If she didn't get out of the marriage, she would end up in a nuthouse—and Jack would commit her, maybe to the same ward as Marvin.

Of course, she hoped to exit with more than the skin on her teeth. Jack could never understand her pain and humiliation.

She would keep cool until after her trip so he wouldn't suspect. And tonight, she would stay up for *"As My Stomach Turns," episode two.*

Catherine set her perfect knit, a St. John luncheon suit, on the bed about to hook it inside a proper valet bag when she heard heavy footsteps coming toward the bedroom. Fluffy announced Gerte's arrival by leaping out of his litter box onto the jacket, kneading its loops with his claws. She brushed the cat litter off and looked up. Gerte, wearing her "bad news to blab" expression, carried a tall basket of linens.

"*Ach!*" Gerte said, "*Frau* Henniger, your *Mann* is angry that you didn't come down."

"Oh?" Catherine asked, her face prickling. Maybe he knew?

"He threw your coffee out instead of leaving it for you to reheat, like usual." Catherine felt chilled. The cheap bastard would never see a whole cup go to waste. He had even shut off the furnace on April 15 to save propane.

"Gerte," she said, holding her head between her hands. "I wasn't feeling well, but I'm better now. What can I do for you?"

Gerte was dressed to the twos in her gray Ralph Lauren II sweatpants and shirt. She wore a bandage on her upper lip where a hairy mole had been. "I saved your buttered toast for later," she said.

"No, thanks. I'm packing for my trip to Chicago. Do you know where my pretty beige La Perla bra is, the padded one with the underwires?"

Gerte nodded. "Someone put it in the dryer."

"Who would do that to my expensive lingerie?" Catherine was certain that she had left it by the sink.

"You gathered it with your towels. It ended up with my bleachables," Gerte countered and smiled, revealing the space between her front teeth.

The ring of the house phone kept Catherine from losing her cool. Gerte, a foot away, gazed at the ringing instrument. Catherine, counting the rings, refused to budge.

Gerte, groaning, picked it up on the fourth. "Hallo?" Maybe Ben was finished with court.

"Who?" Gerte demanded, shaking her head. "Oh, Mr. Williams…" Catherine waved her fingers wildly to signal that she would take the call. "Yes?" Gerte continued, "And from *where* would that be? *Ja, ja*… from Blumenfeld— somebody, and *Williams?* I *see*. Conner, Blumenfeld and Williams. A law firm, then?"

Gerte turned to her, pointing at the handset. "He wants to talk to *Mrs.* Henniger."

Catherine felt the urge to strangle her.

Gerte cleared her throat. "Do you mind if I ask what this is regarding?"

Give me the frigging phone.

Gerte huffed, "Well—if you must know, I am the Henniger's housekeeper." The caller said something and Gerte frowned. "She is standing right here!" She thrust the phone her way. "It's for you."

"I'll call him back," Catherine said with nonchalance.

49
CALLING MR. WILLIAMS

Catherine quietly told everything to Ben from the privacy of her car. He could feel her tears through the phone. "He ripped a hole in my heart." Her crying made him sad. He swung his desk chair around and booted up his computer.

He understood her sense of panic. "The hole is in his head, Catherine." Horndog Henniger was a pro at getting rid of unpleasant problems with cash. Sometime last year, an admin at Zorox had threatened a wrongful dismissal suit. Dolly Maguire had claimed she had found a cache of "no-no's" on Henniger's office computer, like underage social networking and offering cigars to minors. His online nickname was "Hard Candy, HC for short." Miss Maguire had been poised to shoot her story to the press, but Steinhart and his boys were able to disarm her with warnings of her future as a bagwoman. They had offered her a bundle, which she took before walking away smiling. Henniger had skated off as easy as a Stanley Cup puck, while somebody else got the boot. Word was his driver.

The other end grew silent. He hoped she could sustain her momentum and leave the dirty coot. He decided to soft peddle the "D" word. "Some men have a hard time keeping it in their pants."

"I believed I could keep him straight, Ben," she said, clearly distraught. "It would be bad enough if he was only cheating."

His interest piqued. "Hmmm…tell me."

"Do you remember Pussi the Pilferer?"

"Sure, the Bible Camp Flasher."

"It's her again. But she has been with him all along. How could I have been so *stupid?*" she implored. "He's still giving her money. And a *lot.*"

"I'm sure she's working hard for it."

She cleared her throat and lowered her voice. "There are others."

No surprise. Henniger would have a bullpen of babes in training. "He can't have just one, Catherine. Like potato chips."

"It's the same with them all—he says horrible things about me. And they're young. I saw them on his Black-Berry, I lost count."

"He ought to be careful—he could end up in jail," Ben said, scanning through his criminal law site while he listened.

"Exactly," Catherine said, lowering the tone of her voice to a whisper. "He and Pussi were at a dress-up party in masks. She wore a checked peekaboo blouse, her frayed short-shorts were rolled above her bottom. Jack had on his red cowboy shirt, muck boots and overalls. Ellie May and Jed Clampett. She cleared her throat. He left his his barn door open on purpose. "His horse was sticking its head *out*."

Ben hadn't heard that phrase for a while and laughed. "He didn't have to worry about losing face," he said. Catherine laughed, too, and choked a little bit on her tears. Ben picked up his ballpoint. "His escapades at eighty could feed the media for months."

"She wears different colored wigs, tall gold boots and a ratty raccoon coat with nothing underneath. He bought the fur for her at a rummage sale. She sits on a tall stool in her fur and the boots," she paused to whisper, "and..."

It must have been a long night on the dressing room floor.

"Then there is the *really* unsettling stuff."

"*Worse?*"

"Uh-huh. I wouldn't make this up."

"I'm sure you're wouldn't. We don't have admissible evidence for a court of law."

"Please, Ben, I don't want it to go public. He needs help."

"Don't worry, we have our ways. Try to remember as much as you can."

"I can't forget."

"Tell me more."

"He buys the ice cream, half-gallons of Rocky Road and Strawberry Shortcake, and liter bottles of Ginger Ale and diet Mountain Dew. She throws it up, and he—"

"Let me guess." He said, cringing.

"It's quite the cascade," she said with a stifled a laugh. "He buys, it flies." Ben felt himself growing somewhat queasy. "Cheaper than movie tickets and a large tub of popcorn," he said, straining to regain decorum. He swallowed hard and nodded. "Sounds like a case for Overeaters Anonymous."

Catherine's voice picked up. "He names the videos like they were pets: Chocolate Puddles, Vanilla Splash, Chunky Monkey; Green Stuff—actually, that one might have been pistachio or guacamole. I couldn't tell for sure. He calls her his Vomit Comit."

"Guess they like reruns," Ben said, composing himself. "We both know he is not well, Catherine." He took down a note that Henniger saved the videos.

"—and the money, Ben. It looks like he's given her a million. Our so-called investment advisor makes sure that Trixie Belle gets her monthly cash, and I don't find out."

"That, I find interesting," he interjected, web-searching criminal negligence.

"I imagine you have decided on a divorce, then."

She cleared her throat, thinking. "I feel like killing him, but I really want to help him, Ben. The press would have a field day with our divorce. He's getting so sloppy people are telling me. Frankly, I'm thinking of my own reputation."

Sensing that her resolve might waver, his hopes sank a bit. Denial was strange medicine in a sick marriage. He'd seen enough dead ones to know that this one was a goner.

He spoke in a soothing tone, "If he continues at this pace, how bad will he be when he reaches eighty-five?

This is a tough one, Catherine." She was a lovely woman. Henniger was blind and deaf as well as dumb. "Don't admit you heard this from me, but I'm going to put a tail on him, keep track of where he's going."

She shifted forward on her chair. "What?"

"To make sure he stays out of real trouble, while we prepare your divorce documents."

"What if he finds out?"

"Let me worry about that."

"Is there someone out there, a professional, to help him? What if we whisked him away for a while?"

He rocked back in his desk chair. You can't put toothpaste back in a tube. Henniger should be labeled a public nuisance and gelded.

"St. Louis is not D.C. or New York, but there's a guy who reports some success with celebrity sex-addicts. Lonny McQueen. Traveled as a grip with a rock band a while back." She sniffled as she listened.

"They did county fairs, mostly Louisville, Indianapolis, Akron, Dayton and got to know the stars well, I guess," he said, clearing his throat. "He observed a bit of addictive behavior—drugs, sex, booze, whatever. Did a fair bit himself, which was how he slipped off the scaffold during a show and took out the drums before he landed in the lap of a female bull rider. She was sitting in the audience on her cigarette break— Bruiser the Cruiser was her rodeo name. She didn't like being part of the act without being asked and punched him pretty hard. Now he can't get around without his Scooter."

"He could help Jack?" she asked, sounding doubtful.

"Yeah. Lonny had to switch careers. Addiction was a subject he knew and could do from a seated position." Ben thought for a moment and asked, "What frightens you about leaving Jack?"

"That's easy." Catherine blew her nose. "Being alone, and broke. And old."

"I promise you won't have to worry about any of that. Should we get the paperwork lined up, so it will be ready when you are? We'll talk more next time. It's your call, but I must warn you, if he catches wind that you're on to him, he could beat you to the punch."

"Now, that scares me."

"Don't tell *anyone,* okay?" Ben thought of Henniger's greedy, son-of-a bitch lawyer. "The first thing Steinhart will do, is freeze your funds. They would expect you to settle on their terms."

"Maybe you're right," she said, her voice breaking up.

"Stay alert on your end. I'll do the same. You have reason to be concerned, but you will get through this. Do you trust me?" he asked with a smile in his voice.

"Uh-*huh,*" she said, sniffling.

"Good. Then go to Chicago and have a happy time with your friends."

50
SURPRISE!

Jack dragged his exhausted frame down the long hall to their bedroom in the dark. With Catherine in Chicago, the expensive house lights could stay off. It was a moonless night, darker than usual, but he could still shuffle and slide his way around the snoring dogs. Quite an evening it had been—one that, now, unfortunately, required forward planning. Since he had brushed his teeth that morning, all he had to do was hook his BlackBerry to the charger-cord and climb into bed. *Dormez bien.* Catherine had insisted on blowing her whole birthday wad on the 800 thread count Egyptian cotton sheets. They were going to feel good. He had burned a small cigar hole near the top of the fitted sheet while falling asleep last night. He'd tell Gerte to give it a one-eighty in the morning. No one would ever see it.

"Smoking in bed," Gerte will say with her usual arched eyebrow, as if this weren't his bed.

For now, he just wanted to calm his worried thoughts,

sleep, and get the death of the colored girl out of his mind. Tomorrow was another day. He wished he had renewed the security company contract when he left Zorox, but their fees had gone up. He cracked the window open an inch for fresh air. Coyotes in the back woods were bawling over which one would get the dark meat off some tragic animal carcass. With his bad hearing, he was missing the high-pitched chirping of the tree frogs, although he remembered how soothing they had been.

He stood smiling in the dark applying testosterone cream to his chest. Fluffy's head was nestled into Catherine's pillow. All lubed up, he plugged his phone in, as always. Its homepage brightened for a few seconds then dimmed. He set it down and yawned expansively, popping his wax-blocked ears and reached across the pillows to pull the top sheet down. It was crisply pressed by Gerte, fresh off the mangle. He tried to remember how pleasant the fragrance of clean linens had been.

He stretched his tired legs between the cool sheets and let his head sink in the downy soft pillow, feeling release. *"Ah,"* he uttered, expelling the last of a bad evening from his lungs, relaxing—until the evening's dilemma resurfaced with images of doomsday pitter-pattering like a circus elephant dancing a ballet on his chest. Getting back the death video would be critical.

Whenever Catherine was not home, Jack let Fluffy sack out on her pillow to nap till the early hours, when he went on midnight guard duty. Stroking the cat had a soothing effect, something that he needed badly tonight. He turned toward his brave feline sentry guard, patting the pillow for the silly furry head, letting go of his stress when he felt it. The warmth of one feline could provide more comfort than a woman's body ever would, he thought as he pulled Fluffy's furry head to his chest.

Something was *terribly* wrong. Fluffy's head felt so... *light*.

Jack's heart pounded as his fingers searched in panic for the kitty's torso.

Where in the hell was the rest of him?

He swiped the head away. "*Fluffy!*" he cried, horrified by the sound of the thud as it bounced on the floor. Bolting upright, he trembled alone in the dark. A dull sword could not have caused him more pain. The cat's head rolled to a stop. "*No!*"

51
FLUFFY, R.I.P.

"Gerte, when you say, 'Fluffy is *gone*,' what exactly do you mean? Catherine often got bad news from Gerte when she was out of town. "What—pray tell, does "*gone*" mean? To the vet, or for a walk?" The Peninsula's Bulgarian room-service waiter rolled her dining cart to the Michigan Avenue window and locked its brakes. He opened the warming cupboard pulling her order out. It smelled good. She was looking forward to enjoying a strong coffee with sizzling hot over-easies before meeting the mother of the bride in the lobby.

Maggie, her trusted friend, knew that she and Jack were having issues. Beyond that, Catherine did not know what to say. She lay in the buff between the sheets of the king-size bed, watching the waiter place a white linen cloth over the cart and transform it into her personal breakfast table. She wondered how she was going to hold the phone and sign the check without revealing any skin. Her bathrobe hung on hook of the bathroom door. She tucked the sheet under her chin for modesty's sake. She hadn't slept much during the night, and had been feeling cranky, even before Gerte called. And now, the usual. So much drama, so little time. Her esophagus twitched.

"Ja, Frau Henniger—well I'm getting one of my *special* feelings again. You do not understand my unworldly gift." There was more to Gerte's story. Catherine, cleared her throat from habit, waiting.

"I sense that Fluffy... *ist kaputt.*"

"Do you think that he has gone far?" Catherine asked to be polite.

"*Ach!* Like I told you, *Frau* Henniger, this one will not be coming back," Gerte said, using her "you are a schtoopid woman" tone.

"I heard you, but—" The smiling room service waiter held out the leather folder with the check. His gold canine tooth reminded her of, somebody. She nodded, added twenty percent, and signed the tab. Her hot coffee was waiting. She wanted Gerte to get to the point.

"Can you please be more specific? Is Fluffy missing, or what?" Catherine shifted impatiently on the bed.

"Okay, yes—my special sense tells me the cat is dead! I didn't want to upset you while you were on vacation," said the drama queen. Fluffy was probably sleeping under a bush somewhere; it was always something dramatic with Gerte.

"Dead, would be terrible, Gerte. What makes you say that? How do you know?"

"I just have a feeling that we will never see *Herr* Henniger's cat again."

"*Because...?*" Gerte was mouth-breathing over the

phone. She waited.

Gerte blurted with finality, "I found it, *Frau* Henniger! Well, *part* of it—"

Catherine gasped. "Gerte, what are you saying? *Where?*" Silence. "Hello? Where did you find the... ah... part?"

"*Ach*! Why, in *Herr* Henniger's humidor—I was in there dusting his boxes off, as I always do, because dusting is part of my job, you know—it was in with the Gloria Cubanas."

Catherine was aghast, it would be a rainy day in Kuwait before Gerte cleaned out Jack's wine cellar. The room service man closed the door, locking it with a click. Maybe the old girl had been down there filching a Cohiba for somebody's birthday, tipping the schnapps bottle while at it. The found part was probably one of Jack's dead squirrels, like the bushy-tailed one Jack was preserving in the freezer for a redneck joke. Surely it was something like that. Jack was doing odd things these days.

"You're sure."

"Well, the cat looked exactly like Fluffy from the shoulders down."

"What are you talking about?" Catherine's coffee was getting cold. "What about his facial markings?"

"*Frau* Henniger, really, how could I tell that if it was headless? The rest of its body was a perfect match for Fluffy, claws and all, I will tell you. Headless. It was grisly—which reminds me of—-"

"What did Mr. Henniger say?"

"Why, I haven't told him. That is for you to do. *You* are the wife."

Catherine rolled her eyeballs. It had to be another squirrel for the freezer. "Hmm. Well, what did you do with his... remains?"

"I gave them to Virgil to bury next to *Herr* Henniger's pot-bellied pig. We had a short service. But, on another subject, I am very upset, *Frau* Henniger. Your favorite Cutco knife is gone, too. I looked for it, I assure you."

"*What?*" Catherine kicked the sheet off. The Cutcos were her expensive personal knives; nice and sharp, and she wanted to keep them that way. "Look in the dishwasher. Someone keeps putting them there."

"I would never do that. Have a good time living it up with your friends in Chicago. Nothing to worry about here with me in charge."

52
GMO JACK AND THE ATTACK PIG

The delicious aroma of bacon and tempting breakfast dishes filled the hotel's expansive Lobby Restaurant, but after Gerte's call and the cold eggs benedict, Catherine's appetite was off. The head waiter nodded and showed her to a table next to a tall, sunny, window where Maggie was already digging into a spread of well-heaped buffet plates. She was full-figured—but not obese, as Jack often joked. "You look stressed," Catherine said. One should be able to say anything to best friends.

Maggie countered with a mouthful of scrambled eggs, "Well, you look like you haven't slept in days, and skinny. I ordered you some eggs." She aimed a forkful toward Catherine's mouth. "Here…have a bite of this sweet Italian sausage in cream sauce."

"Ah—no, thanks." Catherine managed a smile with closed lips. An invisible waiter removed a small dish of prune pits and the two extra place settings. He reset the remainder to perfection. She settled in and spread the napkin on her lap. The women looked each other over and sighed. They were two old friends with some personal ground to cover.

Maggie was right, her energy level was lower than whale droppings. Gerte's creepy cat news hadn't helped. Fluffy had despised the porcine pet. Catherine prayed a different cat was buried next to Piggywig. The waiter presented her egg plate without interrupting. She took a bite to be polite. She remembered when Jack had brought home the "so-called" Potbelly pig—a cute little piglet at the time. Ever public relations minded, he had proclaimed the miniaturized, corn-eating pet a photo-journalist's dream. The pig was to lend a homey insight into the lives of the rich and famous. The press would love the human-interest aspect, he insisted. GMO Jack would use his own air gun and nails to build an indoor litter box for his tiny indoor house pig; and train the pig to use it when she wasn't sleeping like an angel on his red Corinthian leather La-Z-Boy.

Jack, as she recalled, had pounded the first nail for the camera crew, but had made Virgil finish the big pine box. According to him, when Jack wasn't home, Gerte used her hunting dog remote to administer mild corrections to the pig's training collar. It was no wonder the animal had peed on the floor.

Piggywig, it turned out, resembled great-grandpig's side. Great, was *exactly* what she was after feeding on Jack's genetically modified corn. In less than three months, she had outgrown her knotty pine powder room.

Not only had she turned out to be huge with a super curly tail, but aggressive and mean. During one horrible

206 | DENISE LUTZ

feeding time when Catherine and Jack were away, Piggywig supposedly charged the terrified dogs, resulting in a lot of spilled blood. Gerte had called it a seizure and cleaned up the mess. But in truth, Virgil had used his .22 to finish Piggywig off; it was the one time Catherine had seen Jack cry. The pot belly breeder had ripped him off. Gerte, knowing how much Jack liked pulled-pork sandwiches, had suggested using Piggywig in the crock-pot; but Jack had respectfully declined.

Refocusing on the present, Catherine reached for a wide strip of bacon on Maggie's plate. "You'll like the luncheon room for the shower," she said, trying to be sparkly for Maggie. The wedding meant so much to her smiling friend. The two longtime friends had shared almost everything since young adulthood. The bride was Maggie's only daughter. Tiffany fell into the "difficult to like" category, as a rule, a little spoiled and moody. Maggie explained that the seamstress was in their room modifying the bridal gown to look more like Kate Middleton's. She and her husband were thrilled that Tiffany had finally found a man who could live with her temperment. "The room is a good size with gorgeous views. We have the Michigan *and* Superior corner." She took a sip of ice water to wash down the bacon.

"Tiffany will be so happy," Maggie said with pure delight.

"What are friends for? I have some pretty decorations for the room, gifts for everybody, and a fun surprise— you'll never guess. We have twelve guests, and the flowers are from Stems on Ashland." Catherine glanced at her watch. "I can't get in to decorate until eleven."

"We have time to talk. What's going on with Jack? I'm not leaving this seat until you tell."

53
MAGGIE WAGS
TIFFANY'S TALE

As Catherine talked, Maggie's expression became detached. "What, Maggie?" She stretched across the table to touch her friend's arm, swiping the butter dish with her own.

"Tiffany tried to tell us about him, and we wouldn't listen. Her eyes grew wide. "Catherine, your sleeve."

"Huh?" she said, rotating her sleeve around, discovering it. She had just bitten into a hard roll. They had very good bread at the hotel.

"Do you remember the nasty phase that she went through at fifteen?"

"Of course. Come on, Maggie, *what?* You must tell me." She felt a sudden stiffness in her neck. "Jack? But you never said anything."

"Chuck and I refused to believe her crazy story," Maggie plowed forward. "Why I never said anything? I was too embarrassed. She'd already told a few whoppers, melted my credit cards, pawned Chuck's gold coin collection and her grades were in the pits. She'd been sneaking out on school nights. We assumed that she was lying about Jack, too."

Catherine looked around the room while giving the twisted underwire on her La Perla bra a wiggle. She dreaded hearing the rest of this story.

"We had just grounded her when *it* came up, and had cut off her cell phone, put her on house arrest. She and her stepdad had a screaming match." Maggie lowered her voice to a whisper. "She crossed the line when she called him a 'prick.' Then, he called her a "miserable little bitch' and wailed on her." Maggie took a sip from her coffee cup, then set it down. "It was terrible!"

Catherine was happy that she hadn't had kids.

"After cleaning out my wallet," Maggie continued, "Tiffany ran off for a day and a half. We guessed she had taken the bus to the city from Winnetka. The bus, Catherine! We called her friends' parents, the few whom we knew. We asked our neighbors, called the school. Nothing. We were *beside* ourselves and had to involve the police. They found her at the art museum, of all places, sketching their replica of David," she lowered her eyes and voice, "on the elevator walls. Fortunately, the incident was forgotten." Catherine, placed her elbows on the table, listening with her head cupped in her hands.

"But what did she say about Jack?" Catherine asked, eyebrows furrowed. "Do you think he did something to her?"

"Yes, according to her story. And after what you've just shared—I finally believe her," she sobbed. "My poor little girl!"

Catherine fumed, feeling one of her bee-sting head-aches strike. Her friend didn't know the half of it, she thought, "I'm horrified, Maggie." The breakfast crowd in the elegant dining room thinned.

"She has never forgiven me for not believing her," Maggie said with pain in her voice. Real anger penetrat-ed her face. "Your husband changed our family dynamics forever. And for *you*—" her voice trailed off.

Catherine took a long breath.

Maggie said, "You remember the night Jack spoke for J.R. Henniger at the Convention Center, the Harvard Business School's annual Leadership Dinner. You had invited us to sit at your table."

Catherine did recall the awards ceremony. Jack, the keynote speaker, had returned from the men's room late, keeping six hundred people waiting for him to go on. When he had slipped back in his seat smelling like cigars, she had figured he had been trapped by an admirer.

"Slow flow," he had shared in his usual hoarse whisper.

Maggie went on. "I'll admit that Tiffany was a true *bratinella*. We'd dragged her there against her will and she was missing the MTV Music Awards on TV. We were going pay."

Catherine smiled weakly and nodded. "Who could forget that night." She felt another head stab—the new headaches were doozies. "Jack made a scene with the wait staff over the leftovers." She let out a tiny laugh. "The overdone filets were not a favorite with the crowd and Jack was furious when the server "forgot" to bring a doggy bag to pass around the table. He hated to let all that meat go to waste. The dogs and pig were counting on him to bring home the evening's kill."

"I'll bet the guests at the closest tables remember his meltdown."

Jack, boozed and in a hissy fit, had summoned the manager, griping that his lazy waiter didn't give a rat's ass about the guest of honor, his pig and six dogs. "Health laws," the manager had fired back.

Jack had grown belligerent, and she had wanted to crawl under the table. "Our guests were squirming like worms in their chairs." The conversation nearby had stopped to listen to the brouhaha.

Catherine remembered feeling ashamed. Jack was angry at her that night, sullen and incommunicado as the driver motored them home. He had texted nonstop, leaving her to feel like a bag of dog scraps herself.

Maggie shook her head. "Do you recall when Tiffany vanished about halfway through dinner to go to ladies' room? Her food was cold."

"Maggie," Catherine asked, picking at a hangnail, "did Jack do something to her before dinner?"

"Yes—if you call offering money to a minor, *something*." Catherine shuddered. Maggie dabbed a tear.

"As her story went, the two of them ended up in a stairwell together. He asked her if she smoked cigars. She lied, of course. He lit one, puffed a few smoke rings, and handed it to her for a toke. You know how she takes after me, a little on the pudgy side?"

Catherine nodded, trying to not overreact.

"He called her hot, Catherine. *Hot.*" Maggie had a troubled look. And she felt grown up, special when he told her, 'It's unusual for a woman of fifteen to have such a high degree of intelligence. You intrigue me. Will you be my 'secret' friend?' Next thing, he was handing her three hundred bucks to spend on her first cell phone, and he—"

"*What?*" Catherine leaned forward in her chair, wanting to know, but she didn't.

"When he unzipped his pants and laid out the old *bug catcher!*"

Catherine gulped.

"Tiff was appalled! She threw his dirty money down the stairwell and ran." Catherine noted that her goddaughter's mental health had meant three hundred dollars to the jerk.

"Tiff spent the whole evening holed up in the ladies' room, afraid to return to the table to see Jack. We were worried about her at first, but then we became furious, if you recall. We accused her of making the whole thing up, an excuse to skip out of our boring, grown-up party. What made me the angriest was that my immature fifteen-year-old child would attack the reputation of a successful industrialist, my dearest friend's husband." Maggie's lips quivered and she leaned back. "But for once, don't you see? Tiffany was trying to tell us the truth."

"Trust me, Maggie, Tiffany was not his last," Catherine said feeling a strange coolness come over her. Putting on her reading glasses, she signed the check, more desperate than ever to talk to Ben.

54
THE POLE A
BARE LOUNGE

The Pole A Bare's ebony ceiling and walls made Juno
Fontana think of cocktails, even while eating lunch.
As far as the food in strip joints went, the menu at the club
was good, Italian. A deep cloud of smoke hung from the
ceiling, sliced by bright, strategically placed stage lights.
Juno sat on a plain metal chair, enjoying a Super Slider
with onions. His partner, Viktor Cappellina—or Viktoria,
depending on the day's hormone level—was feeling
feminine today. She was slathering French's mustard on
her foot-long hot dog. She was a refrigerator-shaped
woman with large, veined hands and curly red hair that
tumbled messily around her shoulders. She looked like a
tugboat captain to Juno, who looked like a weightlifter,
himself.

The two professional killers were rewarding themselves with a hearty meal after spending the morning
dumping the runaway's body in a mucky fresh-plowed
corn field. The girl's unfortunate death occurred during
the shooting of the new porn film Richie Zabaglione

was planning on entering in the Columbian Blue Light Film Festival. Word was things got out of control when the director shouted cut. The movie featured the Pole A Bare dancers and Pussi's eighty-year-old benefactor and had ended up good for Zabaglione, who had figured out a new blackmailing scheme using prominent men and immigrant sex slaves.

"Nice place, huh?" Viktoria said. The new venue, just opened, was the latest addition to Zabaglione's Baxter Township strip clubs. The music playing was playing a tune by Doo Doo Brown, *I Wanna Rock,* one of Viktoria's favorites. She did a drum tap on the table with her gorilla-sized hands.

"Yeah, beautiful," Juno said. His eyes were on a dancer swaying toward him. He hoped she would choose him for a lap dance. It was gonna cost him twenty bucks. He pulled out his phone to get to his money clip.

"Hey, keep your fucking phone in your pocket, dildo. No pictures. Somebody will see you." Viktoria said, motioning to a side stage where Brenda, Zabaglione's bombshell brunette of a wife was auditioning new girls for the show. "Richie would punish you."

"Shut the fuck up, bonehead—I ain't taking pictures. I need some money for the lap dancer. I'm gonna stick it in her thong." He grimaced. "I'm out. Got any twenties?"

"I'll look." She-he dug in her purse. "Nope. Anyway, Vinny's the one who owes you money. Why don't you get it from him, wise guy?"

"When I see him, I'm gonna toast that loser for it," Juno said. The girl was coming on to him like he was catnip. "He told me he needed a chainsaw to speed up his clean ups, to help him fit his stiffs in tighter places. I gave him the money." He took a good look around the smoky, dark place, not seeing him.

"Where did that motherfucker go?"

"To the county jail," Viktoria fussed with her hair, "to bail Pussi out."

"*Another* DUI?" Juno asked, stuffing his empty money clip back in his pocket; the stripper moved on.

Viktoria said, "Naw, the camera at Liquor Barn caught her pinching booze, slipping a bottle of Moscato inside that big raccoon coat of hers."

"The one with the giant pockets sewed inside? I seen it. Handy for shoplifting, doing crowds. I like Moscato, don't you?"

"No, Juno. I hate sweet wine—and in the summer, a fur coat is wrong."

"Well, listen to the fashion maven," Juno said. "And let me tell you—for scrubbing blood out of that Escalade, your silk dress and high heels aren't right either."

"You'll have to do it, honey. I'm not splattering my best dress with bleach. I've already wrecked my heels."

55

ATTORNEY REVISITS
THE BAR

"It's great to have you back, man," said Harlan Jones as he filled Ben's glass with St. Pauli girl from a pitcher. The popular sports bar had a bustling after-work crowd. It was a short walk for Ben from the courthouse. The walls inside were festooned by glowing television screens. There was plenty of conversation, laughter, and color. People blowing off steam.

Harlan was Ben's buddy and handball partner. He watched to make sure that Harlan, the landscaper, didn't poke an unmanicured finger through the foam. A few months of therapy, meds and R and R had helped to patch Ben's broken heart.

Now, a year later, Ben felt back on his game, at least professionally.

"A healthy guy like you ought to start making the dating scene." The two other guys out with them nodded in agreement, while observing a couple of attractive court reporters select their bar stools with their eyes locked on Ben. *There he goes again.*

Harlan meant well. He was a hulk-framed, well-stacked guy about Ben's age, mid-forties. Thanks to his old friends from college, the failed law student had made it in lawn and garden. He was a "man's man" beyond a doubt.

Ben didn't consider himself to br clever, or especially good-looking, although he strove to stay fit in the physical, spiritual, and mental sense. His wife would say how he was the kind of man that both women and men noticed. It was his positive bearing, a certain sense of self confidence, she would add. And that the courtroom ladies swooned over his English suits, serious ties and tortoise-shell reading glasses and that their furtive feminine glances had filled the courtroom. She had loved the innocent way that he had seemed unaware of his fans and had further proved her confidence in his love by buying him the killer club ties.

Harlan interrupted his thoughts to badger him until he blushed. "Breaking news: Attorney uses good looks to win case. Today, in Judge Allison Gilbert's courtroom, eyes dilated when Attorney Ben Williams stood before the bench making David Gandy moves with his thumbs in his belt loops."

Ben preferred to think his success had come from treating the clients' problems as his own. He'd been thinking a great deal about Catherine's situation lately.

"You're predators. You don't have a clue, he told them, growing serious. "It's scary taking new chances after losing someone you love."

"Oooh, *scary!*" teased his buddies, feeling their beer.

"It takes time," he continued, feeling a little red in the

face. "I need a woman with depth." The other guys' attention had turned to a Cardinals-Brewers game. "It's complicated," he said to Harlan.

"I'm concerned you are falling over the celibate edge, my friend."

Ben defended himself. "It takes work to break through the surface with a woman. I haven't felt much like it." He scratched an itch on his scalp. *Up to now.* "I've had some 'just lunch' dates and I occasionally run into an interesting woman through work." Ben dabbed his mouth and put his napkin back on his lap. He had a little pride. "I wouldn't mind getting to know one of them better," he said, thinking of Catherine. "A client. An elegant blonde, but she's married."

Harlan, who liked blondes, but preferred brunettes and tomboy types, leaned forward, listening. The guys passed the pitcher around. There was a car commercial on for Volvo.

"Swedish?"

"I don't know, Harlan," Ben said, visualizing Catherine in his office. "She's easy to talk to." He laughed, looking at him. "You wouldn't care about that."

"She's married?"

"Not happily, but you know how I stand on that point," he said, tipping his mug. "I handled her previous divorce years ago. Since then, estate and family issues."

A short-skirted waitperson with a tattooed heart on her shoulder flashed a frisky smile at the men and set the bill between them. Harlan accidentally touched her thigh, without losing eye contact with Ben, who was picking up the tab.

"Free advice sucks, but maybe your client could use a 'go to' guy. She needs to go out and get laid!" The guys laughed. Harlan patted Ben on the back.

Ben shifted on his stool, straining to converse over the pub clatter. " She's a nice person—with money, society, fame, and talent. Besides, she has been devoted to her husband." He took a breath. "Well, up to now, anyway. A powerful public guy—and an old asshole!"

Harlan allowed a gassy burp to escape. Interested. "Who's that, Jack Henniger?" Ben sat up and dabbed his mouth, took a glance at the baseball game.

"Hey," one of the other guys butted in, "somebody say Jack Henniger? My dad, *hell*— my *grandpa,* worked for Henniger Chemical. Met him myself once on a summer job in their lab. He seemed down to earth with us commoners and a ladies' man—*woohoo!* Harlan, you're the landscaping professional—you've got old Henniger to thank for your profitable green lawns."

Ben completed his train of thought. "I'm not mentioning names, but she's taken plenty of crap from him. It's been painful to watch him break her spirit," he told the guys, surprised by his feelings.

56
NOT THE RED ROOF INN

Jack's rare call could not have come at a worse time, five-thirty. The wedding was at six. Catherine's limo was leaving at quarter to six for the First Fourth Presbyterian.

"No one has heard from you," he said, his voice making her think of flies that burrow under skin to lay eggs. She couldn't let on that she knew, any of it, if she wanted to come out of the inferno intact. "Having a good time?" He cleared his throat—too much smoking. "Still in ORD, right?"

"Jack, hello," she said, sticky sweet, with one hand struggling with the zipper of her new lavender dress. She hoped her bra straps wouldn't show. "I can't talk now, I'm getting picked up for the wedding in a few."

"Just wondering when you'll be back."

Something in his voice said he was about to get in trouble. Sneaky Jack was double checking that she wasn't on her way home from the airport. Knowing that he had wisened up after the hot tub, Catherine had removed her itinerary from his desk before leaving for Chicago. *Let him wonder.* Tonight was the well-anticipated "group grope," according to Pussi's text.

"How's the hotel?" he asked. "Red Roof, right?"

Holding the phone, she tugged on the zipper. Up it went, but stopped mid-back, it wouldn't move up or down. "I'm fine, staying at the Peninsula, where my luncheon was."

"Kind of expensive, isn't it? I wish you'd told me, Catherine. I have coupons for the Best Western. Stay three nights, and the first one's on them. Breakfast, all you can eat. You'd enjoy it." No, I wouldn't, she thought, wondering how he would know what kind of breakfast they served.

"Look, Jack, if I don't get the zipper unstuck in five minutes, I'll have to go to the wedding with my dress hanging half open. I can't get it off."

"Hah?" he rasped. "Get some scissors from room service."

"Sure...right. Thanks, Jack, I hadn't thought of cutting myself out of the dress. I can wear my gym clothes to the church."

Jack, ignoring her, asked in an innocent tone. "How does Tiffany look these days? Is she still as large-breasted, or has she fixed them, yet? Give her a hug from her old friend Jack."

"I sure will. Give Fluffy a big kiss from me."

57
BILLY REDD AND VIRGIL

It was a soupy summer evening, and the heat waves were rising off the tractor. Virgil felt limp after the long day of cutting and tedding alfalfa, but was happy to put the Ford 800 in the implement shed and call it a night. He had pushed himself to finish the tedding, because rain was coming the day after next. He would rake tomorrow, and get the hay bales in the barn before they got wet. He would need help tossing the fifty-five pounders on the trailer before they could be stacked in the barn. If he couldn't beat the rain, he'd have to sell the hay to the neighbor as forage for his cows and the Hennigers would have to pay full price to buy somebody else's bales for the horses. Mr. H would go nuclear. Virgil idled the spitting tractor engine in front of the barn and jumped off. He opened the sliding barn doors and brushed off the alfalfa that clung to his weathered face, T-shirt, and jeans.

He looked forward to taking a good shower and watching TV. He dropped his cigarette and ground out the butt with his work boot, then picked it up and added it to the others in his pocket. He flattened a mosquito that was dancing on his neck, and wiped their mutual blood on his sweat-logged blue jeans. Killing bugs was what bats were for, and there were plenty of them diving for their dinner on a hot night like this. His own dinner, would be a Swanson Salisbury Steak and a Michelina Fetticine Alfredo.

The florescent lights were on in Mr. H's car barn. They were bright but needed to be. Mrs. H had saved the big shade trees when she had built the garage for her husband for his 75th birthday. The metal building stored Mr. H's old cars, twelve or so fast ones that Virgil's dear momma would have remembered from her movie-star magazines. Virgil noticed movement inside a window from where he stood thirty feet away. Billy Redd, the new guy, was in there working, he guessed. Both buildings were on the riverbank by the fox den, not far from the bridge that took folks to the back eighty acres and rear entrance. It was after seven o'clock, with the frogs already chirping. Mr. H had driven off hours ago, to a videotaping session, or something like that. Mrs. H was away in Chicago. Nobody else was home.

If he could catch Billy, he might snag him for help with the bales.

A ten-year-old pink Lexis was parked in front of the garage. Hitched to it, was the useful flatbed trailer that he would need for hauling hay. He had been too busy mowing the hay field earlier to notice the pink car in the drive. He scratched at a mosquito bite. That Lexus, he knew, couldn't haul more than a motorcycle with its low-output engine. The dew had come in with the evening, slowing the flight of the bugs. It had also left a sheen of night dew on the Lexus's trunk. Its engine was running. The windows were tinted dark. He could not see the driver, who was no doubt, staying cool.

He walked past the car and trailer to the garage's side door and opened it. Inside, was Billy, pushing a case of 30-weight motor oil and a six-pack of beer on a floor jack across the concrete. Billy looked at him and stopped. He was a sneaky, scrawny kid.

"What the hell are you up to?" Virgil asked, honked. The cold beer bottles were pearling with sweat from the heat. "I need this trailer tomorrow 'cause if I don't get my hay in, it'll be wrecked. What the fuck are you doing with it?"

Billy spat. "Hey man, Mr. H said I could use his shit for Serena. She's moving out of her apartment and needs the trailer for her living room set. You'll get it back, old man. Have a beer."

"No, thanks. Did Mr. H give you the 10W30, too?" he asked, pointing to the very oil he needed for the 800 tomorrow. Billy was Vincent Puziari's nephew. Virgil had seen Billy's type before—a fast talker who needed a job. Mr. H had taken him on when he bragged about detailing cars. He was an ex-con if he ever saw one. His tattoos were the size of his Aunt Pussi's. Oddly today, the cashier at the corner market had asked him when Billy would pay her for the groceries that she had let him take last week. He worked for Henniger, she had figured he was good for it. That was the last she had seen of Billy, who owed him twenty bucks, too. He scowled at Billy.

"I'm doing an oil change on Serena's Lexus. She's leaving for Guadalajara to see family. That's her new car, it just needs a little work. It's only a few bottles, man. His fridge is full of beer."

He worried about Mrs. H being alone on the huge estate at night with a felon running loose. But he didn't want to make waves, he needed his job too bad. "You're working late," he said and coughed. He would ask somebody else to help.

"I'm cleaning cars. There's mold on the leather."

Virgil did some math in his head. "His cars are worth something, you know."

"Oh, yeah," Billy said with a twinkle in his eyes. He laid his hand on the little MGB-TC positioned close to the door. "This one has to be worth a half million."

Virgil's stomach growled. "Don't stay too late," he with an uneasy feeling. But then, it was Mr. H's business, not his.

58
CHEESE PUFFS

Catherine double-checked her ticket and settled into 13B on the MD80 flight to St. Louis. The wedding would have been perfect had it not been for the painful duet of *"Every Breath You Take,"* sung by the newlyweds. The bridesmaids' luncheon had been a success, especially with the stripping waiter. She was glad to have been there for Maggie. Their conversations had been educational, especially with what lay ahead. Thinking of Jack made her remember the addiction counselor that she had been trying to reach.

She pulled the Toste book from her purse, hoping to finish his chapter on chronic cheaters. Her Prada purse was a rip-off, but still a magnet for snatchers. She put it inside her larger Ferragamo tote and confirmed that all was properly stowed under the middle seat in front of her.

Her row mate to the right was a wheezing heavyset middle-aged white guy wearing a green and yellow John Deere tractor hat, who could never reach her purse. He made a sound like a weightlifter at the gym as he struggled to slide open the window sash. There wasn't much other than the steady rain to see. He pulled a gyro sandwich from a paper Quiznos sack. She faced forward, watching from the corner of her eye as he organized his tray table with a large Mountain Dew and jumbo bag of orange Cheese Puffs. She didn't mind going Economy, it pleased Jack. But after hearing Maggie's story, she should have been sipping a Chardonnay in a wide leather seat in First Class.

Behind her, two young men praising Allah, were banging their knees on the back of her seat.

John Deere ripped open his Cheese Puffs and generously offered her one. She shook her head as her cell phone rang. The addiction counselor, who she had tried several times. Being careful not to tip over the large Mountain Dew, she wiggled her fingers inside her tote to get to her ringing phone. A few straggling passengers filed noisily down the aisle and got themselves situated.

"Hello?" she said, noting his number while taking a deep breath of insecticidal air.

"Hey," the voice said, hesitating a second or two. The connection was bad. "It's Lonny McQueen, returning your call." His voice was hazy, very relaxed.

"Dr. McQueen, you don't know how relieved I am to hear from you," she said. Either some smart Alec was repeating every word, or it was one of those echoey calls. The plane's PA dinged, and the captain's voice asked for all electronic devices to be shut down. She would make the call fast.

His voice was low and gritty, a smoker. "Call me Lonny, okay?" He was hard to hear. "Yeah, sorry about that. I had to take my Scooter in for a tune-up. What can I do for you, baby?"

A woman in her thirties in a tidy business suit and sensible shoes set her laptop on the seat to her left. She hoisted her carry-on into the overhead compartment.

"I, uh...need to talk with you about sex, ah...deviants," she said with her lips touching the phone and her eyes shifting left and right. The echo on the call was throwing her off. "I heard you handle the *really* bad cases."

John Deere's hand froze inside the Cheese Puff bag.

"McQueen's the name, addiction's the game," Lonny said. "I see 'em all. Alkies, druggies, pornies, nosepickers. You name it, whatever ya' can't stop doing," Lonny said, chortling. The guy sounded like her man.

"Please," she begged. "Nose picking is a minor issue; my biggest problem is sex addiction."

"Each case is unique, ya' know." This guy knew his material. "Your voicemail said you were worried about your hubby. While there's always hope for a partial cure, baby, the recidivism rate for that is high. Your addict must want to stop."

"Excuse me," she shouted, "The connection is terrible, you have to speak up."

"It would help if I had specifics. What worries you the most?" The lady on her left seemed to be bending an ear her way. The two guys behind her were yucking it up, projectile coughing.

"Hmm…it's so hard." she said, speaking up, letting it out. "Child molesting, I guess. S&M, sexual device hoarding, some unconventional, as you might expect." She wanted Lonny to know it all. "Doctor, I need help."

The guy next to her took a large bite from his gyro and wiped off some yogurt sauce with the back of his hand. He gave her a slow, dirty grin. She covered her knee with her skirt.

"Good," Lonny encouraged, "tell me more." The woman next to Catherine rudely yanked her elbow from their mutual arm rest, crossed her right leg over her left and stared up the aisle.

Finding that talking about it wasn't as hard as she had thought, Catherine continued. "I've lost count of the infidelities. Of course, the obsessive pornography, masturbation, and ah… group sex." She sighed. "It feels good to get this off my shoulders. I guess that just about covers it."

"*Whoo*-ee—it sounds like you've got yourself a cowboy, Cath! *Yahoo!*" Lonny seemed excited about the case.

"Doctor, it has to stop, or I'll do something I'll regret," she begged. "Please be the answer to my prayers!"

The snarly Economy Class attendant had made her way up the aisle with eyes that burned holes in soft tissue. "It's time to shut it down," Cruella ordered. "Or your ringy-dingy will go *bon voyage.*"

59
DUNKIN' DONUTS

"Forget your raise, Dubrowski," said Grey Day, taking a bite from a raspberry crème-filled donut. Day was a fit man of about forty, with slightly protruding ears. "You heard the sheriff, the recent crime is our fault." Lieutenant Detective Grey and Sergeant Leon Dubrowski were discussing what to do over coffee at the Dunkin' Donuts counter. Dubrowski, like usual, needed a shave.

The election was coming soon. Lately, Mayor Womble's crime map had been smattered with yellow dots. Baxter City was looking more like a spilled bag of buttered popcorn than a safe, exo-suburban tax magnet, whose votes he needed for re-election. He had been cranking up the heat on Sheriff Nixon for his department to self-correct. The extra help they needed was not in the budget.

Dubrowski and Day had hoped to move up in the department this year. But with the recent increase in murders, assaults, and arson, they dared not bring up a promotion. If their department failed to land a big one before the election, they would be filling out online job applications soon. Nixon had made that clear as a siren. Baxter's two-fold rise in crime coincided with St. Louis's spillover of gangs and illegals—the increase was, in fact, so bad that the regular felons had been rushing to Baxter County so they could live and work in a safe environment. Because not many county businesses outside of waste management and the strip clubs took a chance on ex-cons, there was a tendency for the crooks to resort to illegal means of support.

"I'm more concerned with what the Zabagliones may have up their sleeves," Day said. "With Pole A Bare open, they have three strip clubs in the county. Wombles is as tired of hearing about the underage dancers and sex trafficking as he is about their drug deals and armed robberies. He doesn't want the rest of the public to know how bad it's getting."

"We're not the quiet farming community we used to be. We could use some new muscle." Dubrowksi set his empty cup down for a refill, his eyes focused on something outside.

"Take a look—there's pa-part of our pa-pa-problem," he said, they both stifled their laughs, making fun of stutterers was bad for morale. Deputy Clarence Peters rolled his patrol car into the lot off Main and parked. They watched the older officer, a man much on the hefty side, wrestle out of his patrol car and enter the donut shop. He removed the cover from his head and hurried straight toward the Men's room, nodding as he passed.

"What we need around here is less dead weight," Dubrowski whispered.

"That's what I mean," said Day. "It's about time Peters hung it up. All he does anymore is ticket jaywalkers and pick up speeders along with his paycheck."

60
CRUELLA THE COLDHEARTED

As Catherine's plane inched through the downpour toward the gate, she watched a long line of planes waiting to take off through a window across the aisle.

Lambert-St. Louis Approach had kept them cycling their flaps in a twenty-minute hold. A confused private pilot had landed his small plane on the parallel taxi strip, wheels up. The passengers had not been allowed to budge from their seats. With the plane circling in wind gusts, she had somehow made a run to the lavatory with the seatbelt sign on and was about to step into the placemat-sized head when Cruella the Coldhearted Economy Class attendant spotted her from her crew seat, where she sat with a salad on her lap, chatting with the Business Class steward. Cruella set aside her lunch and rose, phone in hand, citing an FAA regulation about seat belts. Catherine, bobbing up and down with her knees locked, had pleaded, "Emergency!" Several concerned heads had turned to watch Cruella approach Catherine like an animal trapper. "Get back in 13B," she fired from her lipless mouth. "Or else."

234 | DENISE LUTZ

Catherine made an obedient one-eighty and tapped the sleeping passenger in 13C. Unable to wake her, she had been forced to navigate around the tray table, knocking the Mountain Dew on her seat.

Jack's new admin had hired a black car for her. He was somewhere on business with his new personal driver. All Catherine had to do was look for a sign marked Henniger outside baggage claim.

"Which door?" she had asked Darla McPhoy, the new assistant, who hadn't traveled much.

"Opposite the carousel." There were fifteen.

The ground crew opened the exit door to the ramp and the passengers ahead of her started moving like slugs at a slugfest.

Her carry on, heavy as a cinder block, had shifted to the back of the overhead bin and crushed her good Burberry trench coat. She stretched on her tiptoes, hoping for a helping hand. If she were only a little taller, she could pull it out. John Deere kicked his trash under the seat and collected his belongings.

As the first-class passengers inched closer to the exit, the two guys in back advanced themselves in the battle against inertia, pressing her ahead of her bin. Extending her torso to its max, she stretched behind her to reach her things, while Mr. Deere extruded himself from row 13, delighted to be of help. His scratchy hand wandered up her skirt, giving her butt a squeeze. Jumping high, she reached her bag, and punched him in the gut with it on her way down, impaling his foot above the top of his dirty sneaker with her four-inch-high heel.

"I've been bad. *Punish me!!*" he said, burping up his gyro's onions, grinning as the passengers cleared the aircraft. His teary eyes blinked with desire.

Cruella flashed a wicked smile. "Glad you enjoyed your flight. Thank you for flying the friendly skies." Catherine disembarked and hobbled down the ramp to the Ladies' Room ahead of Mr. Deere, who limped in hot pursuit behind her.

Peeking out from the restroom minutes later, she was surprised to see a man holding a sign with her name on it, obviously the driver that Darla had ordered. Somehow, he looked familiar, yet she could not quite place him. Jack had likely used him as a driver before, she decided. His olive-toned complexion was deeply pock-marked. His long black hair was slicked neatly back. He wore expensive looking shoes and a well-cut suit made from shiny fabric.

"Need a ride, Mrs. Henniger?" he asked, coolly reaching for her carry-on. He wore a gold pinky ring with a diamond. Everyone had a story. She wondered about his.

"I'm so glad you're here!"

61
A KILLER RIDE

Catherine rode down the escalator, her driver a step below, his eyes straight ahead. Hers eyes were on the four-inch scar on his neck which was ugly enough to make her knees tingle. It ran side to side across his neck. Pehaps a battle wound, or perhaps, bad plastic surgery— certain questions, a lady didn't ask. Catherine tapped the dirty rubber rail for balance. Her heavy tote bag dug into her other shoulder and slipped off her arm. The smarmy man stepped from the escalator, and she followed.

"So, you had a good time in Chicago, Mrs. Henniger," he said without using facial expressions. The hatch to the large baggage claim area dinged. It opened with a kerchunk, and the belt began to move. She felt icky when his hand touched the small of her back. He guided her through the passengers and their roller bags to the belt. "You went alone, eh?"

"Ah, very nice, yes, thank you," she said, juggling her shoulder strap while twisting away from his hand. "I attended a friend's wedding." She felt off-kilter with this man. There was something about him that wasn't right; his forwardness—the unwelcome touch. She shook the feeling off. But he did seem polite, and she was grateful for the ride.

"There," Catherine said, relieved. She pointed to a scruffy set gliding toward them on the belt. "The bags with the striped neckties tied around the handles are mine." His steely eyes looked up at her intently. There was nothing about his face she liked. She nodded anyway. "Caution, many bags look alike," she said, failing at sounding jaunty. She rolled her wedding band with her thumb, preparing for the confrontation with Jack. It was late and he would be home by now.

"What are the red and green paper clips for?" her driver asked.

"My husband attaches them when the zipper pulls fall off," she answered, pointing. "The colors match the ties." She could feel her face flush. "It works."

The driver reached for her two heavy cases and set them down, examining their ties before he rolled them toward the door. "Stay here," he ordered. "I'll pull the car up front first." She formed a question mark with her hands. "It's a black Chrysler," he said, taking her tote. "Look for me."

62
DETOUR TO THE COUNTRY

The driver sprayed rain puddle roostertails as he pulled his Chrysler 300 up to the baggage claim. His headlights cha-cha'd hieroglyphics on the brim filled potholes. He opened the back door, muttering something impatient. He had waited a long time for her tonight, but wasn't that part of a limo driver's life? It was too bad he was getting wet, but the weather was not her fault—professional drivers keep umbrellas in their trunks. She stepped into a cold two-inch puddle and climbed in, her shoes as soaked as her hair and silk suit. She kicked them off.

Reading the time on her watch was futile without her glasses. They were in the tote bag on the front seat. She patted her frizzing hair.

Her aching calf muscles would be worse tomorrow after her one heeled quarter-mile jaunt from Gate 4. She sank into the Chrysler's thick leather seat and released the world's longest day from her lungs.

The doors locked with a solid kerchunk, and the driver

drove on. Paying vague attention, she noticed that instead of the usual ramp to Ladue, he chose an odd exit, which before long, turned into a dimly lit road. A short-cut. She hoped he knew where he was going. The rain continued to fall hard. She hoped he could see better than she could. The windshield wipers shuffled off rain as fast as they could. She would have pulled over by now. She brushed the water off her wrinkled trench coat and pushed her shoes under the seat with the balls of her feet which were tender from the day.

A heavy scent of watermelon air freshener clung in the car, worsening her headache. Cracking the window an inch would help. She toggled the window control, finding, with mild irritation that the child lock was on. She pinched her lips together. *Just one breath of fresh air.* The driver's noisy defroster fan was blasting.

She tried to catch his attention. "Hello?" She said and cleared her throat. *"Hello?"* she repeated, upping her volume a notch, but gaining no response.

It was dark without lights, way out wherever they were, a long way from town. She pressed her nose against the cool window, trying to calm her nerves. She could check the weather and catch up on the news; take her mind off her fear of seeing Jack. She felt the seat bench for her bag, and the floor next to her shoes. Nothing. Her heart sank an inch in a moment of panic, maybe she had left it in the terminal.

She felt the seat bench for her bag, and the floor next to her shoes. Her heart sank in a moment of panic, thinking she had left it in the terminal.

Then she remembered. The driver had taken it from her at the baggage claim and put it safely up front with the tote. Breathing a sigh of relief, she looked out the windshield. There was still no traffic on their road.

"The weather's awful," she shouted, making conversation. "My flight was delayed in Chicago. Scores of planes were already backed up by the weather when a private pilot making a go-around forgot to put his wheels back down."

Again, there was no response up front. She did not like this man.

"We must have circled for an extra half hour," she continued. Still, the man did not answer. Maybe he wasn't the type for small talk or couldn't hear with the radio on. It was opera, an interesting choice.

He was possibly Italian.

But one thing was sure. He was focused on the set of taillights ahead. He added speed, rapidly closing the gap. She picked away at her cuticles, thinking about the scar on his neck. Their car was moving up on the sedan, fast now—*too* fast, and was almost touching nose to tail. He was nodding his head, blotting a runny nose with the back of his hand. Why would he want to follow that close? She desperately wanted out.

Looking ahead, behind, and to the sides, there was nothing but darkness. Clenching her stomach, she stomped on an imaginary brake with her bare right foot. Two cars passed that she wished she could flag. There was no one else on the road but their car and the sedan ahead, now starting to slow. Her driver moved up on the sedan and laid on his horn as he slammed on the brake, hard enough to throw her head and upper body forward, shocking her. He yanked their car off to the shoulder and rolled it to a gravel-scattering stop. The sedan ahead did the same. Two black cars, in the middle of nowhere. Something was terribly wrong; soundless, except for the Pucini playing. Her driver was a maniac. What could the other car have to do with them?

"So," she asked, her heart picking up as she tried for light conversation, "have you worked for this limo service long?" Her driver flicked on his courtesy lights and turned his upper torso to look at her, his black eyes, penetrating. His facial expression was ugly, menacing. The lights inside the car ahead went on. Two men got out, and now were walking towards them. Her palms felt clammy.

"You know I'm not a limo driver, Mrs. Henniger," he said, sending a chill up her spine.

She felt her good high heel on the floor. A sharp blow between his eyes could save her life. Her heart pounded. "I'm sorry, I didn't get your name."

"Oh, geeze, Mrs. Big One, I thought you would remember. You and me go way back through your husband, my wife. You have deeply offended my feelings." His voice was crude, rough. She knew this man, all right. Her situation was now painfully clear.

"You are *Vincent*," she said with a trembling voice.

"Very good, your memory is back. You are too young and pretty to lose your brain," he coughed, "or any other part." His gold front tooth glinted with the yellow glow of the dome light. He chuckled cruelly. "I'll bet you won't forget my face again." She gripped her good shoe by the heel.

Vincent waved off the men. Obeying, they returned to their car. He turned to her.

"You and me's about to get to know each other *real* good."

63
TAKE ME HOME, COUNTRY ROAD

The ride home was long. But there was nothing left to say; besides, she was too frightened to speak. She was grateful he wasn't talking. The Pucini had been followed by a gramophone recording of *La Traviata* played the archaic hit filling the space of the Chrysler 300 with Pauline Donato, warbling her tragic fate as the "fallen" woman, Violetta. Vincent's back up, the men in the other black sedan, were doing some serious tailgating. She rode with her eyes closed tightly, eventually recognizing the road surfaces and stops, relieved that they were *en route* to the estate.

Vincent slowed as he finally approached their gate. The rain had fizzled down to a drizzle. He carefully positioned the car as close to the call box as he could without scalping his side mirror.

She was almost home, but would he let her go?

The hangnail she had been rocking with her front teeth hurt more than expected when she pulled it free. She picked her other fingers over, thinking—praying that he would let her go, hoping that this would be one of those Soprano-style warnings where the victim could stay alive if she agreed to play along.

Vincent had been clear about the rules. By Friday, he wanted a million dollars for an embarrassing and legally incriminating video. Would she cooperate he had wanted to know, and she had begged him to let her go. What if he took her into the house to murder in front of Jack?

"What makes you think my husband would care if you killed me?" she asked him boldly, striking a chord. Vincent grunted.

It was 2:00 a.m., foggy and moonless. The quiet estate looked eerie through her child-proofed window. If only she had more information. If Vinny let her go, she could grab Jack's BlackBerry and leave with her bags in her own car, go to a motel, call Ben in the morning. Or she could face the music and go in, hiss Vincent's demand to Jack. But she wasn't safe, yet.

Vinny lowered his window and reached for the call box; he turned, gave her a look, his eyes, black and vacant. She glared at him, hesitating to give him the access code, the default. Nobody since Pussi had known how to change it. But Vinny was no stranger here. He groaned and stretched his fingers out to the keypad, making the speaker beep.

"Enter access code," the digitalized voice ordered. Vinny pressed, *one, two, three, four.* "Access granted," the call box confirmed, and the big brown gate opened slowly. Catherine shivered, ready to run through the woods, if necessary.

64
THE DROP

The rain came down harder as the Chrysler rolled to a stop by the door under the deck. The driveway and garden lights were timed out for the night. One light burned in the house, a lamp glowing in their bedroom. It was unlikely that Jack had waited up. But she wanted only one thing now, to leap from the car with Vincent's phone and be free.

Numb from the long trip and queasy with fear, getting this monster off the property was her most critical goal.

The trunk popped open with the engine still running. A duet from Carmen softly played. Her abductor slithered from his seat and out, then moved efficiently around to the back. The rain pelted the roof of the car. He lifted her two extra heavy bags and rolled them to the door under the deck. He returned to the car and opened her door, offering her a soft, squishy, hand. She jerked her hand back in disgust. He reached behind her seat, for something.

The touch of a cockroach would have disgusted her less. She stretched her stained silk skirt to cover her knees and gathered her shoes and raincoat. Heart pounding, she stepped on the wet driveway with her bare feet, ready to dash to the door. Vinny grabbed her arm, stopping her motion, his fingers painfully digging in, freezing the very breath in her lungs. He held something in his hand. Vinny was the mob, she reminded herself as she waited for his blow to come. Taking her by surprise, he opened an umbrella and positioned it over her head. He dipped his underneath, giving her a cheek a slippery kiss. Catherine stood stock still as his hot tongue twirled on her skin. She shuddered, going weak in her legs, making Vincent smile, his gold front tooth glittering from the taillight.

"Remember what you promised, little girlie," he oozed, making smacking noises with his lips. "I will."

She stood by the door in the rain with her suitcases, watching him shake off the umbrella and toss it in the back. He climbed in and closed his door. When the Chrysler pulled forward, she let out a small, exhausted breath, relieved; he was letting her go. A second later, he braked, lowering his window. She clenched, cringing, as his eyes fondled her body in the same way as his tongue. He tossed her leather handbag at her chest as if it were a week-old diaper. It thumped against her wet suit and dropped to her feet. "Friday," he said, one jaunty last word like they were planning a date, then slowly drove away. With her eyes on his taillights, she retrieved her leather purse and listened to the splatter of his tires until he was gone.

Craving sleep, she did not have the strength to run to anything but the couch for what was left of the night. She rolled her heavy suitcases through the furnace room to the dumbwaiter. It took all she had to hoist the awkward giants inside and push them to the back so they would not cause a jam. She closed the door with a click and hit the top button. With a creaky rumble, the small lift rose to the bedroom floor, where the dogs were going wild, surely waking Jack.

Her head was filled with images of the murdered underage runaway, a decapitated cat, and Jack's secret sex. She climbed the stairs, feeling her 125 pounds, and followed the hallway to the bedroom and the light switch. She lightly patted the rushing six dogs and pointed to their dog beds.

Jack, still out cold, lay sprawled in his thunderpants on the bed, snoring soundly. Catherine flipped on a light and patted Jones, who purred a hello.

She reached for a sleeping pill but stopped herself. This was insanity. Tomorrow was Vincent's deadline and time was running out. She needed her lawyer. She went over the facts to tell him, first thing.

Jack wasn't as clever in his old age; she would start with that. His pungent hormone gel grew hair on women's faces, but he insisted it enhanced his reflex time—his *BrickBreaker* score was sensational.

The gel may have reawakened his irrational teenage self. He would have been self-centered and conceited back then, but now, he was ensnared with the mob and the death of a runaway girl. Her geriatric man-boy was a serial adulterer, but not a murderer. Vincent, on the other hand, was a professional killer. She could thank Jack for putting them both in deep trouble.

His bare legs spasmed as he dreamed, talking gibberish while escaping from gangsters, dead girls, and cats without heads.

His phone would have been locked several hours. The only one she would check tonight, was her own.

She needed Ben, now, more than ever. She typed him a fast SOS and hit 'send.' First thing in the morning, she would call his office, leave another urgent message, and hope that it could reach him while he was on his fishing trip.

Too weary for a shower, she shed her wet clothes on the dressing room floor and stepped into a warm flannel nightgown. *A million bucks?* She would never sleep tonight without a pill. She swallowed a whole one, brushed her teeth, and flossed. She washed her face and slathered on her anti-wrinkle crème.

With some satisfaction, she yanked her pillow from under Jack's head, watching his head flop back on the mattress. She grabbed a throw blanket to take to the couch where she studied her phone until her eyelids grew heavy. There were several new texts and emails. She would deal with them in the morning.

65
THE MORNING AFTER

Gerte's Teutonic voice erupted over the intercom. Catherine catapulted from her makeshift bed and charged toward the phone like a freight train with its wheels in need of oiling. The housekeeper was wrestling with telephone buttons while verbal abusing a contractor.

"*Na, ah, ahh!*" flooded the house on "all page," as if Gerte, in rare form this morning, was about to crack her crop. "Leave your filthy shoes at the door!" She cleared her throat over the all-page. "*Frau* Henniger! I need the soiled underthings on your closet floor for the dry cleaner."

Catherine, wincing at the airing of her dirty laundry, continued in a sleep-dazed wooze toward the phone on Jack's nightstand. Now that she was awake, all she wanted to do was wring some necks.

10:45 a.m. The dog beds had long since been abandoned.

"Toto, we're not in Chicago anymore," she said to herself, picking up the receiver, cutting Gerte's announcements short. Courtesy of her miracle sleeping pills, she had been dreaming of Tiffany's wedding. Gerte picked up her handset. "That's better, " Catherine said, tapping her fingers on the receiver, trying not to tip her hand. "No clothes today, Gerte. Where is my husband?"

"Gone for hours." Her implication was that stupid questions were unnecessary when one did not over-sleep. "He drove himself." She yelled at the workman, "I told you *not to* set your bucket on my carpet!" Gerte pronounced her W's like V's. "*Frau* Henniger, the window wiper is here—*Ach! Nein, a mouse*—behind the drapery. Drop it in the bucket!" Gerte thrived on chaos. "Frau Henniger, the window wiper and his two brothers are ready to do your balcony doors and bedroom windows."

"Gerte, please, I just woke up. Keep them busy for a while…show them the German way of cleaning nose prints off the front storm door. Give me a few minutes to put something on and I'll be down."

"Fine. Leave your clothes on the floor, like always. I'll go tomorrow, but you won't get them back until Thursday." Catherine was alert to Gerte's cunning maneuvers—the housekeeper had something better to do this afternoon, anyway, and she had more pressing things to worry about, like hired killers who were threatening life and limb.

Jack's enormous ego had sucked her into a world where young girls died and cats were beheaded, and his reputation and assets, if not their lives, were destroyed. This was not how she had imagined her marriage would end, full of fear.

Yearning to talk to Ben, she wished that she had reached him hours before. Once again, she was late. Today, there was no time to relax with a Nespresso to watch the morning unfold. Puziari and his monkey squad were about to conduct a tactical strike. If she didn't act now, too much would be lost. She threw on her robe and rushed back to the sofa.

Ben's call waiting played a scratchy Vivaldi with too much volume. Catherine grew more anxious by the moment. Finally, his line rang. A recorded voice came on. "You have reached the office of...*Benjamin*...*Williams*. Your message is important. Please leave a detailed message after the tone and...*Benjamin*...*Williams*...will get back to you soon. If your message is urgent, please push zero to return to the operator." She sucked her lips.

"Ben, it's Catherine, and urgent. Jack's in so much trouble, I don't know what to do! I uh, hope you get this. It's—" she put her hand to her head, thinking for a moment, "it's

Friday morning. You know my number."

And Jack—where was he off to? Oh, yes, his *Integrity in Leadership* conference, what a joke. She returned to her own unread emails. She stiffened. Two were from brenda-zabaglione@hotmail.com., an address well etched in her brain.

Let me know if you want to meet tomorrow night—Brenda Zabaglione, the woman Linda Anderson had seen in the car with Jack. Catherine scrolled to the earlier message from the same address:

You don't know me; I'm married to Vincent Puziari's boss. You'll want to own my adult entertainment video, starring your hubby. I'd like to discuss how to trade it with you for cash. If

you're interested, I'll meet you at the train station at 11:00 tomorrow night. Will you be driving the white SRX?

Catherine paced between the sofa and the bed. A woman doing threesomes with her husband and his mistress had *chutzpah* to contact her. It was clear why Jack would not sign her postnup, she was never meant to be "permanent."

Brenda, the local Godmother, probably did have the goods. Puziari worked for her husband, Richie Zabaglione. Maybe, Catherine thought, she could turn a rotten lemon into zest, she would get the video for Ben—the hell with helping Jack. She would call the police, take her dogs, and move the hell out. A sinking thought struck. Brenda's emails were already a day old.

Catherine typed as fast as she could and hit "send": *Interested. Yes, the white SRX. I'll be at the train station. What will you be driving?*

66
ROCKING THE
FISHING BOAT

"Doesn't get better'n this, buddy." Harlan swung a bare foot over the side of his small bass boat, dangling his toes in the water. The vessel rocked back and forth, nearly tipping. Ben held on.

"Hey," Ben shouted, "I'm not that thirsty, take it easy, man!" He laughed and threw his weight to the opposite side to counterbalance Harlan. The bass in the bucket were splashing their way out. "The fish will have their revenge." He had been daydreaming again about saving Catherine, his mind, on drafting her divorce. It was 72 degrees, with warm sun and fresh air. The lake had gentle ripples and smelled like heaven to him, a precious mixture of seaweed, gas, and fish—worms, even. The rocking motion made him feel a little sleepy. He yawned, cast out on the downwind side, watching for telltale rings.

"No cell service, no women," Harlan remarked. "We're free men and flawless!"

Harlan would have his share of texting to do once he got back within range. Girlfriends, lots of them; Ben wasn't sure how he did it.

"I thought you couldn't live without a constant dozen," Ben said, and smiled.

"*Baker's* dozen," Harlan corrected him with a silly grin and swished the ice in their small beer cooler. He came up with a bottle. "You want another one?"

"A woman?" Catherine was only one in his thoughts at the moment—he couldn't seem to stop thinking of her these days. Maybe it was time for a relationship, maybe, someday with her. But there was the pesky issue of getting rid of a cheap bastard with his bottomless assets and legal team of hungry werewolves.

"Ben, my man, have another beer."

"Naw, I'm good, thanks. Yeah, it's been terrific being up here," he said, gazing across Lake Ozark to Harlan's log cabin and dock. Besides having the fishing boat, his old friend had a vessel for every occasion, kayaks, a pontoon, a sleek MasterCraft for skiing. Ben shook a dragonfly off. "I have to get back to finish the divorce I'm drawing up for a beautiful lady in distress."

"Come on, man! We were just starting to empty this lake." Harlan belched with his mouth closed and winced.

"Like to, but can't, I promised to pick up Bumbles tomorrow by ten. My neighbors can't keep her over the weekend. Bumbles was an active Jack Russell, a dog who liked to dig. Ben cast another throw, getting a nibble. "It's a long drive back to civilization. I need to leave tonight," he said, feeling a tug on the line. He gave his pouting friend a sorry smile, "but not till after our fish fry!"

67
FLUFFY'S REVENGE

Jack stepped outside the packed auditorium to place a call. He was the keynote speaker at the sold-out annual leadership conference at the Sheraton complex. His integrity speech was one he had given a dozen times, freshened up by new jokes and a plug for JR Henniger stock. The economic and industry panel discussions afterwards would take up a good part of his day, so it was critical to reach his investment guy to bring him the cash for Puziari, now.

Felix Butmann was a good Jewish boy, smart, and strategically responsive to his high-profile clients, among whom Jack was the most prominent. He counted on Felix for personal service and expected him to deliver with a smile on demand.

In a weird way, he knew that he was getting high off the excitement; was reckless, even, but he had always liked the thrill that came with balancing on the edge. His life was one that most people living boring lives would never understand.

He wasn't paying *a million bucks* for any video, forget the death threats, he wasn't stupid. Vinny, the pissant, was in no position to negotiate. The low-level hoodlum would have to be dumb and crazy not to take his deal. He thought of Fluffy and wiggled his middle finger.

Vinny would get five-hundred grand, half of the demand, more than enough. Felix would bring it and he would meet the blackmailing little ratshit later and take possession of the video.

"I'm sorry, Mr. Henniger," Felix said over the phone. "The market in Europe has been closed for two hours. Time difference."

"Hah?" People were streaming out the double doors for the lunch buffet and the noise was rising. The place had incredibly bad acoustics.

"I said I can't get much today, Mr. Henniger," Felix answered with a cracking voice. "If you'd like, I can request a sell order for first thing Monday."

Jack's mouth opened to protest. What the *Hell? Golden Rocks* was Golden Rocks, wasn't it? He deserved better service. Felix was starting to smell like an over-ripe Yuppie. "You're telling me that Europe is closed for the weekend," he said thinking fast. "All right—then, what can you do on *this* side?"

"I can put in for a domestic funds transfer. Your cash balance today is roughly... $250,000." He cleared his throat.

"Pull some funds out of Europe ahead of Monday," he told him, pacing with a hand over his bad ear. "Float some from another account till then." He would not take this lying down.

"Impossible, unfortunately. Boston closes early today for the holiday," said the messenger delivering bad news to the king. "Two-fifty is the best I can do." The crowd's collective body heat was making Jack's nose glow. He pushed up the gold aviators that had slipped down his nose from their weight, thinking of where he could get more cash.

68
NUMBER TWO WITH FELIX

After delivering an excellent speech, Jack held court outside the men's room, regaling a triple ring of aspiring youth with polished tales while he kept an eye out for Felix. He hadn't lost his touch. The fans waved their programs hoping for an autograph. He rocked his chin, said a few words, and signed each one with a Sharpie, something he never left home without.

"Glad you finally met me! —Jack Henniger."

He had figured it out. He still had the money for Pussi's new house in his safe. He could use it, she would never know. Vinny would still have half of his blackmail money later tonight from Pussi, and half was all he needed—no *million* bucks—and if Zabaglione was unhappy with Puziari, he might make their mutual headache disappear. It would be better for Pussi to present the bad money news, the least she could do considering how she wanted the house and needed her allowance. He had been withholding it until she agreed to plant her butt back in rehab.

He would hand her the cash from his safe with Butmann's two-fifty and give her a tip.

"Mr. Henniger!" Felix Butmann shouted, approaching the swarm. Butmann, a short, balding man in glasses, was waving a brown lunch sack two fan rows out, trying to catch his attention. Jack motioned toward the men's room, thinking how Butmann would never make it to the top in his badly fitting suits.

"Ladies and gentlemen," he shouted. "It's been great talking to you. You'll have to excuse me, but both my schedule and nature are calling." Giving a jovial laugh, he parted the sea of sycophants and swam upstream to Butmann.

The countertop in the men's room had been splattered by water. Butmann held the bag of money between his knees to keep it dry. He sidled up to the closest urinal so he and Jack for a private conversation.

"This is a royal *pain* in the ass," Jack barked with an echo. "You're closing early for the holiday? When I was a young exec and our customers needed something, I fucking *made* it happen."

"I know, Mr. Henniger, but Boston makes the rules. I'm just a bozo on the bus, at your service," he said in a stage whisper, gripping the bag with the money.

"Yeah," Jack said, thinking of the numerous "wifeless" transfers and skillful deliveries that Felix Butmann had made for him over the years. He shook himself and zipped up. "Thanks," he said, and took the bag.

69
THE GREEN ROOM

Jack relaxed on the green room sofa waiting for his driver, trapped in the rush hour. He was chatting with a new "friend" on his favorite sex site. The TV was tuned to the local news. A child advocacy group was offering a large reward for tips leading to the arrest of a dead girl's killer, a runaway. He knew who. The body had been found in a Baxter County farm field. Jack loosened his necktie and unbuttoned his collar. He had pegged her for way over fourteen, besides, they were supposed to have been professional actors. By the time he had figured out the film's special genre, it was too late.

Choosing to reflect in silence on his speech, he typed a quick goodbye to his new friend and reached with the usual muscle twinge for the remote. "Setting the tone for leadership by example" had been his theme. It was gratifying to know that his message resonated so well with the young.

The janitor swept lazily around him, bagging the left behind coffee cups. Jack kept his hand on the briefcase

Felix had filled with cash. There were still a few people milling outside the green room, but for the most part, folks had already gone home to their sad, mundane, lives. Once his driver showed up, he would get home, retrieve the money from his safe, grab another cigar, and leave in the BMW. He would only need a few minutes. Catherine would barely notice. "Hi, sweetie, another interview—got to go," was all the dimwitted gold digger needed to know.

Jack's aching feet had been steam-wrapped in brown Naugahyde all day. Kneading the ball of one foot, he reflected on how Catherine was fortunate to have the use of it all at his expense, a beautiful house, top society connections, private jets. But naturally, she wanted more. But what had *she* done for him, but bore him to death? *Wives!* He was sick of her postnup drafts and all the money the two law firms were costing him. Life was too short.

She had quit her bible selling job to "tough" it out in the rough world of luxury. He was tired of the complications. Of her, and them. He would leave the problem of Gracies's step-shark twins to Catherine when he died.

He opened his briefcase to reconfirm that Felix's paper bag of cash was still safe. It was nestled next to his silver flask, engraved with one word, "STIFF," a divorce present from that first bitch, Irene. He had never been hard around her either.

He rotated the flask ceremoniously and poured its contents into a plastic cup with ice from the hospitality table. It would do just fine without an olive, he decided, as he gulped in a satisfying mouthful. He opened a free bag of chips and glanced at his Navitimer. Six thirty. He liked to keep Catherine in the dark about his ETA, because he could. He wished she had stayed in Chicago. He disliked confrontation, and being an honest person, he hated when she made him lie.

By his best calculation, Puziari had been waiting for the payoff, stewing in his own garlic sauce for over an hour. It was time for Pussi to start the gentle letdown. He texted her:

Those dipsticks switched our speaker's lineup; why I'm late. How about, after the swap, you meet me alone for some toe-curling orgasms? xoxoxo

Pussi fired back. *U Know how late U are?? Vinny is gonna kill us both, and UR thinking sex! I'm scared shitless, baby. Vinny threatened me. He's scared of Zabaglione, who no joke, will take him out if he don't get his million. What do U want me to tell him?*

Jack was nimble for an old guy. His thumbs could keep up with his brain, to which he credited Brickbreaker. Vinny could make do with half a million. Jack wrote: *Tell him I'm late from complications beyond my control—I'm good for the money and still good until midnight. It's coming, Puss. Once you're sure he has the video, call me and I'll meet you both at the fairgrounds for the swap. Later, you and I will make time for a hand job in the car!!! I'll have a twenty-five-hundred-dollar bonus for your trouble, which I believe you can use! xoxox*

OK. I'll tell him I'll be there soon. And see you at 10:00. The usual place.

So far, so good, and the evening would not end without a proper tribute to the old weenie. He replaced his flask, patted Butmann's money sack and latched his briefcase.

Hunched from all the sitting, he stretched his arms over his head until he felt the right pops, and then headed for his car and driver.

70
THE BRENDABERRY

The tall trees to the west blocked the last of the daylight. Catherine stood on the large deck above the back driveway, nervously turning shish kebob on the grill. From there, she hoped to see Jack's driver bring him to the furnace room door. He would be asleep before she left to meet Brenda. The dogs were positioned between the wrought iron dining set and the grill, with their attention divided between the meat and Jack's garage. Except for Otis, salivating on her flip-flops with his eyes on the grill, the other dogs did not like intruders.

There was a light on in the distant garage. Other than Billy Redd detailing Jack's cars, she was alone on the large estate. The guy's sneaky demeanor frightened her. Drug-skinny, with multiple tattoos and a black goatee, he was the kind who did not look you in the eyes, although his right eye did stray. She flattened a mosquito with a swat. Every night at eight, the little darlings showed up lusting for her blood. As if she were not miserable enough, one bit her ankle and another skewered her neck.

The brown bats swept at buzzers from above. Ducking, she nudged Otis with her foot and plopped the half-done shish kebobs on a platter to take into the house.

Tonight, she would negotiate with the *donna* herself. Once she had the video evidence—*she* would have a bargaining position.

It was only eight o'clock and she was heavy with fatigue and dry-mouthed from nerves. It would be critical to stay alert later. She was so tired...two solid hours of sleep would help. There would be time for a nap before she left for the station.

Upstairs, she crawled on the bed, set her phone alarm on, and reached in the nightstand drawer for a little red pill, swallowing half, enough to put her out for a bit.

71
FUNNY MONEY

The driver passed the evening traffic with ease. Holding the cigar with his teeth, Jack opened his briefcase and patted the paper lunch sack with Butmann's cash. Catherine, peeved that he was late for dinner, would be lurking in the kitchen, waiting for him to come up the basement steps. To avoid her, he would enter through the front door and tiptoe up the stone staircase open the safe's five-inch door. He would take the money and leave the same way. The combination was his social security number cleverly penciled in reverse where no one would think to look or could read with the refrigerator watt bulbs that Gerte, the Princess of Dust and Darkness, liked using. He had been smart to install the safe in his closet, where he could rest assured that the contents were secure, not just convenient.

He had set the money aside to buy Pussi a small place of her own, a house with a white picket fence for the toy poodle. Big Daddy coming through for his baby.

The home of her dreams (technically, his) would be

a step up. The new house had some minor glitches, but other than some radon and dry rot, there was nothing that couldn't be remedied with money, the sellers insisted. Considering the fantastic low price, he was ready to buy—with a small *quid pro quo*. All she had to do to get it, was do rehab. The last time, instead of signing up, she had blown the money that Felix put in her account on drugs and cheap Chianti, which she had shared with her mutt of an ex-husband.

72
CASH N' GO

Finding Mrs. Henniger asleep was good fortune for Billy. It allowed him to shop unbothered in her husband's closet for free loose cash and watches. His only threat now was the loudly snoring blonde. His girlfriend waited anxiously over the hill by the campsite, for some gas money to put in her new certified used car, which was packed for their long trip to Mexico.

73
TEA SANDWICHES

The sky was almost dark. It appeared that Catherine was not home. The SRX was not in its usual space. Good. No need to use the front. Jack's driver pulled under the deck in back to let him out. The dogs zoomed to meet him at the lower-level door, wagging and whining. He patted their heads and lured them into the garden room with his Ziplock bag of leftover conference food. He fed each one tea sandwich and leaving them longing for more, closed the big glass door and flipped on the kitchen wall switch. The power was annoyingly out. They lived on the edge of the power grid, where it happened with some frequency, why they had bought a commercial generator, a finicky piece of machinery. Fortunately, his BlackBerry cast all the light that he needed. Jones sat on the counter picking at dry cat food in a bowl next to a platter of licked shish kebob. He tapped the extra sandwiches in his pocket.

74
CROWDED CLOSETS

What the *hell?* Billy quickly camouflaged himself as a Nehru suit. It, and a bush hat, coverered all but one eye. The old fart had come from out of *nowhere.* Something must have gone wrong with Henniger's meeting with Uncle Vinny, Billy thought as he stood immobilized in Henniger's closet, taking care not to rustle the dry-cleaning bags or budge the metal hangers in the closet. He held an amazing two hundred fifty thousand dollars in his hand, and he'd just been looking for gas money when he'd noticed the fingerprints and the safe. A dyslexic, he couldn't believe his luck when he had read the safe combination scrawled on Henniger's shirt shelf.

Uncle Vinny was the guy he owed this shit-hole job to. It wasn't fun for a felon to have to check "yes" on a job application after the *"Have you been arrested?"* box. Ex-cons learned to lie after getting kicked in the ass enough. Billy, a triple-felon, belonged to an exclusive fraternity that nobody wanted to join, and nobody got to quit. Not that he hadn't appreciated the work here, thanks to Vinny, who deserved respect for coming up with his drug bond. That, and Zabaglione's lawyer had gotten him this far. *And now, goodbye USA.*

Henniger's wife was still sound asleep on the bed, sawing some fucking big logs.

His immediate thought upon hearing Henniger's car had been to bolt with the money through the backside of the pass-through closet and scram down the hall to the front stairs. The money would get him and Serena out of the country and buy them a good-sized plot in Mexico for growing weed. If he woke the sleeping bitch up, she would try to call the cops. He'd have to make sure she and the old guy, slowly making his way up the back stairs, could not do that. He scanned Henniger's highboy for a weapon, finding nothing sharper than some plastic sword-shaped toothpicks.

Billy's heart pumped fast Henniger's irregular footsteps closed in. At the first whiff of cigar, Billy reached out from behind the plastic bags to grab a fistful of the swords. He would stab them in his eyes when the time came.

A cell phone dinged. Henniger's footsteps stopped. Billy, thinking pure Mexico, hoped the old man would stop at the bathroom, so he could get out, blow this pop stand with Serena, who was waiting by the campsite in her pink sedan. *He hoped.* He had promised to come back in ten minutes. Surely, she was smart enough to stay quiet until he came out, so they would *vamoose* together before his court hearing.

Fuck. The drugs hadn't even been his— they were hers, and she had been with him. But he was the one they had wanted. The canine unit had pulled him over for running a stop sign. The fucking liars had had their eye on him and when the dogs sniffed the coke in the glove box. they had impounded his truck. His plan for now was to start a new life at her cousin's place in Guadalajara. First, they had to get there.

Serena saw the good side of him. She didn't even call him stupid when he got caught. It was simple bad luck, she told him. It was also a way of life she understood. Like the rest of her people, he had done time. His was for breaking and entering, possession, stalking with a firearm and assault and battery—although that charge was his ex-wife's fault; she had asked for it. He tried not to think of what he had done to her face.

His bank account was closed. There wasn't even a debit card left to trace him. But now they would have plenty of dough. He grinned, squeezing the fat wad of Henniger's bills against his chest. Serena had good wheels, the used Lexus, a former cosmetic rep's car, had new retreads that she had bought with US dollars earned from cleaning houses. He would buy himself a new truck. The old man owned some very good watches. Billy was sorry that he couldn't stay longer to browse. Fortunately, the ones already in his pocket would bring a good bit at the pawn shop.

Henniger's closet was about to get crowded. Billy stood statue-stiff, clutching the money, until his fingers felt numb. He wiggled their tips and waited for the old guy to come and go.

75
SWEATING THE
SMALL STUFF

Jack, finding Sleeping Beauty home and snoring on their bed, celebrated his luck with a grin. In the dim light, he made his way to his closet where he peeled off his clothes, leaving only his knee socks and Jockey briefs. It would take him days to stretch the leg holes large enough to get comfortable again after their last sanitizing in the Miele. They were clean enough for tomorrow, he decided, giving the restrictive waistband a snap. He was getting a little soft around the middle from Catherine's "gourmet" dinners. Fortunately, he wouldn't have to pretend to like her cooking much longer.

His tan corduroys hung on the hook by his Nehru suit. He stepped in both the legs, then unsnapped the red cowboy shirt from its hanger, putting it on. He wiggled his mocassins back on, and chose a pair of brown plastic shoes, setting them aside to carry downstairs. Never completely dressed without a cigar, he selected a Gloria Cubana from the mahogany mini humidor a female employee had sent as a gift. He winkled the *robusto* snuggly into his chest pocket and pressed the snap shut for later.

The clock in his closet announced the quarter hour. He was running tight on time for his meeting with Pussi—so now, to the two hundred fifty. He loosened his fingers and knelt by the safe on the floor, his knees crackling slightly. Using the light from his BlackBerry he pushed his gray suits aside and pried the pseudo heating panel away from the safe.

There in its loveliness, was his repository of dark secrets and very good things. Wasting no time, he wiggled the dial until the little red light glowed green and the safe beeped, then he covered the red indicator up, and pulled hard on the handle. The heavy door clicked open. He reached inside, for the money on the middle shelf. *What the fuck?* The shelf was empty, and it couldn't be. He cleared his throat and swallowed.

Holding his breath, he laid everything inside the safe on the Berber wool rug, taking a fast, frantic inventory: his cousin's yellowed vibrator; a used monogrammed hankie; a foot from his old Steiff teddy bear, and the faded black-and-white photos of his uncle's naked girlfriend, who had instructed him on female anatomy at the manly age of thirteen. He wiped the empty shelf in disbelief that the tall stack of thousands that he had left there in front, had vanished.

He felt clammy.

The image of himself dying in prison forced him to get a grip. He needed that video. He drew in some long breaths. That kind of money didn't just evaporate. Somebody had it; but who would leave behind the vibrator and photos?

He doubted that Catherine was guilty. But Gerte, on the other hand, perhaps. Opening this safe was too hard for an average woman to figure out. He could hear Catherine snoring as his thoughts scattered further. He could wake her up, but this would be a bad time. You don't keep the Cosa Nostra waiting over an argument with your wife about money for your mistress's new house.

There had to be another explanation. One of the girls could have noticed his cleverly hidden numbers and found the safe. *Naw.* The crime had clearly been the work of a professional. It was only money, right? He would worry about it later.

The good thing was he had the Felix's two-fifty. He would tell Puziari that it was as much as he could get them tonight. He didn't like sweating this small stuff, why should Zabaglione? Anything could be straightened out with time. Besides, if Zabaglione were to whack Puziari, how bad could that be?

Pussi would be waiting with Puziari and the video. Suffocating the little slut had been an accident. Whatever it took, he would have the video tonight, and pay the balance to Puziari the later…maybe never. Toting his plastic shoes, he took a last look at Catherine and departed, as swiftly as he had come, for the fairgrounds.

76
RAMBLING AMBIEN

The sound of the BMW pulling out woke Catherine before the alarm on her phone did. The dogs were barking, he must have let them in the house. She felt groggy from the sleeping pill and had a wallop of a headache. But now she had to pull herself together, take the $250,000 from the safe, and go buy that video.

She found herself swallowing hard several times, thinking that she should have thrown out Jack's vintage turkey soup with his pasta water. She rose, quickly checking her text messages. Not a word from the sneaky, geriatric bastard.

She splashed water on her puffy eyes at the bathroom sink. Lipstick would help. There was a bit of the broken still piece left in the tube. She used her finger to dig it out and ran a hairbrush through her hair.

A car with a rumpy muffler started up out back. It would be Billy leaving late.

Once she was on her way to meet Brenda in the SRX, she would feel better. She wondered how the Mafia mama looked wearing clothes, Armani or Piani, perhaps.

She stepped unsteadily toward Jack's closet, stopping at the bed to allow herself to lay her heavy head down for a moment. She closed her eyelids and breathed in deeply, as her brain continued working. Her eyes flashed open wide. She would buy the video back—but there was a safe full of bills to open first.

Forcing herself to move, she resumed her route to the money. Facing his Saville Row suits, she pushed the summer two-buttons aside to reveal a false panel that concealed the safe that only Jack (and she) knew about. She popped the panel off with the same shoehorn that she had used in the past.

She blew out a long breath and wiggled her fingers. She didn't have to look at Jack's numbers penciled on the bottom of his sweater shelf, which she knew by heart, his social security number, backwards. With her nose twitching from the dust, she cranked the dial back and forth. When the blinking red light turned green, she covered up part of the dial. Hearing the double beep, she pushed firmly on the handle, and the thick door opened.

Feeling inside for the fat stack of thousands, her jaw dropped. Except for Jack's eclectic collection of "personal items," the safe was bare. She swallowed hard again. So, this was why Jack had come home. After the blackmail video, too, he beaten her to the cash. Brenda would have to take a check, but she couldn't have her Cartier watch. She checked the time on it and slipped it off.

Otis was downstairs in the garden room with the others, howling for madly for attention, begging to go out. They would not have to suffer until she returned from the train station. On her way out, she passed Jones on the counter eating the rest of Jack's shish kebab, and freeing the dogs, let the wood screen door slam behind her. Checkbook in hand, she assumed a brisk walk toward her usual parking place, only to stop short when she saw that her vacant parking place. Virgil had taken in the SRX for service. It was gone. She bit on a nail, thinking. Brenda would be looking for that car. She paced for a moment, calming herself. There was no need to panic—there were plenty of cars in the big garage where she climbed into a metallic gold sedan, closest to the rear, a fifteen-year-old Plymouth that looked it.

Jack expected everyone to leave the keys in the vehicles, a rule that would come in handy tonight. She unplugged the Plymouth's battery-tender, stuffed the little wires and clips back in, and closed the hood with a clunk. The engine started with a satisfactory purr.

Her phone battery was very low, she realized with a start, its charging cord was in the SRX—and it was too late to do anything about it. As she backed out the Plymouth, she felt inside her purse, hoping to find extra cord, then grimaced, her face prickling. Old Plymouths were never made with charging ports. To save the phone's remaining energy, enough for one important call, she would have to power down. She would not be able to call Brenda Zabaglione until she reached the station.

Arriving, she circled the lot, all the while clenching her teeth. Brenda hadn't said what she would be driving. Catherine realized, she didn't know what to look for, a luxury car or maybe an SUV? She was sure of one thing, Brenda's car would likely not be gold with two rusting quarter panels, like the Plymouth that she was driving tonight. She wound up and down the half-filled rows, looking for a woman who looked like a mob moll.

If Brenda missed her late response, she would have to go home empty-handed. But it was only 10:50, still early. She hesitated to call yet. She sank into the car's crushed velour seat and watched the last train of the evening pull in. The parking lot lightened as the drivers found their passengers and left. She yawned. Besides being a burgundy brunette, what would Brenda look like? She could only remember those breasts on Jack's phone, not the face.

Fighting another yawn, she pinched her thigh to stay alert and continued to look. The seats in the older cars were so darn soft. Soon, she would call Brenda. She opened her fluttering eyes every few seconds to check for new cars coming in. There had been no bottle brunettes, so far. Her last conscious thought as she drifted sweetly off was of a car circling the lot like a second hand, looking for a white SRX.

77
HUMAN ATM MACHINE

The overhead lights cast a ghoulish veil on the closed county fairgrounds. The pothole Pussi had parked in was full of yesterday's rain. She was applying additional mascara in the rearview mirror, waiting for over an hour for her eighty-year-old ATM machine to show up. Vinny wasn't coming. He was yelling at her on the speakerphone.

"Relax, baby—okay?" she said, craving another drink. "So, you couldn't find the video, and you want me to squeeze... *how* much from the geezer without it?" The brush wand missed her lashes, stabbing her eyeball. She jerked her wrist away in pain and blotted the teary mess with the back of her hand. "I'll let you know how it goes."

"Get the fucking million to me, bitch." Vinny feared Zabaglione. "You'll figure it out." The tone of his voice grew mean. "Unless you want to see me get whacked."

She could visualize that. "Look, I want my money too, but Henniger wants his goddamn video and he's expecting it." She laughed lightheartedly. "This might cost me my virginity." She repositioned her tube-dress, the one

Vinny had bought her on Nastydress.com. Jack loved the way her nipples peeked through the holes.

"Sweet Mother of *Jesus*," Vinny's voice shot back. "That would be a cold day in Hell." Pussi hung up—she'd taken enough guff from Crater Face. Back to waiting for Gramps, who would come, just like Christmas, and she had a snow job to do.

The BMW's lights appeared in her rearview mirror and wove through the parking lot, dodging the largest puddles. Jack pulled beside her car and rolled his window down, gesturing for her to get in. His engine was running.

Pussi made a clumsy grand *jeté* across the pothole between them. She would get the business portion done quickly, pleasure the old guy, and get the hell out. Jack leaned across the center glove box to open her door. His brief- case was on the back seat. She breathed a sigh of relief.

"Where is he," Jack demanded angrily. He was supporting an unlit cigar with his teeth, "and my video?"

"Something happened, hunky-bunk, Vinny won't have it till Monday." She tickled Jack's inner thigh. "But listen—they're after him for their money tonight, or else! *Tonight*, Daddy. Please don't let your Pussi down!" She watched his face closely for clues of weakening, seeing little progress. She would coo the line that always worked on him. "I'm not wearing... my panties, *see?*" He looked to confirm the absence of that undergarment through the holes in her dress. *Got him*, Pussi thought, smugly.

"All I want to see is my video. No tickee, *no* washee." She reached for his briefcase, smiling a toothy grin. "Is that the money?" He smacked her hand, sharply.

"I filled my part of the bargain. How about you?" She said nothing. He looked at her with glinting eyes. "You're drinking tonight right, and this is a joke? Where's my video?"

"Come on, Jack!" she pleaded, shifting her tactic.

"How about just some of the money, then?" She would peel off some badly needed thousands for herself, get some booze. Vinny would be too dumb to catch on. "You're gonna get it, baby. Don't you trust me?"

"I could only get part of the money tonight, anyway," he said, touching her shoulder with a finger, "but now, you're not even getting that." He poked his finger through one of the holes in her dress for emphasis.

"S'cuse me?"

"We agreed on the terms. Now both you and Vinny are ripping *me* off like I was as stupid as the rest of the men in your life." Jack lowered the window again and tossed his cigar out.

Pussi, weighing the odds of performing a successful grab and go, hooked the handle of his briefcase with two fingers. She could outrun the Gimp.

It happened so fast. As she tugged on the case, he caught her hand and pried away her fingers while popping open the passenger door to push her out. Resisting, she screamed and dug her full set of rock-hard acrylic fingernails into the meat of Jack's palm. A tough buzzard, he kept pushing until she lost her grip on the briefcase. "*Hee-haw,*" Jack hollered and shoved her from the car with all his might, and she tumbled out and landed in a puddle.

"See ya' *Puss*. Call me when you get the video!"

Jack spun the Beemer off in the darkness, plowing through ruts on his way out, leaving Pussi sitting up to her waist in the puddle, furious. She reached for her phone.

"Siri...call...Crater Face." Vincent answered right away.

"Did you get the money?"

"Not exactly, Vinny. I told you Gramps wouldn't produce without the Follywood flick. The son-of-a-bitch lied. He said he only had part of the cash. He's headed home from the fairgrounds with, my guess, five-hundred grand in his briefcase...Go for it."

78
VINNY AND THE TRIGGER

Vinny left his Chrysler on the one-track that ran up the wooded east side of Henniger's land from Baxter Road. He parked it far enough back to be out of sight when Jack approached the property. The glow from the bright full moon filtered through the fat burr oak trees, lighting his path. He made his way with his rifle through the thicket to the killing site that he'd chosen at the top of the hill.

"Your time is up, my friend," his boss had said with sociopathic coldness, taking a smooth drag on his cigarette. Zabaglione sometimes used that tone with others and Vinny knew what it meant. "…unless you take the right action." He looked him in the eyes, puffing it out like he wasn't blowing smoke. "You'll produce by midnight tonight, right, Vincent?"

He had nodded and said, "I believe we understand each other."

Vinny practiced lining up the sight, a muscle twitched in his face. Her allowance couldn't keep her in booze for a month. Even a week. She'd planned a much bigger bonus from Henniger, obviously. Pussi planned to marry Henniger for his money.

Henniger had to have the cash in the car, and it would be in Zabaglione's hands tonight. He only had to intercept it on its way back to Henniger's closet.

"Vinny, baby, please believe me," Pussi had shouted over the phone. "I'm sorry, I *tried!* The old fart won't give it up!" She'd sounded breathless. "He wants to see the master first. Can you blame him? Can't you try to get it back from Brenda? I flunk when it comes to squeezing blood out of turnips."

"*Fuck your bimbo clichés, Pussi.* You're about to be reminded who can."

79
WHEN CARS FLY

His long wait for the *mortadella* was about to pay off. Coming fast, was the sound of the old BMW's gearbox, whining through second to third. Vinny rolled his shoulders. People in his line of work needed the occasional hit to help maintain proficiency. He lined the sight with the rifle's notch. He would relish logging this kill in his diary under the entry for the cat. From high above the road, it should be an easy shot, over and done with quickly.

This was going to feel good. His adrenaline flowed as he watched the headlights bob with every downshift. His pulse painfully pounding trigger finger, he took a full breath, letting out half as he nestled the nine-pound rifle into his shoulder, forming a straight line from the weapon to the center of the highway below. In perfect position, he braced and waited, his injured finger trembling a millimeter over the trigger.

Now, he told his finger, ignoring the pain from the rifle's sharp retort as the butt jerked across his shoulder, smacking him hard in the jaw, busting another tooth to pieces. Flinching, he pressed on, delivering bullets until the shatter of glass and squeal of brakes sounded and the fucker's car chattered in the gravel. Vinny sucked on his finger as the black and white car flew airborne.

80
BOBO DOC
AND THE SALT FISH

It was Friday night. Bobo Doc was warming up their black and white telly for a rerun of America's Got Talent, his favorite show. The telly was his source of pride. He and Digger had rescued it from oblivion on a recent run to the company dump—a place they had affectionately named 'the shopping centre.'

The brothers were impressed that after so many years, the vacuum tubes still worked. All it had needed was a pair of rabbit ears wrapped in tinfoil. They found a small antenna there.

Digger tuned in a local station while Bobo Doc browned the plantain and salt fish in a darned good electric skillet that they had discovered under a blown-out tire. He reached in the icebox for the Howe's Hot Sauce to top off his beans and rice which was steaming to perfection in the reclaimed microwave. It was their first meal of the day, and their last, they were hungry. Besides, the ganja was beginning to kick in.

"Smells nice, Bo." Digger was already drooling. "Make

shore dat you pu' tin enuff rice!"

"I *know* dat, Bro, but we don't got *mo!*" Digger was getting in a rap mood.

"In de street ya' go!" Digger roared with laughter and drained his can of Wadidli Ale. The frying pan was sizzling and popping oil spits.

"*Bro* go?"

"Met a man name Mo," Bobo Doc continued, chuckling. "*Heh, heh, ho.*"

"Den, Bro—he sock ya' in de nose!" Digger grabbed his side, which was about to split from laughing.

"Another Wadidli, and down de gutter, ya' go!" *This was good ganja!*

Bobo Doc decided on no more intoxicants for them tonight. Tomorrow was Saturday, and after work, they could lime all they wanted. It was a Rasta holiday, although that meant zip to their boss, who needed their help due to a breakdown this week. There was a rubbish pileup. The customers got mad when they smelled stuff like "fish and shit," the boss liked to say. The Daley brothers would have to get up extra early, too.

Bobo Doc was happy for the extra pay; the rent on their room was overdue. Last week, he purchased an advance on tomorrow's pay. He handed Digger a steaming plateful. They settled on the floor in front of the telly.

The medicine Auntie Ella needed for her liver disease was experimental and expensive and the insurance company had said 'no.' He and Digger sent her half of every paycheck. Digger complained loud about it, too. Bobo Doc had to remind himself that Digger had been too young to fully know their family. The little boys had lost almost everybody in the volcanic eruption. When they escaped to the safety of the British Navy ship, his little brother had not felt the same desperation about leaving the dead behind. With no other place in the world to go, the boys had gone to the States, to Auntie Ella, their only adult relative. Auntie Ella was already a mother of seven children and a hardworking motel maid.

She could have said no, but she hadn't. And now, they could not deny her. He cried when he thought of how she had collapsed, wailing from relief, the day they had offered to pay for her pills. She had praised the Lord for sending her dead sister's miracle sons to her.

Helping her made Bobo Doc feel important. The best part was that the medicine seemed to be working; she was beginning to show signs of strength again and might get the needed surgery.

"There's big money in show biz," Bobo Doc reminded Digger. He was transfixed on the Las Vegas juggling act that had followed the Cadillac ad. After dinner, they always jammed with the fine, custom-made instruments Digger had assembled from other people's trash. One day, his musical treasures—the metal garbage can lid turned into a steel drum, and the pieces of PVC pipe that he had turned into a xylophone—would lead them to stardom. All the brothers needed now were a few more instruments, more practice. And faith.

"Digger, we go' work to do."

81
SWEET ANTICIPATION

Vincent slid from his perch and trekked single-mind-edly down the hill on his way to Henniger. His rifle swung from his shoulder with every step. The hit had exhilarated him. He could almost see the body and his money. The raspy leaf blades of the cattails brushed against his face as he waded with determination through the frigid water in his expensive Italian leather shoes and dress pants. His satin track jacket was wet up to the elbows. He wasn't happy that his good clothes would be ruined. A Thornberry branch snapped him in the face, scratching his cheek as he walked.

He could see the roofline of the BMW a full fifty feet from the highway ditch. With childlike pleasure, he could hardly wait to see his hit. He hoped he would be lucky and find the pig-dog alert enough to recognize him, see the missus's knife in his hand. Vincent hoped that Henniger would react with the appropriate level of fright. He would enjoy watching him die, but not before carving him up a bit with the fuckin' sharp Cutco. He would only take one part at a time..souvenirs for the lady. He liked the concept of show and tell to demonstrate what happened to cheaters.

By the time he reached the sinking car, he was sweating under his cold wet clothes. His jaw smarted. He wiggled what remained of his tooth with his tongue, which jolted him, lighting up his brain with the poke of a cattle prod. He shone the light from his cell phone inside and smiled. So far, he was pleased with his work.

82
NICE WATCH

The *vecchio sporcaccione* was still breathing, barely. His thick white hair was turning a deep, rosy, pink. Vinny, whose chest puffed with pride, congratulated himself, satisfied that had not lost his touch.

At least one of the bullets had left a dark little bull's eye dead center in Henniger's forehead, rendering him motionless except for his eyes. Henniger blinked up at his face. His lips looked gluey as he tried to form words.

"Hey, Mr. Henniger, can I get you anything? Gin martini? Ambulance?" he asked as he reached through the open window to remove the BlackBerry from the old man's hands. First, he would have to unfold his thumbs, which were frozen in place on the device's tiny keyboard. "Texting and driving, eh?" Vinny tsked in mock disapproval. "A smart guy like you oughta know how dangerous that can be."

Henniger couldn't speak, but his eyes remained impolite.

"What was *that?*" Vinny asked. "I'm very sorry, can

you speak up? You say you're craving a Rocky Road ice cream sundae with a Diet Dew?" He wanted to sound sincere. "You should reset your lock on this thing." He whistled. "Looks like you have a text or two here from my wife—*ex*-wife now, thanks to you—that would be more correct, wouldn't it?" The vein in Vinny's neck pulsed as he read a few texts for fun.

Vinny pulled the door handle with his injured hand, noticing how the car's poorly maintained hinges creaked. His surgical gloves would guarantee against tell-tale fingerprints. Her Cutco had sliced cleanly through the latex, causing his wounded finger to drip, but the car was awash in blood, and his own would blend with Henniger's. The briefcase which had landed in the footwell was still dry. It would have plenty of green bills inside. Red and green put him in a celebratory, out-of-season, holiday mood. He whistled a bar of Deck the Halls and noticed the fucker's eyes widen when he realized he had seen his last holiday. Vinny unbuckled Henniger's platinum Navitimer watch and slipped it on his own wrist, a memento for himself.

83
TOO CLEVER BY HALF

Vincent climbed the stumpy bank, his socks squishing inside his mud-caked shoes from swamp water. He continued through heavy thicket to the two-track logging road at the top of the hill where he had left the Chrysler 300. The sky brightened with the first hint of dawn. He figured he had a half hour to get the funds to Zabaglione and he would make the tight deadline. His kill had taken the edge off his stress. *Fuck*, his finger hurt. A hot shower and a whiskey would feel good right now, but later. He stood the trusty rifle against his car so that it wouldn't fall. An expert marksman, he had not had to use the extra rounds and was ready for the next job.

Henniger's fat gut had merged with the steering wheel. To reach the briefcase, Vinny had been forced to wade to the other side in the knee-deep muck, smelling up his suit pants with swamp gas, a pain in the ass. After removing the body parts, he had placed the old Blackberry back in Henniger's chilling fingers and tucked them smoothly around it.

The first traffic of the day whizzed past on the highway below. If Zabaglione was still waiting at the Waffle House, he would be pissed—he didn't like to wait. Vinny set a mud-logged shoe on the 300's running board and balanced the vinyl briefcase on his thigh. He gave the latch a light jostle, and the snap unlatched.

With heavy breathing he counted the neatly packed cash. Two hundred fifty. Blood rushed to his feet from his brain. He shuffled through the bills. *Where was rest of the fucking money?*

Death meant the most when it was personal. He squeezed his eyes shut. His own death was *too* personal. He could have sworn the whole million would be there—or at least half. Obviously, he had not intercepted it in time. Unless that lying little bitch had snitched it.

From out of nowhere, a car's engine roared, its headlights bouncing on the sandy trail, bearing down on him—Zabaglione's men in the Escalade. *Shit!* He had to scram. A few seconds too slow and he would be joining Henniger.

He slammed shut the briefcase, grabbed his rifle, and disappeared into the ferns and oaks, flying through the familiar woods on foot.

84
SHIP AHOY!

This was a high holy day for the Daley brothers and their Rasta brethren an ocean away. Bobo Doc and Digger were looking forward to the celebration tonight after work, during which they would properly honor the second coming of the Messiah. God spare life, they would roll and enjoy the special ganja they had grown in their black-lighted garden box at their tiny St. Louis flat; eat goat water and pray. They'd talk about blessings, and how to save enough of their pay to keep helping Auntie Ella. Bobo Doc knew in his heart that one day the brothers would return to their beloved, volcanic island home. Their dream would come true if they continued to please God with their obedience, he would continue to protect them from the dark one, who had nearly nabbed them as little children and still desired them.

The atmosphere this morning promised Spring, its warm air lifting Bobo Doc's mood with the ground fog. Their truck rattled onto 167. A mile or two ahead, was the entrance to the big gates where, as the Lord now told him, he and Digger had witnessed the hand of the Devil himself. From his crow's nest at the back, Bobo Doc scanned the morning horizon, praising the Savior. He dreaded the next stop.

"Just pick up de cans. Dump dem fast, and jump back on de truck, Bobo," he told himself, biting on his chapped lip, shaking slightly as he did his job. He was counting on his younger brother to make it quick, too. Digger could peel the last of the rubber from the tires, as far as he was concerned. The brothers were not getting yanked into Hell today. Digger spooled up and off they went again.

So far, everything seemed normal this morning with the usual man-made debris of scattered Bud-Lite cans and 7-11 "Big Slurp" cups in the ditches, American style. Bobo Doc inhaled a grateful breath, feeling the new space between his teeth with his tongue.

His eyes focused through the brightening mist on something out of place in the wetland—something had gone aground over the gravel shoulder and deep drainage ditch, fifty yards to the starboard. It was black and white, and half-submerged. He held his breath, at the omen dropped from the heavens, or perhaps a lure cast by the Devil. His heart began to race. He banged ferociously on the truck's steel hatch. They had no choice but to find out which one. Digger screeched the lumbering vehicle to a halt and locked the doors. Gripping the wheel, he froze still as a pillar of salt with thoughts of eternal damnation. He knew the special-painted car, too, one like most people had never seen. Bobo Doc knocked wildly on the window in a vain attempt to catch his eye.

"Open the goddam door, and you come out now. I say right *now*, girlie. We are both going down there! Somebody may be hurt!"

Digger rotated toward him and stretched his frame across the duct-taped seat to pull on the broken door handle. With his eyes open wide and his head swinging he said, "I cannot swim."

85
RASTA WATER

The two men slipped down the sloped bank of the road burn and plowed with painful determination through the thicket of shoulder-high cattails until they had closed in on the wreck site. A rattled gaggle of geese squawked indignantly at the intrusion and scattered off. "Jesus, man!" Digger warbled as his Wellies melted into the swamp. "I sinkin' in dis quicksand!"

"You're okay!" Bobo Doc shot back. His teeth chattered as his Carhartt overalls swelled with icy marsh water. "Keep goin'! We're in dis together, Digger, it just muck, move onward, princess!"

"No man, my boots fill up. It stinks. I'm freezin'!" Digger cried. His voice lowered to a loud whisper. "You know dat it be what I know, Bo! We got away clean de first time, thanks be to Jah!"

"Don't you see?" Digger lowered his voice. "What if it gets us now? I can't swim, and I can't run in dis shit—*Oh, Jesus!*"

"Just shut up and move, Digger, come on—we're

almost dere!" Bobo Doc gripped his phone, and holding it high to keep dry, he plucked and sluiced each foot in front of the last. He trembled at what would come next. The faint sound of morning traffic was beginning to rise. What was the chance that a driver, harried to get to work on time, would notice the abandoned garbage truck, see the wreck in the swamp, and bother to call for help? Fate could not be changed.

"Unless de Lord decide we worth de fight, we *done!*"

Bobo Doc nodded. Digger was right. On he swished, without concern for his soaking armpits or the swamp muck filling in his boots.

He was sure that the sinking car was the black and white one with the old man and girl. The inside was awash in red. His shaking fingers punched 911.

86
ZOMBIE CAR

Digger sank in the bog like a spoon in cold soup. "Help!" he cried as he went down. Driven by the Spirit, Bobo Doc grabbed a hold of the thrashing man's soaking wet uniform and plucked him up, pulling him close to save him from the watery Hell.

"Keep *moving!*"

"Oh, Lordie, spare me!" his little brother cried, chest heaving. "I don't wanna drown!"

"I got you, bro. You *good!*" he shouted in his commando voice, holding his splashing brother's shoulders. He turned him so that he faced the bloody scene and poked him with his elbow. They would have to crane their necks to get a look inside without falling over.

It was early dawn, yet light enough for the Rasta men to know pure evil. The Devil had paid a visit to Route 167 all right and was grinning as they moaned and swayed. The two brothers wailed a cacophony born of repulsion and fear.

Bobo Doc's mouth dropped open as wide as his eyes.

He ripped the gold chain and Coptic cross out from under his T-shirt and waved it high, as this was no accident. Inside the car sat a mutilated, half-naked body. An old white fellow with his head turned face down. He was not just an ordinary "cloud" sitting dead inside his high-class wheels. Bobo Doc's breathing accelerated, he'd seen this man before, in this very same car.

The dead man was folded in right angles, his clothing saturated by blood. His red shirt partially covered his belly, revealing suntanned flesh, which popped through the steering wheel in Pillsbury dinner roll portions.

Bobo Doc grew cold-skinned and light-headed and wanted to run but couldn't feel his feet. Satan dropping by for a holiday visit, pointed his bony finger at Bobo Doc. "Look closer—you'll like it!" Bobo Doc didn't want to look. Pure evil was about to burst through the window and grab another sinner. *Him!*

Digger wobbled unsteadily and turned his head away. But Bobo Doc, who under the Devil's spell, took a closer look. What he saw, made him drop like an anchor in the frigid muck. Wild-eyed, he looked to the sky through the rising morning fog and pleaded to Jah for mercy. "Please save us from de evil spirit da' ha' somehow come upon us!"

87
COLORFUL SKY PIECES

Seconds after Deputy Clarence "Pops" Peters received the dispatch, Baxter was awash in swirling waves of blue and white. He secured his coffee *au lait* in a full donut bag between the passenger seat and his clipboard and reversed out of the Dunkin' Donuts parking space marked Officer of the Month, while switching on the sound and light show. Squealing, his patrol car rocketed off at high speed toward an incident reported on Rural Route 167.

He was sixty-six but could move when he had to. He didn't mind admitting he was out of shape and that the younger officers called him Flat Butt, something he'd earned from years of full-time sitting in patrol cars. If they were as lucky, they'd have one someday, too.

From the safety of his car, Pops observed the strange sight. Two pasty-faced, dark-skinned guys sat like bobble-art bookends on the running board of a garbage truck. Both wore Medusa-like dreadlocks. The taller one waved wildly at him with a colorful crocheted hat which stood out against the grayish-brown wetland. As he pulled up, Pops lowered his window to hear a blend of hysterical laughing, crying, praying. The men's heads were bobbing as their arms swayed like the end was near. From thirty feet, he saw the whites of their eyes. The men, in their early twenties, wore Waste Management uniforms—mustard-colored Carhartt overalls which were bog-filthy black and soaked to mid-thigh.

Pops took in the scene, dumbfounded by its weirdness, until he saw the black and white automobile in the swamp. This was not going to be an ordinary day on the job. The one-of-a-kind BMW 507 had obviously gone airborne and was half-submerged in water—the former Pebble Beach beauty queen was now headed for a landfill. Urgent work was ahead for him. If the driver, he presumed Jack Henniger, was alive, he would need help.

88
STIFF ONE

Pops shook his head, remembering the night he had seen the valuable car on the Henniger estate, after one of those crippling mid-March ice storms. The house, a standout at the end of a long curving driveway was a mile from Baxter Road on 167. A stately home in the middle of a hundred-and-fifty-acre wooded wilderness was unique. The enormous European style chalet had balconies and lots of glass in front. There were several garages, presumably filled with the "good" stuff.

The BMW, its vanity plate STIFFONE, had been parked under some wind-creaking oaks in front of a smaller, similarly styled guest house. Its engine cover was cold to the touch and an inch of ice had accumulated on its wind- shield, but its interior lights still dimly glowed. If the car had been his, he would have stored it in a garage on such a night. *But that was affluence for you.*

The dispatch had come at exactly two a.m. He had nearly slid off the bridge on the driveway trying to get to the house. It had been authentic domestic dispute, in his opinion, yet he had had no choice but to write it up as a false alarm.

He had pulled in and parked, taking note of a bedraggled brunette huddling outside the fortress-like front door. She wore a large hotel bathrobe and stood shivering in the pelting winter weather. He had punched through the slush-covered walk to reach her. Her bare feet had been piggy pink in the glow of the Henniger's porch lights.

The woman was clearly distraught and had looked like a dog's dinner. She wore two or three cheap necklaces with small stones, and a gold-toned wedding band. He remembered the stench of alcohol and vomit. Her damp, brown hair had been as dry as cotton candy. Rivers of dried mascara had run down her cheeks.

"Good morning, ma'am, I'm Deputy Clarence Peters. You look like you could use some help. I'm answering the emergency call regarding an incident at this residence. Are you OK?" She nodded. He watched. "What's your name?"

"Pussi," She answered in a surprisingly high-pitched voice.

"Last?"

"Puziari." A familiar name.

"You all right?" he asked, clearing his throat, noticing marks on hers. "You look like you took a fall. What happened to your face?"

"Oh, sure! I'm okay—really. It's my damn allergies," she'd said, looking down at her feet. They were long. "I'm just a little tired this time of night," she said, stuffing her hands into the robe's deep pockets. She shifted her weight from one frosty foot to the other. Her toenails were orange, sparkly.

"Somebody here pushed the 911 button and screamed the words, *'HELP ME!'* Now, was that you?"

"Ah, no, Mr. Officer—not me," she burped slightly "Oops…!" she said, covering her mouth with her hand, clearly imbibing. "*Excuse me—*"

"Sure. Do you have any idea who might have made that call from this property?"

"Dunno, there are security boxes everywhere—one in the barn, another in the guest house. A prank, sir. Everything's *good!*"

"May I ask why you're out in this weather clothed like this?" Her rosy toes wiggled.

"Uh…yeah. I was in the sauna. I come out to cool off."

"Right. It gets hot in those boxes. How old are you?"

"Thirty-five—uh, well, okay—thirty-eight." Her robe slipped open in a revealing way, he recalled.

"M… m… married?"

"Yes, sir."

"Is your husband inside?"

"Oh, no," she answered, eyes drifting, hesitating some.

"Who's inside, then?"

"Mr. Henniger. *Jack* Henniger," she said, sounding the syllables out emphatically. He made a note.

"Anybody else?"

"Just him and me, officer."

"What about Mrs. Henniger? There is a Mrs. Henniger, isn't there? Where, is—"

"I wouldn't know, sir."

"So, as far as you are concerned, everything is fine, right?" Pops remembered it all. She nodded. "Do you work?"

"I'm an *Executive Assistant*."

"A secretary," he had said, making another notation.

She had shaken her head. "I'm really much more than that."

"Then you will need to go to w-work in the morning? Where do you work?"

"Ah, here, sir." she answered, tightening her robe belt.

"I need to talk to Mr. Henniger. Why don't you go get him, and put some shoes on those feet, ma'am?"

"Ah, sure, officer," she said, trying the door. It was locked. She banged with the big brass knocker…inside there was silence. Mrs. Puziari's lip curled in a crooked smile as she shrieked through the door, "Jack, please. Would you just come out?" Several dogs barked inside. "A cop's here, wants to talk to you." A man's muffled voice said something on the other side. She cleared her throat and shouted even louder through the door, "I told him how *everything's* okaaay!"

Pops had been intrigued. There had been some obvious trouble that night, maybe even physical. Women sometimes called, then changed their minds from fear, mostly.

The heavy door opened wide enough for Pussi to slide past the emerging homeowner, the famous Jack Henniger, who pushed his way out, flashing a million-dollar smile. It was surprising how much older he looked in person. The big one had come out to slap a little praise on small town Pops Peters. Henniger clipped his phone to its holster and extended his hand. "How are you doing this evening, officer? Officer...?"

"Clarence Peters."

"Can't thank you enough for coming out, Officer Peters. Fortunately, there is nothing going on here except a little too much red wine drinking by our houseguest. Heh, heh," he laughed. "Everybody is just *fine*, seriously. But I do thank you for coming. I assume you got a call from our security firm?"

"No, it was a direct 911 call. Took me less than ten minutes to get here from the station. Are you the person who called?"

"No. Nobody here called. Maybe our houseguest, just fooling around? Must have seemed like a joke to her after all the booze, officer, but, honestly, everybody is fine."

"Mrs. P... P... Puziari is a...houseguest, then?" Pops stuttered when he got excited.

"Yes, very good friend of the family."

"Do you have any idea how she got that abrasion on her f... face?"

"Well, officer, no, I really don't." Henniger had stiffened slightly.

"Have you noticed anything unusual going on... someone uninvited on the property lately?" he asked. Mr. Henniger shook his head. "How... a...b..bout now? Anybody else home?"

"Just our dogs and cats." His shiny eyes danced behind his glasses. "Catherine... my wife...is out of town," he added, taking a step forward. "You guys are doing a fine job of keeping the community safe, the crime rate down—taking care of business so efficiently on a night like this! You can count on me to make a call to the sheriff tomorrow to let him know how happy I am with your high level of professionalism. Of course, I'll also be making a donation to the Widows and Orphans Fund."

"Well, thank you for that, sir."

"*All right,* then," he said in a dismissive tone, extending his hand. "Considering this horrible weather, we ought to call it an evening. I'd like to say good night, unless you have any more questions."

"No, that should do it," he said and shook his hand. "If you don't mind, I'll look around the property to be on the safe side." He'd touched his hand to his pistol. "By the way, Mr. Henniger," he said, pointing at the BMW, "Is that your black and white car? Nice one. I'll shut its headlights off."

There was something manipulative about them both that left Pops feeling he had been "managed." Without a formal complaint, all he could do was turn off the headlights and try not to slide off the driveway on his way out.

89
TIGHT BLACK
DEPUTY BOOTS

"Stay where you are!" Peters ordered them as he hoisted his stiff hulk from the car. The trash men looked like they had been planted on the truck's running board. He had seen enough accidents to know that they were traumatized. "Don't budge till I say otherwise. G…g…got it?"

He adjusted his trousers above his belted midriff and shuffled his shiny black deputy boots along the dew-covered, cracked, asphalt. He had laced them lightly to go easy on his corns.

He determined that the wailing men were too pathetic to be a threat as he passed them on his way to a path of broken cattails, where he paused to assess a slippery looking steep ditch. As his boots shimmied for a hold, he lost his balance and he slid into a stump, smacking his pistol holster hip. Cursing under his breath, he trudged ahead through the quicksand-like bog, wheezing from exertion. The trick to not sinking, would be to keep his legs jiggling in the mucky cattail nursery. When he reached what he believed was Henniger's car, he shook the sticky mud off his radio and called in.

90
CHOPPER DROPPER

"Peters."

"Dispatch. Go ahead, Pops."

"Ah, send medical. I've got a vehicle ca-rash. Two miles west of Baxter-Davis, RR 167, north side."

"Wilco. Will you need back-up?"

"10-4."

He was not of the best of health, but he wasn't the best patient, the clinic had been trying to schedule his overdue physical, but he hadn't made time to call back. His extra pounds troubled the doctor as much as his prostate issues, and like the hemorrhoids, slowed him down. The sitting and eating didn't help the Type 2, either and a good night's sleep wasn't in the cards anymore.

He never thought he'd get to the point, where counting the days to retirement, he prayed to get by until then without losing face. Soon, he'd be able to move to God's waiting room in South Florida to pick up golf and look for a wife.

For forty years, he had been a loyal officer in the department. He had respected his fellow workers. He would never call it quits without letting them know how much he appreciated their willingness to work around his speech impediment. He only stammered when overwhelmed.

He had been stuttering more lately. Before the Zabaglione family moved their headquarters to the township, Baxter's worst crimes had been shoplifting, fender benders and cherry-bombed mailboxes.

Unprepared for what he would see, Pops bent stiffly at the waist to peer inside the driver's garnet-splattered window.

The victim had been struck by more a bullet. This was not just a terrible auto wreck or hunter's wayward shot.

Pops' words rasped into the handset, "One dead." He fought with the difficult door handle. "Ja-Jack... ah... Henniger," he blurted.

The dispatcher's voice intensified. "Ten four. Jack Henniger dead."

Pops ignored his irregular heartbeat. Henniger's well-manicured fingers were stuck with blood to his phone. He had squeezed in a message that could not wait.

The man's bony knees had steered his well-treaded tires down their last lonely road. Pops shrugged his shoulders. The radio squawked. The murder weapon would have been a military-style assault weapon, he was familiar with them all. The station had an arsenal of weapons and ammo. This one, was most likely an AR-15. A bullet had pierced through the sparkling-clean windshield at sonic speed, penetrating the prominent man's suntanned forehead and lodging in the shoulder of seat behind him. Henniger's high-class brains had become spin art on his Armoral-shined dash.

Pops followed that angle, looking to the knoll above. The best he could figure was that Henniger, shot, had lost control. His car had flown off the cambered road and done a bellyflop onto its marshy wetland deathbed.

The assassination had the mark of the mob, with a message. Henniger's thumbs had been removed with a sharp implement; the stumps remained. Pops, gagging on the taste of recycled donuts and coffee, counted the remaining fingers. Henniger's right hand bore deep claw marks from long fingernails.

When Pops saw it, he spit a loogie in the water. Another appendage was "gone."

"What, in the holy name of Jesus," Pops cried, "happened to his *d-d...dick?*"

91
CLICKERS ARE QUICKER

The sun peeking over the train station jolted Catherine from her pill-induced sleep, mortifying her with reality. She had missed Brenda and her chance at the video. Excuseless and rumpled, she drove the old Plymouth home, not expecting to find police and media gathered outside her gate wanting in. She would need to get her wits about her fast, something bad had happened. The driver of the news van was pushing the gate's call box buttons. Gerte would let their calls go into voicemail. About to turn in, Catherine caught the eye of a female officer glancing up from her radio. Changing her mind, she drove on, taking Baxter Road east and turned north for the last half mile to go in the back. Passing through the soybean fields and woods, she finally reached the back of the house, where, hoping to avoid being seen from the front, she parked under the deck behind Gerte's car with the groceries. Needing to avoid Gerte, she climbed the stone steps to the side garden room, where she slipped in past the dogs, and tiptoed up the back stairs. Quietly, she slid open the pocket door and stepped in the large upper foyer for the front staircase and halls, where she stood, deciding her next move. Someone had to let in the police. She rushed into Jack's study and hit the right buttons on the phone. With no time to change her clothes, she ducked into Jack's bathroom, splashed water on her face, and ran his metal comb through her hair. Within a few minutes, there was heavy pounding on the front door with the knocker. The dogs were barking fiercely.

Her face prickled as the heavy front door creaked open. Gerte opened the door and was now talking to a man. From the window, Catherine saw the police car parked by her Hosta lined walk.

92

BAD NEWS

Gerte, in the kitchen, was brewing a rich smelling European-style coffee and looking forward to a well-deserved cup and her horoscope. It was nine-thirty, and her Saturday grocery shopping was finished. She had just unloaded and sent the last bag up in the dumbwaiter. She would put it away later.

The Hennigers had not touched her precisely set breakfast table.

She was returning the half and half to the fridge when the phone rang, giving the dogs in the garden room a reason to bark. When the Herr was home, she tried to answer, *mach schnell*. But the phones rang all day, and the calls interrupted her coffee breaks and work. She had to let some go. Nobody ever called for her, anyway. Sometimes, a visitor got stuck outside the gate, but they repushed the call button when important. Now, she noticed the phone light flicker and go out, her cue that a delivery truck or visitor was about to show up in front. Somebody had answered upstairs. She patted her thinning hair and straightened her comfy sweat suit. Stepping to a curtained window by the door, she watched with interest as a county police car arrived in the circular driveway and parked.

The police showing up before noon could only mean trouble. Three men, one uniformed, walked up the sandstone walk and pounded on the front door. Her throat felt grippy, her blood pressure pill was overdue. Contrary to how her horoscope might have read, the day had begun to look like work.

The sixty-four-year-old housekeeper shook her head and tugged open the weighty front door. She motioned for the officers to enter and examined them suspiciously and looked at their shoes. Her left eyebrow peaked like the St. Louis Arch.

"Mrs. Henniger?" the older one in the uniform, asked with a bit of surprise in his voice. Upstairs, she heard a flurry of light footsteps. *Frau* Henniger was scurrying down the maple-floored hallway from *Herr* Henniger's bathroom.

"Morning, officers." Catherine called to the men in the large foyer from the landing. "I'm Mrs. Henniger." She descended the wide staircase, relieved that she had rinsed off yesterday's makeup and combed her hair. She gave them a weak smile.

"The gentlemen might like some coffee," Catherine said to Gerte. She was conscious of her dry mouth and pounding heartbeat. The female officer in front had seen her. She did not have a credible answer to where she been all night. She wondered if they had learned about the dead girl and Jack. An alibi came to mind. "Please, come in," she said and motioned the officers to come in. Catherine smoothed her hair with her clammy hands. "I was out doing research on the habits of migrating birds with nesting Canadian Geese at dawn... *fascinating*, really! Did my husband send you looking for me?" Their eyes darted this way and that, filling her with dread. "Is something wrong, officers?" she asked, reading the uneasy expression on the Deputy's face. "Does this, have something to do with my husband?"

Gerte was focused on the officers' footwear and about to say "it." Cops didn't like to walk inside people's homes in their socks. But Gerte saw the mud on the older man's boots. Her chin twitched belligerently. "Shoes off," she ordered. Sliding open the pocket door, she disappeared into the kitchen. The men looked at each other and removed their shoes.

"Please, gentlemen, have a seat," Catherine said, despite her tapping teeth. She had seen zero signs of Jack upstairs.

"We have upsetting news, Mrs. Henniger." Her face prickled like a wildfire. The older man guided her to a chitz-covered chair inside the cavernous living room.

"I'm officer Clarence Peters," he said in a business-like tone. He introduced the plainclothes men. "This is First Detective Leon Dubrowski and Lt. Grey Day, Baxter Township. We wish we a better outcome to share. We're so very sorry to inform you...."

The men watching her face and reading her body language.

Mrs. Henniger impressed Pops as a handsome woman, not the lace and ruffles type, too elegant for this countrified part of the world. She was also not the type to stay out all night—or study birds in a swamp at sunrise. Her tired eyes showed dread. He'd try to be delicate. His boss, not a talker, always made him do the dirty work. "Early this morning, a body was found in a black and white automobile registered to your husband." He cleared his throat. "It happened off Baxter Road, about a mile from here. I answered the call myself." He took in a breath, watching her expression. "Unfortunately, we have a positive ID on the body, it is your husband, ma'am. Jack Henniger."

Catherine swooned from angst. "Oh, no—my Jack?" If she hadn't fallen asleep, she might have saved his life. Jack had been right; she was always too late.

"We are very sorry for your loss," the three said in unison. She felt limp and helpless, frightened. Hot tears filled her eyes. Deputy Peters offered her a tissue that had been in his pocket.

"Thank you, officer," she said, staring out the picture window, clenching hard. "I don't understand, how, or why, he was such a good driver. He loved that car." The moment she spoke, her jaw locked down, making it impossible to speak except through the tiny openings between of her perfect rows of teeth. As the dentist had predicted, her teeth were clamped together, stuck. "I didn't get to say good-bye." she mumbled through her lips.

"Excuse me?" Deputy Peters said.

She tried again, baring her locked teeth. "*Bye-bye!*"

"Forgive me, ma'am—gee, this is really awka—awka—awkward." He paused, then continued, "I'd like to ask you some preliminary questions. I'm sure you under...*sstand* how important ti-t- time can be in a criminal invest—"

"Preliminary...*criminal?*"

"Well, yes, ma'am, that's right."

Catherine slumped in the chair. She had reason to worry. Her heart and brain were in a race with fear moving up fast on the homestretch. The police had seen her drive in. It would not be long before they asked where she had spent the night. Her brain spun and her face felt frizzy. She pried open her mouth, using two fingers to dislodge her jammed upper mandible. *I was zonked out on sleeping pills, alone, in my car.* There were floating, sparkling spots in the room. "I... don't understand what you're saying, officer," she managed to say.

"He's sorry about his stuttering, ma'am," said the one with the hole in his sock.

She rubbed her forehead in little circles with her fingers, her breathing was fast and shallow. "This is unraveling," she said, looking at their faces for subtle cues. "He was so healthy—well, compared to other men his age. Are you *sure?* Please tell me what happened," she cried, leaning forward, her jaw slipping in and out.

"This is unpleasant, and we do apologize. Ma'am, your husband was shot by a rifle."

"Oh, no..." she whispered. Her thoughts spun in circles. "A hunter?" For a second, she hoped it had been the Dunlap brothers—the old farmers next door, using the geese for target practice. In her gut, she knew who, and *why*.

"We will explore all the possibilities, Mrs. Henniger," Deputy Peters said in a subdued tone of voice, "Ma'am, the body was mutilated." She swooned, gasping through her lips. "You mentioned you hadn't said goodbye, ma'am. Please. Was your husband out last night?"

Catherine thought of Fluffy and knew, her jaw ratcheting tighter. *Mutilated?* She could force out two words, shorthand for 'he'd never come home' and she 'hadn't seen him last night.' "Never... home."

"Was anything out of place, recently? Something unusual, troubling your husband?"

She stretched her jaw muscles causing a pop. "No," she said, rubbing her jaw. "Nothing I noticed."

"I apologize for being personal." He lowered his voice, "How was your relationship? Your marriage?" Catherine's face was motionless except for the rapid blinking, she could not hide the truth in her eyes. "This may be as hard to answer, but was he having an aff—?"

"I'd rather not say." Catherine looked at the floor.

"Understandable. Can you tell me if you noticed anyone *s-s-suspicious* hanging around lately?"

She rose, shook her head, and said, "I feel uncomfortable answering your questions."

"You certainly have the right to to contact an attorney, but Mrs. Henniger, we will need all the help we can get to find out who did this horrible thing to your husband. Did you ever sense that your husband might be in trouble?"

"Officer, I don't want to be rude, but I just lost my husband. I don't want to say anything else." Pops pushed.

"As I mentioned, there was a gun was involved. Did Mr. Henniger own or keep guns in the house?"

"Ah... well, yes, he has some rifles. Likes to hunt on the property. Deer, geese."

"You probably cook what he shoots, right? Do you like to cook?" Catherine shrugged. She could not speak much about cooking.

"My sister," he said, "she likes those Henkel knives from Germany. *Swears* by them. What brand do *you* prefer?" Catherine tapped her foot self-consciously and stopped to look at their eyes.

"I like Cutco, Deputy. Only Cutco—the sales rep sharpens them like razors for free, here, whenever we call. "They're guaranteed to do damage. Why do you ask?"

"Because, Ma'am, there was a large one found on the floor of your husband's car, a chef's knife. Are you missing one?"

She felt another wave of facial prickles. "Not that I know of."

"We'd like to ask you to come down to the station with us for some further fact gathering— if you don't mind. It will help us to move the *c-case* forward."

Her stomach flipped. "I'd like to talk to my lawyer before answering any more of your questions, officer— make a phone call, if that's all right." She stood up, staggering a bit.

"Think you're going to be, okay?" he asked.

"Oh, yes, thank you," she said, remembering her life insurance policy.

Suctioned to the kitchen door like a satellite dish, Gerte's ear received most of the transmission. By now, she had forgotten about coffee. The appalling news made her reel in disbelief, unhinging both bad knees. She steadied her pudgy self against the kitchen door frame. This development would change everything. She struggled to the liquor cabinet. Her plans to become Gerte the Fourth had just shattered, she realized with burning tears. Who would do such a horrible thing to her man, to their plans? *Die Liebe meines Lebens.* She poured herself a glass of schnapps in tribute to the great man. She was the only one who would miss him. She had known his needs better than any woman on Earth, *especially* the present *Frau.* She dried her tears before anyone could see. Gerte Schmaltz, child of postwar Germany, had kept his home for twenty years with unwavering loyalty. She had been his sole informant and principal source of secrets, the wisest purveyor of opinions.

Serving the finest man of the Greatest Generation had been her life's most important accomplishment, but it had not been a walk in a *Biergarten.* Her job had required the vigilant surveillance of others. It had been important for the *Herr* to know what the people in the house were doing—to assure they remained honest. She had tackled her task with determination, especially when sprinkling tidbits of suspicion here and there. Her days had been lonely, as it had been impossible to fraternize. Her dream had kept her going through *years* of cleaning up from his spoiled and lazy wives and their dogs, cats, and disgusting pet pig. While perspiring from heat, she had ironed thousands of bed sheets on the steaming hot mangle, and had even pressed the ungrateful bitch's cotton underpants, folded, and stacked them with precision.

Before long, her unhappy *Herr* would have realized that looking beyond her for sexual relief was fruitless. A dominant female, ready in the event of the slightest masculine need, was every man's fantasy, surely his. While he had not yet expressed his interest in her as a mate, outwardly, under the circumstances, it had been awkward for him to reveal his festering desire. But he had admired her quick wit and womanly ways. Now, her beautiful plans had become a waste—a tragedy of inconvenient timing for them both.

His females had come and gone, some faster than others. Each had been a misfit in her own way. This crazy *Frau* had outlasted most and had acted stranger than usual the last year, so weird, that Gerte had often had to bite her tongue. She was the one who washed their dirty laundry— the one who knew the secrets.

Her new life was supposed have begun when she became the final *Frau* Henniger. She would have made a fine one, too, because she knew how to live like a fancy lady should. Her preference for quality, the best things in life, had come from somewhere...certainly not from her *Mutter*, the pathetic whore. Her unknown father had, surely, been somebody important. She would have spent the *Herr's* fortune on jewelry— the good *Schmuck*—mani-pedis, massages, expensive clothes, and fine Italian handbags—and would have shopped at places beyond the grocery and drug store, had the 24-hour dry cleaners pick up. But thanks to his murderer, her dream was chopped liver without onions.

Wild suspicion crossed her mind. The couple naturally had experienced some problems, and she knew what they were—but murder? Perhaps the *Frau* had discovered the others and decided to destroy her comfortable retirement plan.

The *Frau's* odd behavior made sudden sense to Gerte. She had learned about the floozies and had killed him in an act of revenge. Premeditated murder! Catherine Henniger had enjoyed slicing her husband to death.

Gerte felt sick and disgusted. She would help the officers and tell the world the truth. She would become a heroine in the news. This was urgent—the authorities must know that the "refined" society woman was a disturbed, unworthy fake. Striding to the cook stove by the granite center island, she threw open the knife drawer. Just as she had suspected, there was an empty slot on the Cutco cutlery block. *Jawohl!* She smirked with smug satisfaction from being correct. The *Frau's* favorite butcher knife was missing from its usual place.

93
KAPUT

Deputy Peters leaned against the kitchen island, sizing up the housekeeper. Gerte Schmaltz was five-foot one, average height for a southern German. She was plumper than typical for her age group, perhaps making up now for what she couldn't eat as a child. She twisted the pockets of her apron and moved as if the bones in her knees rubbed together.

"He was such a good man! *Und* now, he *ist kaput!*"

"You've been with him a long time, then? Have you detected unusual activity here lately?" he probed.

Displaying a prominent dental gap, she smiled. *"Ja wohl* officer!" she said, clicking together the heels of her boiled-wool house clogs. Cracking her knuckles, she reached across him to the knife drawer, throwing it open with a dramatic clatter. *"Gone,"* she shouted excitedly. "The favorite knife of *Frau* Henniger! Her special Cutco knife has been removed!" The housekeeper leaned closer to hoarsely whisper. "She allows *no one* to touch it!"

94
FREEZER PARTS

Later that morning, during a search for evidence in Henniger's basement, Sergeant Leon Dubrowski discovered three human appendages as he dug through the deep freeze looking for ice for his diet drink. What he had at first mistaken for chicken fryer parts, was upon closer examination, Jack Henniger's missing "goody" bag.

By 11:00 a.m., the sergeant had officially declared all of Mr. Henniger's parts present and accounted for.

"What the *hell*—" Dubrowski stiffened and dangled the bag by two fingers. *"Eww!"*

Henniger's manicured thumbs and his essential male organ had been meticulously packed inside a small, zippered freezer bag, air-sucked, and stuck in a gallon-size bag with a kielbasa, or maybe, Italian sausage, he could not say for sure without the lab. The remains were laying in state on top a stack of well-marbled Omaha steaks. Perhaps a surprise for someone special?

"They were vacuum-packed by some really sick fucker's lips," the incredulous Dubrowski said to his homicide partner, trying to maintain decorum. "Strange, the parts bag was handled with care. The other one has some mileage on it."

"What's in it?" Lieutenant Day asked, interested, and taking notes.

"One partially freezer-burned sausage…Italian, looking more closely," he said, turning it under the ceiling light. "The zipper part is worn out." He handed the bag to Day. "Take a look." Its contents were covered by frost. The two concluded that older bag had been opened and closed numerous times. Inside, there was a neat note, penned in with a Sharpie in block-style writing. It said nothing especially noteworthy. *DELICIOUS! MILD ITALIAN SAUSAGE—HEAT AND EAT!*

95
FISHHOOKS AND
BICYCLE TIRES

Ben, back from the fishing trip, pushed up his shirt sleeves and reached across his soapy sink, smacking open the stuck kitchen window. The tip of his silk tie skimmed across his dishwater. A dew laden breeze filtered in through the old bronze screen, smelling good. The squadron of yellow daffodils that Jeannie had planted before she died, stood at attention along the backyard privacy fence. They brought back a blend of rich memories and reminded him that she had been gone for two long years. His tie dipped in the dish soap deeper.

The weather that day had started out clear, but an afternoon storm was predicted. He and Jeannie were taking their mountain bikes to a secluded place outside the city limits, a grassy spot off the beaten path— very private. They would not stay as long.

"Will we still have time for a romp?" she asked from the kitchen, where she was busy packing peanut butter sandwiches. He was in the garage lifting the bikes from their hooks for the ten-mile ride.

"Absolutely, yes," he answered, noticing that his MGB was parked too close to the cabinet to open the drawer where he kept his tire pump and pressure gage. Jeannie's car was parked behind his, and her keys were in the house. She emerged from the kitchen, locked the door, and loaded her saddlebag with their lunch, ready to go. She looked so darned desirable in her tight little black bike shorts.

The tires looked good enough.

They had made a pit stop at a coffee shop half-way to their favorite spot. He was faster and could easily outlast her but liked to lag back to watch her perfect butt sway back and forth. They would laugh out loud with the lively spirit of competitiveness.

He felt a lingering tingle as he remembered as he set a clean pan in the drainer. *Two long years.*

There had been no reason to suspect their trip would end as it did.

If he had acted more responsibly, her tragic accident would not have happened. If he had only checked the tire pressure like his conscience had warned, he would have noticed when he rolled out the bikes that his bass lure was stuck in her tire. And if he hadn't left his cell phone in the men's room, Jeannie would still be alive. Instead of safety, his thoughts had been on turning his saucy wife into a helpless female love machine on the picnic blanket. The sandwiches would have waited while they made out like hormonally crazed teens.

They had never even eaten the sandwiches.

She had spotted the large timber rattlesnake first and

braked— but something was wrong— her front wheel had wobbled wildly, and she had lost control, going off path. The snake struck her leg, and she had screamed sharply.

Growing weaker by the moment, she had lain immobile with her snake-bitten, badly broken leg. He had yelled for help into the silent, remote woods as the murderous snake pulsed away. There had not been a soul within earshot.

"Please, call 911," she had pleaded. *"Where is your phone?"*

96
BEN AND BUMBLES

Ben put away the last pan and patted Jeannie's aging Jack Russell, the only female in his life. "Good girl. Need to go *out, Bumbles?*" The happy dog gave him a wide, fangy smile. With Bumbles, he was never alone in the kitchen—or in bed, for that matter. She had taken over Jeannie's side the day she had died.

He shoved his towering pile of mail toward the dish drainer and reached for Jeannie's watering can. The kitchen clock said it was time for the local news. After watching, he would ride his 12-speed to the office and finish the draft of the divorce papers to go over with Catherine on Monday. He pursed his lips, deep in thought. Henniger had lost his mind along with his manners.

The plants were praying for a drink. Jeannie would have watered them before the fishing trip. She had had a personal relationship with each and had even named the spider plants: Jumper, Tarantula, Widow, and his favorite, Biting-U. He groomed them and sighed. The dwindling few survivors would never make the Garden and Flower

Show. He filled the watering can to the line and started with the philodendrons, which were as dusty as Harlan said that he was.

He had finally made partner at his law firm and was happy to be useful once again. Especially, to Catherine.

97
CALL FROM THE CLINK

Ben poured a second cup of Columbian and settled in his chair, propping his feet on the ottoman for the morning news. The tan leather moccasins Jeannie had given him were growing dog-eared around the soles.

He wished they would last forever, like his memories of her as the pretty new girl on the block. She had had freckles, short auburn hair, hazel eyes; and a laugh, so contagious that she could make him beg for mercy. From his bedroom window, he had watched her walking door to door raising money for the garden club by playing her school violin. His heart had fluttered when she rang his parents' bell. Her neighborhood price was a dollar a song, but for him, two songs. He had scraped his coins together.

"How do I get to Carnegie Hall?" she had asked, applying some resin to her bow. He had grinned and reached in his pocket for quarters. "Practice, practice, *practice!*"

He missed the music they had made together.

The homecoming dance had been their first date.

Jeannie, a stunner in her new party dress, had returned from the ladies' room with the backside of it stuffed in her underpants. They had enjoyed a good laugh.

They were married while undergrads. She was a talented music student, and he was good at law. After plenty of practice, she had landed the position of first-string violin with the St. Louis Suburban Orchestra. He had found a law firm job.

Bumbles' whine returned Ben's attention to the present. He set down his coffee cup and patted her. Jeannie's books were still on the dusty maple bookshelf with her hardback copy of *"The Joy of Sex."* More than a few pages had been marked with folded corners. Although they couldn't have kids, they had enjoyed trying. The dogs had become their family and their marriage had felt complete.

He set his laptop on the lamp table and tuned the TV to Channel 7. He liked to watch the local news and read the financial report to begin each day. The red banner rolling across the screen, catching his eye. He sat up straight, letting a foot drop to the floor.

"Breaking News...Chemical Tycoon...Jack Henniger... dead...." He clicked to the front page of the Journal with his brain completely tuned in. "API: American executive, former Henniger Chemical International Chairman was found dead in his car this morning close to his Baxter, MO estate. Henniger, known as the father of Agent Brown, has been credited for masterminding the concept and production of genetically modified food. Several persons of interest are being questioned."

Ben choked on his mouthful of coffee as he processed

the blast of dumbfounding news. His phone startled him. He grabbed it by the second ring. It was Catherine, choking back tears, struggling to say that she was at the police station.

"I heard the news. I'm speechless," he said, with a reassuring voice. "Are you okay?" She was hyperventilating. "Do you have a paper bag?"

She spoke in hushed tones. "Ben—I'm scared and can't think. He was... dear God, he was *murdered!*"

"Murdered," Ben repeated. If anyone had asked for an axing, it would have been Henniger.

"Shot," she whispered, "and dismembered." Now, he felt her terror. "I should have called the police days ago, but I felt confused. I don't know what to do now, I'm afraid," she sniffed. "I need you."

He had already slipped into his bike shoes and laced up. "Where are you?" His suit was rolled up in his backpack.

"At the station downtown," she said in the tiniest voice, "being questioned." His heart sank. Nothing about it sounded good.

"Do not say a word until I get there."

Catherine whispered a quiet confession, "Ben, I was out last night before dawn."

His heart sank. She needed to talk. "Yeah?"

"It's a long story." She paused to breathe. "I have no one to confirm where I was." He pushed his glasses up his nose. "And Jack was killed before sunrise," he said, his hands perspiring. His English muffin was smoking in the toaster. He unplugged it.

"He was being blackmailed for a sex video...a young

girl died. They were planning to kill him for the money. I thought I could buy the video from Brenda Zabaglione." Ben gulped, barely believing her words. *Mafia.* "While I waited for her at the train station, I fell asleep from a pill I'd taken earlier. I can't fall sleep without them anymore." He knew. He had taken his share.

"You shouldn't be saying this over the phone."

"When I woke up, it was already morning. I never saw her. I drove straight home," she offered. "But two squad cars and a TV van with reporters were out front. One officer saw me. I drove the mile around to the back entrance to avoid them."

Ben cleared his throat. "Then, what?" he asked. This was trouble.

"I parked under the back deck. Our housekeeper showed the police to the knife drawer. My chef knife was missing. She stood with the police, glaring at me, like I had killed him. I was sick. They turned my home into a Hollywood-style crime scene their rolls of yellow tape and gave me five minutes to make this call. I'm glad you answered."

"Have you told them anything, yet?"

"They saw me at the gate. I told them I had been ob- serving the mating habits of geese at dawn."

"Don't say another word. They can wait. We can figure it out together," he said, trying to soothe her, feeling her innocence deep inside his gut. "Remember, don't talk to your friends— and especially, to the help. The media's all over this." He stuffed his work folders in his backpack. "Sit tight. I'm getting on my bike now. I promise to get there soon."

Her breathing sounded more even, but her voice was low and intense. "My future is at stake. Please, hurry."

98
BOBO DOC AT THE POLICE STATION

Bobo Doc slouched on the bench closest to Deputy Peters' desk and bobbed his leg, trying not to cry. His soggy pants, socks and shoes were still damp from swamp water and clung to him uncomfortably, as did his nervous sweat, making him shiver. He was waiting to be interviewed in the small interrogation room by Peters and the detectives. The hands on the electric wall clock showed they had been torturing his brother for thirty minutes so far. He wanted to stand up and walk around, work off the fear—run away. It would be harder for the Devil to focus on him when he made himself a moving target.

He rose a foot, craning his neck for a peek through the blinds, hoping to catch a glimpse. The stern lady officer who had taken his fingerprints and hair sample stopped him. When he called 911 from the Devil's place, he had not imagined they would be treated as suspects. He had done the right thing. He was a peace-loving vegetarian who had never even hooked a worm, and the sight of blood made him swoon. As God was his witness, Satan was trying to frame him for somebody else's 'bad.' He couldn't take his mind off the horror of the slaughtered old man. Only the Prince of Darkness would have mutilated a human being like that. There was nothing in his belly to throw up, but he wanted to.

His head spun with dark thoughts. What if he and Digger were charged with murder? What would Auntie Ella think? They were law-abiding, innocent, believers in the golden rule. He had seen stories about racial problems with the police. Perhaps they would toss them behind bars and throw away the key. He needed to play it cool, stop his shaking, be a man. But he was scared. He and Digger might never see their beloved Montserrat again, he thought, beginning to cry. He could not stop, but nobody in the station seemed to notice. If they went to jail, how could they help pay for Auntie Ella's liver operation? He closed his eyes and prayed for a miracle. He would let Jah be the ultimate judge.

The door to Digger's interrogation room opened a crack, spilling out voices. Bobo Doc opened an eye. A detective emerged to pluck a handful of hard candy from the dish on the lady's desk. He looked him over expressionlessly as he unwrapped the candy and popped it in his mouth. Without a word, he returned to the room and closed the door behind him.

Bob Doc glanced around again, killing time. There were desks in several small cubicles with busy looking officers. A beautiful blonde woman had been escorted to the room next to Digger's ten minutes before. He watched the nice shape of her silhouette on the window's bubble glass. Inside the room, someone stood up, the voices were muffled. To distract himself, Bobo Doc counted the black and white floor tiles but stopped. They reminded him of the dead man's car. A notice with a photo on the bulletin board caught his eye. *Murdered Minor Female, Human Trafficking, $10,000 Reward for Information Leading to Arrest or Conviction.*

He studied the picture of the victim. She was young— early teens—a Negro, like himself, and there was something familiar about her face. He could almost place her, but not quite. A thought crossed his mind; he sat up a little taller. Could she be the girl that the old guy had been groping in the car? Bobo Doc could never forget. He looked toward the ceiling fan, hoping that Jesus was listening. "Is this a connection?" The car windows had been steamy, so he wasn't entirely sure—still, reporting it would be the right thing to do. He would tell them that he had seen the murdered girl with the old man as he was emptying Henniger's trash. The same car, same girl, same man.

Bobo Doc thought on. There was a reward. If he could get his hands on the reward money, (providing he did not go to jail) he would pay for Auntie Ella's surgery—and repay his cousin for the new brakes and fan belt on the $800 Plymouth Neon that he and Digger co-owned.

He traced some crude graffiti that a whacko had carved on his bench. His chest heaved at the thought of nutjobs with knives. Hearing some voices, he looked up to see a wild-looking white guy in padded shorts and a helmet pass through the metal detector, another weirdo. The man stopped at the lady officer's desk. Busy with a phone call, she directed him to the bench, then resumed her conversation and writing on a notepad. The man with the helmet paced the floor. Bobo Doc made room for him on the bench. He nodded thanks, and unbuckled his plastic sky piece, setting it, and his backpack, on his other side. He fidgeted with his shoelaces, then tested his breath with the palm of his hand and patted his hair.

The crazy man seemed okay, he decided, a nervous city guy. Most people had a reason to feel anxious at a police station. The man took a pair of tortoiseshell reading glasses from his pack. Bobo Doc thought. Had Jah sent them a lawyer? The gentleman stood up, then walked to the bulletin board, where he examined the law enforcement notices and the headshot of the girl.

Maybe the man could help him to get the reward money. Taking a chance, Bobo Doc blurted, "I saw de girl, ya know." The man raised an eyebrow. "Could you be a solicitor?"

The man handed him a business card. "Yes. I'm Ben Williams, and you?"

"Garbage guy. Both me and my bro down the hall. I'm Alfonso Daley, please call me Bobo Doc." He held out his hand and they shook.

"What did you see today, Bobo Doc?" He closed his eyes and shook his head, recalling it. "We found an old white man, dead, in his black and white car. It was *ugleee*, man—he was missin' his junk."

Mr. Williams gasped. "Do they believe that you and your brother killed him?"

He nodded and pointed to the poster. "But last week, *that* girl was wit 'im."

"You saw her with the man? Bad, huh? Maybe we can help each other," the lawyer man said. "Can you describe the girl?" He lowered his voice, looking around like good people did.

Bobo Doc formed large circles with his hands. "Jumbo boobs." A naughty laugh burped out. With his face flushing, he told Ben what Jack Henniger and the underage runaway had been up to the morning when he had seen them in the black and white car.

99
GUINEA PIG

Lieutenant Day emerged from the interrogation room, clearing his throat as a polite acknowledgement to Bobo Doc and himself. "You're up," Day said, nodding to Dubrowksi as the phone rang. Amanda Hernandez, the crabby female officer, wrote another note on her pad.

"First," Dubrowksi said, "we need to talk, Lieutenant. His eyes motioned toward Bobo Doc. The two officials stepped far enough away from Ben to be mostly unheard. Ben, listening with a cupped hand, understood that they were talking about the girl Daley had seen in Henniger's car. He listened harder, watching their body language.

Fernandez hung up the phone and approaching the others, dropped her note on Peters' desk. She motioned to the poster with a stern expression. The three officers were speaking in hushed tones. Day called Peters over to say something quietly. Dubrowski and Fernandez scattered to make phone calls.

"Williams," said Day, calling him over.

"We have a positive ID on the runaway now.

Nobody gave a shit about her. Thanks to the Rasta man, we're connecting the dots, getting a picture. The dead girl was an unwilling guest of Mascarpone's human trafficking ring. Henniger's mistress worked in his house, at least for a while, Peters tells us," Day continued. "He remembers seeing her there a couple of years back—a domestic dispute call, without an official complaint. She was Mrs. Vincent Puziari then, divorced now from that son-of-a bitch felon."

"What else?" Ben asked, quickly tying his bike shoes.

"Puziari is Mascarpone family. He moved up to their porn division since his recent round in the clink. We would do anything to throw him back in."

"Didn't Puziari get extra time for assaulting the chaplain with a metal coat hanger?" "Yeah, the chaplain told him to go to hell—Puziari didn't like it."

"Okay, listen—I have an idea," Ben said, and the authorities listened to his plan.

Providing that it doesn't kill her, it will work, Ben thought as he entered the spartan interrogation room where Catherine waited. The space had two glass ashtrays and a Dixie cup on the table. She was biting on a cuticle, staring at the wall. He walked over to her, rolling a chair. The change in her appearance was startling. Without saying a word, he grasped her rigid hand and pulled it away from her mouth. He held it until it warmed. She'd grown three shades paler since he had seen her last.

Her expression was exhausted, dull. He wished he could have been in on the conversation if he had only pedaled faster.

Catherine had not waived the right to have him present during her interrogation. They had pressed ahead without him, anyway. The problem was the facts were indisputable. The police had the knife, one of the two weapons used. It belonged to the victim's wife and was covered with dozens of her fingerprints. She had a motive and did not have an alibi, a reality that was hard to ignore.

The firearm was out there, somewhere. Maybe they would find it, but then, maybe not. One 5.56 bullet was embedded in the seat. A thinking person could see that Catherine was not the type to wield an automatic weapon with the accuracy of a crack shot.

She was a good girl, a quality Jack Henniger had not appreciated. Old Scratch had finally paid a visit to the twisted narcissist whose lechery had sealed his fate. And now, Catherine was the key to luring his assassin, who wanted more revenge. If everybody did their job, his plan would vindicate her. The police would guarantee her plenty of protection, but the truth was, she would still be in peril. He looked at her beautiful, frightened face. She was vulnerable, the way Vincent Puziari liked them.

After Bobo Doc's revelation, the police had reason to believe that Henniger had been intimate with the teen. They could also connect him to the mob and to the Baxter County porn business that they had been trying to bust. He tried to calculate what to say to Catherine first. He didn't want her to be in harm's way—there were bad guys involved in this. If she agreed, and all went well, she could help the police put the Mascarpone kingpins away for good.

Her husband had died for a personal reason that reached beyond money, but Puziari needed his dough, and believing that it was in the house, he would be back. The chance was slim that he would come tonight. Puziari was too smart to show up before things cooled down. Tomorrow, or the following night, were most likely.

Catherine moved her water to make room for Ben to sit closer. She touched his hand. "I told them every-thing, Ben," she said, rubbing her eyes. He looked at her, stunned. She hesitated a second, and added, "Well... not *everything.*" He had a good idea what she meant by that.

"Did you tell them that Jack was being blackmailed?" he asked with a sinking heart. He would have stopped her from talking with his foot under the table.

"Yes. By the mob."

Ben managed to squeak a small smile. "Catherine, the police know more now." He watched her color improve. "I think they'll let you go, but there's just a small catch." He glanced out the window. It would be dark before long. "How would you feel going home to an empty house tonight?"

"Somebody," she said, smiling slightly, "has to let the dogs out."

100
AND TODAY'S
GATE CODE IS?

The lieutenant's unexpected demand for overtime came as he was packing it in. Pops would be babysitting all night for a Mafia target, after a grueling long day, the most disturbing of his career. He hadn't fully recovered from this morning—if he ever would. In thirty-six years of law enforcement, he had never seen such gruesome butchery—never so personal and up close. He badly wanted a hot bath and some boiled pierogies. But his job was to uphold the law and protect the innocent. He had to suck it in.

He would take Mrs. Henniger home, then circle to the back entrance and hide the patrol car and would sneak back to position himself in the trees behind the guesthouse—on the off-chance Zabaglione or his guys would make trouble tonight. His stomach growled. The digital clock in the squad car read nine—way past his seven o'clock dinner time. He was feeling a blood sugar slump.

In his mirror, he watched the widow dozing in the back, exactly what he felt like doing himself. She hadn't said much, which was understandable considering the re-al-life nightmare she was living through. He hardly knew what to say, except that he was sorry for her loss. Nice as she was, she wasn't off the hook with the law yet. She was a clean-cut, good-looking woman, the opposite of the barefooted babe who had come to the door wearing

Henniger's monogrammed bathrobe that icy cold night. Pops wondered how the missus had put up with his cheating and all the rumors. Maybe she had stayed for the money—who knew? She seemed to have a fair bit of class, not the gold digger type. She was shy, unassertive, something that he, with his lifelong speech impediment well understood.

She was to be a *Mafioso* magnet, good idea or not—it wasn't his, but deputies don't get to make the rules. The Zabaglione clan was a rough group.

He pulled onto Henniger's private road and lowered his window, stiffly twisting his torso for the gate code. The cool air woke her up.

"One, two…three, four," she said, sitting up in the back seat. "I know I should change it, I don't know how." She rubbed her eyes. "Nobody does."

This had been a sheltered little township. The average citizen couldn't imagine how much evil slithered about unseen. Most of the TV crime stuff, like what Pops couldn't watch, stayed under the radar of the ordinary person's life, thanks to law enforcement.

He drew a deep breath of her expensive cologne, a rare treat for a working man's nose. He, of all people to be put on this case. He hoped he could keep her safe. He rotated his head, cracking his neck. *Guaranteed Pest Control, at your service, ma'am.* He would be up to a fight with them if it came to that.

If he could put those bad boys out of business, he could hang up his badge with honor. Every time he drove past the Zabaglione gravel yards, he wondered what they were up to behind their barbed-wired privacy berms. He could be about to find out.

"Peters," Day had assured him, "you're the best guy I have. Your reinforcements will reach you in minutes, providing your cellphone works."

Pops was feeling his age these days, especially with the kinks in his back from vegetating in his car. He was a little overweight, but proud that he could still coldcock the average creep. Underestimating him, would be their mistake. He tested his bicep. He was just as ripped as always under the fat, and confident.

Zabaglione's guys were not just petty shoplifters, although they did plenty of that. The local business owners turned a blind eye. This was different. Thinking of the killer's horrific slicery, he squeezed his legs together. He slowed to a stop over the bridge to scan the house and grounds. The fountain was the only visible sign of motion. Mrs. Henniger had fallen peacefully back to sleep. He hated to send her into the cavernous house alone.

She would be safe. He would stake out the grounds and then surveil the house from a distance. He knew the estate and how to make himself undetectable. He would make sure nobody came in or went out. If necessary, he would rush in and rescue her.

It would be tough for him to stay alert until the shift changed in the morning. Eight hours. Java and food for his diabetes would keep him awake. His stomach growled again. Before getting to work, it couldn't hurt to slip out for some fast food and coffee, then quickly return to the rear entrance. He would need more energy for the walk through the woods to his post behind the guest house. From there, he would be able to see both the front and back of the main house. He rested his hand on his pistol. She would be alone on the estate, except for her guard dogs, but for only a short while.

The lady, sensing that they had arrived, stirred in the back. He cleared his throat. "You're home, Mrs. Henniger. Are you awake? Things look ca-calm and quiet... ah... quite *quiet* here."

He pulled up to the basement door and they talked until the headlights shut off, then he helped her out of the car. "Now, remember, ma'am, I will be within rr-range throughout the night, if... if anything appears out of place, you know you ca... ca... *can* call me, right?" he looked at her, attempting a smile. The frogs were chirping. He opened the heavy door and she entered. It would not be as scary with the furnace room light on. She would be fine.

"Thank you," she said, giving the pool and shadowy shrubs a quick scan.

"Do you have your cell phone handy?" he asked, smiling.

She patted her side pocket, "Yes," she answered simply returning his smile before disappearing through the door.

"Turn on some lights."

"I will."

The Hennigers' dogs were quiet and well-behaved.

101
GOONS AT THE GATE

Returning to the estate, Pops listened to the Cardinals-Tigers game with his Biggie Burger fast meal wedged between his legs. Cardinals were three and four, game tied, top of the ninth. The French fries were still warm and tasty with just the right amount of salt. Because he had been thinking about losing fat and finding a girlfriend, he had skipped the second burger and ordered a bacon-gorgonzola-cranberry salad with Paul Newman's creamy ranch to go with his fries. He would have plenty of time to eat it later. Driving while eating salads was messy.

Justin Verlander had just pitched a strike when Pops noticed taillights outside Henniger's gate. He cranked off his headlights and slowed to a stop, staying far enough back to observe without being seen, thinking. He washed down a fry with another swallow of coffee, barely feeling the brew when it dribbled. His mouth dropped. The vanity plate on the black Chrysler 300 was 'CUTUP.'

Two men with refrigerator-sized shoulders were trying

to enter the grounds. The driver opened his window and reached for the call-box buttons. A moment later, the large gate opened. Pops replaced his cup in the holder, freeing his hand for a radio call and continued past them, lights off. His challenge now was to beat them to the house and get his reinforcements to block the road at the bridge.

"How about a *cc-couple* of guys with some fire... fire-power?" The vein on his forehead was pounding. "Mrs. Henniger is about to gg-get some *cc-company.*" He gave the dispatcher the specialty plate number.

Pops accelerated to eighty-five, holding that for the half mile to St. Louis-Baxter Road. Turning right, he pressed on for the next quarter mile to the estate's back entrance, where he entered the rough two track, head-lights off. The coffee splashed from his cup. The unsavory pair in the Chrysler was not there to read electric meters. It would be a race to beat them to the house and they were in the lead. He was counting on their surveilling the house before making their move.

From out of nowhere in the moonless dark, a parked Volvo wagon blocked his path. He steered away and braked hard, avoiding it by inches. No one was inside, not even teenagers making out. The estate was getting crowded fast, he thought, trying his radio once more.

"What else you need, Pops?"

"Got another p-p-plate for you to run, sss... ah... stat," he ordered, spitting out the numbers from the car. What'd...what'd you g-*get* on the first one?"

"Registered to a Vincent Puziari, St. Louis, MO. Numerous arrests, time." The dispatcher's voice was all business. He gave her the suspects' descriptions. Pops faced a quarter mile jog through the dark woods to head off Jaws and Odd-Job. He set off on foot in the direction of the main house, his chest burning and heart hammering wildly, making good time until his boot caught on an unseen root. He flew off course, his head hitting a stump. Dazed, he picked himself up, ignoring the bright spots and dizzy feeling long enough to type a message to Mrs. Henniger without delay: *THEY'RE HERE. HELP IS COMING. STAY INSIDE.*

He prayed she would read his words and stay safe until he got there.

102
"GOING UP"

Fourteen hours and some newsworthy happenings earlier, the former farm boy sprinted through the woods in the early morning light, dodging obstacles, and ducking behind trees. In hot pursuit behind him, was Zabaglione's search party, crashing through the brush with the goal of putting him where the "sun don't shine." Vinny spotted a handy fox burrow and dove in, camouflaging himself with a tree branch. Like two blind rats, the goons sailed over him and ran on. They would eventually search the house for him and the money. But he would beat them to the big game prize. He climbed from the hole and nimbly backtracked around them.

Vinny stood, now, by the basement broom closet waiting for his chance to move upstairs. Unfortunately, he had spent more time inside the house than desired, stuck most of the day in the fucking dumbwaiter (a cubic yard in size), between the basement and kitchen levels without food, water, or bathroom facilities. On regular days, the housekeeper used the stifling little lift to hoist her cleaning and groceries, used breakfast trays, and Hennigers' fancy luggage to the various floors where it was controlled by a panel of buttons that worked only when the door was "firmly" closed.

He had just placed Henniger's dick and thumbs in the basement freezer chest as a surprise for the missus when the ruckus between Juno and Viktor began. Dropping the freezer lid, he had scrambled inside the dumbwaiter and folded his short arms and legs up like a pretzel. Nobody, especially those two, would guess that he and his rifle, could hide, or fit, inside a pea-sized elevator.

He wiped his brows, they dripped from the heat. A million bucks could take him a long way in style. Why not keep it? The hell with Zabaglione, and them all. Nobody would stand in his way. Except, for the Gestapo housekeeper. Despite the police warning her not to touch nothing, Fraulein Schmaltz had clicked the dumbwaiter door shut and pushed the green button, sending him to level three for the dead man's laundry. He wished he could get his hands on her.

If the sleeve of his best satin track jacket had not gotten jammed between the door and the elevator shaft, he might have made it up there to kill her.

Halfway to the kitchen floor, the lift had come to a screeching halt, pinning him down like an addict in a straitjacket. During his last stint in jail, he had complained of claustrophobia, and they had put him in a better, bigger cell—of course, he had only been shitting them, then. Today, his panic had been real. The only good thing about the solitary confinement was that he had learned they had taken the missus to the station. Once the cop show had left, Gerte Schmaltz had taken the dogs. Recognizing that his only chance for escape was to cut, or gnaw, off the sleeve of his racetrack jacket, he had patted his trouser pocket, finding the large toenail clippers Pussi liked to use on his feet. With a toothache and a bleeding finger, he had spent hours extracting small pieces of satin from the dumbwaiter door. The clippers had worked. Once freed, the dumbwaiter had returned home...good thing that it had happened before the power outage, he thought, thinking on. So there would be no chance of the power coming on, the first thing he did when he got out was throw the main switch off in the garage fuse box.

Now, he and his AR-15 stood motionless under the basement stairs, wishing for another knife, thinking that the smaller Cutco chef in the kitchen drawer could work even better up close.

Outside the door, he heard a man's steps running away. A minute later, a car and two people showed up, one of them, the missus. Interesting, that they had let her go. He ducked in the broom closet, squeezing himself behind the bubble wrap and boxes, brooms, and cleaning supplies. The singing rubber fish served as a useful distraction when she entered the house. She continued upstairs in the dark.

The broom closet had been a safe place, he thought, stepping out. He would visit the pretty lady in the bedroom when the time was right. He was sure that she would help him find the money. He waited a few minutes, listening for the creak of steps as she climbed the second flight of stairs to the bedrooms. Now that the coast was clear, he could think about stretching his legs, getting something to eat, and rape.

103
BAD TO THE BONE

Catherine found she had another problem. The ceiling lights didn't work. Either the storm had caused another outage, or someone had intentionally shut it off. She put the latter out of her mind, refusing to think the worst. The house was eerily quiet, no barking. Jack's animated motion detector, a mounted rubber bass, suddenly jerked its head toward her, its eyes flashing red as it belted out a bar of *"Ba-ba-ba-bad to the bone!"* Her heart ricocheted in her chest. Tomorrow, she would toss it back in the lake. In a few moments, the fish stopped, and the house returned to quiet as before.

"My God," she whispered to herself, "where are the dogs?" She felt drained, alone, and worried as she wondered whether Gerte had taken them, or not. Her teeth closed vacuum tight. She opened her mouth, hoping to stop her jaw from locking up again. She had counted on the dogs for security tonight, especially the Dobermans. She double checked the door lock behind her. The alarm system control was mounted above the light switch.

No one since Pussi had known how to set the alarm, or bothered, because so many people and dogs came and left during the day. If ever she had needed the alarm, it was tonight. Fortunately, the system had a battery back-up. On a hunch, she tried the default, same as the gate box, and hit STAY. After thirty seconds, anyone coming in through a window or door would trigger an alarm. But the flashing message said, COULD NOT BYPASS. Frowning, she slipped off her shoes and reminded herself that Deputy Peters would be within range with his backup. She crossed the long hallway to the stairs, lighting her way with her phone.

Stopping in the kitchen, she filled a glass with cold water from the tap and drank half. Her knife drawer, she could see, was ajar—Gerte, the disloyal bitch, who had been in such a hurry to leave, would have plenty of time to watch soap operas after she fired her in the morning.

Catherine paused, deciding to put a knife under the mattress tonight...

But the image of Jack's gruesome death haunted her. Unable to even look at a knife, she closed the drawer. Nothing would happen tonight, she assured herself, pushing aside a curtain for a last look at the guest house. There was nothing as far as the bridge or the bend in the drive.

Puziari could have somehow taken money since it had not been in Jack's safe. She prayed that the police would capture him, so she would never again fear the sight of his evil face.

The message light on the house phone blinked madly

with voice messages. As long as Puziari was still lurking about, she could not talk to anyone. Not even Jack's funeral arrangements could be made. In the morning, after finding the dogs, she would give Gerte the boot and look for dark clothes. She drew the curtains closed and climbed the back staircase, dreading tomorrow.

For now, her flannel pajamas would help calm her nerves. She would go straight to bed, pull the covers over her head and call Ben to keep her company. If only for a few minutes, the sound of his soothing voice would take her mind off how frightened she was. His strong arms had comforted her at the police station. Before she could reach for the bedroom doorknob, a message dinged on her phone.

104
SHARPENING CLAWS

"Hey, there, Mrs. Henniger." Catherine swallowed hard as the voice from the bedroom squealed like blackboard chalk. *Pussi!*

"Fuck!" Catherine shouted, eyes spinning toward the sofa next to her beloved antique Steinway piano. The phone dropped from her hand and skated like a hockey puck across the hard maple floor. Her imminent danger made her feet turn to lead as her mind scrambled for something in the room that could serve as a weapon. It had been foolish to come upstairs without a knife.

"Guess who, Titties?" No one since middle school had used that cruel nickname. *Jack had sweetly shared.* Pussi threw back her head, cackling. Catherine trembled from the familiar feelings of unworthiness fighting to take her down. There was nothing good about this visit. She had often fantasized about killing Pussi, but when given the opportunity, she only wanted to gallop away. Her real nemesis still lived in her own heart. Fear. She knew that if she didn't kill it, it would crush her faster than Pussi ever could. Peters' text to stay put had been clear, yet she remained conscious of the long hall behind her. Help from the deputy and other police was on its way; she needed the courage to hold herself together until then. Her rising heart rate matched the shaking of her hand as she patted the wall for the closest light switch. Still no power. Fortunately, the rain had passed, and the sky had cleared, allowing moonlight to send dim light through the windows.

"Someone gouged the side of yer precious piano with one of them sharp metal church keys." Pussi announced with a loud cluck and sympathetic shake of her head. Her large gold-toned earrings flip-flopped on her neck. "Such a rotten shame!" Pussi caressed the shocking damage that ran along the entire length of the century-old instrument. With a wicked smirk, she pulled a bottle opener from her pocket and waved it at the ivory keyboard. "Hmm, lookie what I found."

Catherine covered her gasp. The cords on her neck were as tight as the piano strings. *"Don't touch!"* she hissed like a hot steam engine, turning the fear in her heart into strength.

It was her piano, her room, her house—and it had been her husband, *dammit*. It was time to put a permanent end to this bitch.

105
VINNY AND THE BISCUIT

Vinny emerged from his understairs hidey-hole and stumbled up the stairs in the darkness to the first floor: kitchen appliances, knives. The goons were on his mind. Zabaglione wasn't the kind of guy who liked to leave a job like killing him, unfinished. So, where were they? What in hell had happened to Pussi...where had she been all day? If she had took the blackmail money last night, she would be drunker than a skunk in a bunk by now. But on the off chance the shameless cheater didn't steal it, she would have stopped by the safe on her way to the liquor store.

Vinny opened the fridge and pushed aside a jug marked 'pasta water' He slipped a nice smelling salami into the pocket of his soiled sharkskin trousers. If Pussi tried to call, he wouldn't have known, trapped as he was all fucking day in the stupid dumbwaiter with an unworking phone. He had not eaten or drunk a drop since the *Pasta e fagioli* last night. His bowels were gassy from having had nothing inside to digest since then. He grimaced as he relieved himself with pleasing results. Another *peto* would feel even better, but he should stop as a personal courtesy. A dog barked off in the woods. Two gunshots fired. The goons were close! He checked his rifle and set it down again.

He knew his way around the kitchen. A ceramic cookie jar conveniently rested on the island. He took the lid off and helped himself, dropping a handful in his other pocket. He glanced at the door to the redwood deck, expecting to see Juno and Viktor peering in the window with their pistols. Not yet. He switched his attention to the knife drawer.

A dim light would have been helpful for selecting his next implement, but his damn cell phone was dead. He would have to use the Braille method without slashing a finger.

The lovely missus would want to lead him to his money. The thought of holding her and the money made him smile. His looks seemed to earn him extra respect with her. He visualized her womanly figure. She would be frightened when he pressed himself on top of her. He frowned a little, knowing he only had time for a quickie, but it *was* going to happen. The lady would have some thrills before she died.

Quiet footsteps on the deck caught at his attention; he crouched on his knees, snapping his eyes between the knife drawer and the door. A dim light on the outside pointed at the door, a fit-looking figure tiptoed up. Taking him for a cop, Vinny raised his rifle, about to let out his breath and press. But he hesitated. A change in plans would be a shame, but the missus would make an easy and valuable hostage. The man, shining his phone on the handle, bent forward as if his eyesight were bad. Vinny got a good look. Cops did not wear ties and bicycle shorts.

Another person snooping around the house would complicate his plan to get the money. He scowled and caressed his rifle. He would deal with him, too, if he had to.

The man rattled the locked kitchen door, and failing, disappeared in search of an easier way in, Vinny guessed. He grabbed a knife, smaller than the chef's knife, and ducked into the small laundry room off the kitchen. The room was still warm from the clothes dryer from hours before. His cheek brushed against the laundry Frau Schmaltz had strung on a line from wall to wall. He felt the delicate fabric and the start of an erection. The missus' panties were pinned to the line. He took a deep nosey breath from habit, but her panties were big and roomy clown pants—they smelled like Gerte's Borax. He would not have guessed that the missus would be so sensible. Killing time, he sat on the floor to listen for sounds of more company. The house had been built like a brick shithouse; its walls as thick as a straw bales.

The back stairs and the upstairs floors were made of maple. He thought of the time he had hidden in the loft above the bedroom watching Pussi and his highness, he had discovered from experience what was creaky. Plan B, using the front staircase would work better. He would creep up the silent stone steps and take the missus by surprise. He had a good feeling. What the hell, have fun, kill the rich bitch, too. She would not have a chance to scream to anybody in bike shorts outside. He adjusted his trousers, maybe she wouldn't want to get away.

In the meantime, he was hungry. Eating anything would help his stomachache. He shoved a cookie in his mouth, chewing greedily on the side with good teeth. He rolled the mash around on his tongue, swallowing half. It tasted dry, more like a dog biscuit. He spat it on the laundry room floor. He fucking hated dogs.

106
CIRCLING IN
SHARK SUITS

"*Psst!*" Viktor whispered, alarmed.

"*What?*" Juno asked, perhaps too loudly. There were no lights on in the house—not even in a bedroom. They'd been watching it for movement from the woods on the west side of the house. Other than that, it had felt like they were alone, until it hadn't.

"Shh. *See* it?"

"See—*whut?*" Juno asked, looking all around, straining. "Sumpthin' moved! "Viktor pointed to the bushes, at something rustling toward them, coming up fast, splitting the sea of thigh-high ferns. *"There!"*

"Gray wolf, maybe," Viktor continued in a dramatic stage whisper. "They travel in *packs* and circle around their kill—"

"*Bullshit.* It's Vinny, sneakin' up on us," Juno warned him hoarsely. "That *fucker!*" Juno fingered the trigger of his firearm and motioned for Viktor to brace.

"You think?"

"I'm gonna finish off this pockmarked douche bag before he does his happy knife thing on you and me," Juno said, cocking the pistol in his hand.

"What about dusting Mrs. Hotsy-totsy, Juno? We're supposed to wait till Richie tells us to act on her."

"*Shut up, I said!*" Juno fired right back, waving him off. "Keep it *down*, Bonehead! This isn't Bambi we're hunting, you wanna wait for his bullet in your brain? We make our move now in case Vinny still has the dough! We tell Richie we couldn't get no coverage." Juno hadn't figured on not having phone coverage. They started to run.

Several meters into the thicket, they saw the menacing creature, crawling toward them with a loathsome purpose; its long fangs bared, saliva dripping. It was black, brown, and white and had a long tail, claws, and large flat. And was spotted black, white, and brown.

Behind the dog, propped against an oak tree with one hand clutched his chest, was a cop. His other hand waved a pistol.

"*Shoot!*" Juno shouted at Victor. "You kill the dog! I'll get the cop!"

Two pistol cracks followed. A yelp. And silence.

107
BEN AND THE
DOG DOOR

Ben, seriously regretting his hair-brained idea, slipped past two bickering thugs stationed in the woods. The men were as wide as they were tall, matching bookends down to their revolvers. Expecting them to enter the house through the lower-level door, Ben ducked behind the waterfall and pool pump room and braced himself for action. His breathing broke in and out, still as stone as he waited, except for his shifting feet. The deputy's pre-planned whistle should have sounded already. It hadn't. This was crazy, and dangerous. Ben swatted away some annoying mosquitoes. Was Peters asleep at the switch? Where was the Security they had promised?

He scanned the length of the big house fretting about his next move. It was odd that the entire house was dark. He would expect at least one light—the bedroom. Zabaglione's men were armed and had a purpose. Catherine was in the house. He could not live with himself if anyone hurt her.

The boys were too big to take on. Shaking some tightness from his shoulders, Ben knocked his tortoise shell eyeglasses off his head to somewhere in the hydrangeas. Legally blind without them, his heart pounded as he patted around the plants, sweeping his fingers back and forth, coming up empty-handed. He would do anything in his power to protect Catherine, but his best weapon was not his eyes, it was his mind, and it didn't take a particles physicist to realize that he had to get her out of the house. Every minute was crucial. He climbed the multiple steps from the hot tub to the large deck off the kitchen and garden room, stepping lightly on the wood to avoid making noise. His instinct was to enter the house from that level and beat the killers to bedroom floor. He flicked his phone light on and off, aiming it at the kitchen door handle, hoping to not attract attention. The ornate bronze handle would not budge. He paused to analyze his options. The kitchen windows were designed with decorative, wrought-iron bars, with the spaces between them just large enough for a cat to squeeze through. His breathing was shallow and rapid, but he would not allow himself to fail. Catherine needed him. He would not let down the woman who had trusted him with her protection. If there was a way in, he would find it.

Ben hoped he would make the alarm would go off but expected the Dobermans to bark. As his panic tried to take hold, he tried the garden room door, but it was locked. On the opposite side of the house was the massive front door, but there was no guarantee it would open, and it was visible from upstairs. He squinted as he studied the casement windows around the floor of the large garden room adjacent to the back hall. It was full of tropical greenery. Its windows were too small to fit through. He took a closer look, blinking. All, but one window, appeared to be locked. This one was different than the others, made of plywood instead of glass. Someone had turned one window into a dog door with an opening made with a swinging rubber flap for the Jack Russell and Basset Hound. Ben studied it, closer. If only he could remove the board—maybe, he could pull himself through the window without getting stuck. Two wooden blocks served as latches that rotated smoothly around a screw in its center. He pulled hard on the board, relieved when it popped into his hands. Two gunshots fired close by in the woods. Without delay, he began to squeeze himself through.

108
THE CATFIGHT

The smell of booze suggested that Pussi had been waiting in the sitting room for some time, it twisted Catherine's colon like an old garden hose. A discarded Chianti bottle on the floor close to her phone. "Notice the dreamy carving on the piano's other side," Pussi said in a syrupy tone. The puffy-faced brunette in her blonde Farrah Fawcett wig smiled and pointed gayly at the precious antique, enjoying the little bubbles before the boil.

"You," Catherine snarled, feeling newfound confidence, "are *toast!*"

"Hmm...." Pussi said, taken aback, certainly drunk. Using the piano as a handrail, she swaggered toward the keyboard, punching depressions in the maple floor with her five- inch spike heels. Catherine cringed at Pussi's sweaty handprints marking great-grandma's priceless grand. Bracing herself against its side, Pussi pointed to her artwork with a long, hot-pink fingernail. Her eyelashes batted provocatively, one of them dangling loose. "Jackybuns and I carved our initials, right here." Pussi tossed back her shoulder length blond wig and enjoyed a deep belly laugh. "*JH + PP.* Them big block letters was his idea. Romantic, huh?" Catherine's stomach turned like a gym shoe in a dryer, she could not bear to look.

"Oh," Pussi said, feigning empathy, "I see why the sight might upset you." She smacked her over-filled lips. "Especially when ya' consider the difficult way he passed—*tsk tsk*—but he didn't pay his debts, ya' know." She lowered her voice and traced a sad face on the piano with a finger. "He so hated listening to you play," she taunted with a smirk. "It got easier, the deafer he got."

Jaw set, Catherine approached the enemy slowly, nothing could sway her from her target, Pussi's tiny new nose, which was so wrong, especially the tip that looked like the tail of a perky female goat in heat. The best noses were the ones that fit the face—there was a reason why horses had large noses. Pussi's surgeon had made a mistake, but she was going to fix it. Catherine threw back her shoulders, ready to level her punch. "Get out of my house, or I'll call the police."

"You're as good as dead if you touch a phone." Pussi's nose was running freely. She sniffed, wiping it with her bare arm, and scoffed, "*Your* house?" What did you ever contribute except for huge piles of vet bills?"

Catherine knew that if she wanted to land a square one, she would have to draw her prey away from the piano. "So, Puss, have you come for his other girlfriends' dildos? Jack had a trunk full, help yourself, plenty of AAA batteries, too. Unless you would prefer something less mechanical like a sweet Italian sausage?"

Pussi was too drunk to be flustered, "I came to get my money from the safe, Dry Gulch! But it ain't there. What did you do with it?"

"Oh, *that*," Catherine lied matter-of-factly. She had had her share of bullies. "I have that money, come on over here, we'll get it together, okaaay?" She spoke like butter wouldn't melt in her mouth. Catherine's newfound *chutzpa* felt good. "We can watch his snuff video together while we're at it."

"Soooo…you know all about that, do you? This changes everything!" Pussi edged closer and shoved Catherine painfully on her sternum. "I want the money you stole from his safe, *Miss Titties*. It's for my new house."

Catherine ripped Pussi's *Charlie's Angels* wig off her head and flung it like a long-haired frisbee across the room. Pussi was the original pinhead. Her real hair was secured under a hairnet with bobby pins that wouldn't budge without taking hair. "It is not your best look, Mr. Blower!" she said, shaking her head. "Name's *Dick* Blower, isn't it?"

Pussi drunkenly launched herself off the piano, banking to final approach, her nose lining up with the numbers, Catherine's four knuckles, coming up fast. *Crack* went the tiny nose.

"My *beautiful* nose-job!" Pussi cried, red blood splurting everywhere. Catherine laughed out loud, loving the moment as the two mortal foes tumbled to the floor, gel tips gouging, bobby pins with hair yanking.

Heavy footsteps thundered toward them from down

the hall. "Which one of you C-words has my money?" Vinny yelled, brandishing the small chef's knife. He dove into the fray, grabbing at slippery arms.

"She has!" Pussi shrieked. "Baby, Vinny, help me to kill the bitch first, then you can have all the money!"

"I believe you, baby, Daddy's here to help." Pussi covered her gushing nose. Vinny shouted to Catherine, "*Nobody* touches my Pussi! Got that?" Unfortunately, he would have to finish the missus ahead of time. The three enemies rolled and screamed, kicking and slapping. The missus wasn't making it easy. She smacked Vinny's rifle butt hard with her foot, sending it flying toward her cell phone and a liquor bottle. Vinny danced around the Tilt-A-Whirl, his knife searching for a soft spot like her heart. He grabbed her and held her down. She yanked his hair—hard with his greasy pomade—and held on like a drowning victim. "Want your Cutco back?" he shouted at Catherine, laughing. "Here—*take it!*"

Mustering her last ounce of strength, Catherine grabbed Pussi's nipple and pinched, twisting it hard. Pussi shrieked, her arms went limp. Catherine spun from the path of Vinny's thrusting blade, and the knife kept going, striking Pussi, who flinched, and gasped, her eyes wide open with disbelief. Vinny stared at his knife and at his beautiful bride, watching her color grow pale as she bled through her lacey black top. The knife, a Cutco chef, had gone straight to her ticker.

"*Pussi!*" he sobbed, caressing her face, picking off her last dangling eyelash. "Don't *go*—I love you, baby girl!"

Pussi lay dying, her lips struggling to form her last

words. Her eyes stared coldly at his. "You never did nothing right, you *loser!*" she whispered, and was gone.

Vinny's eyes grew as wild as a poltergeist's. He spun toward Catherine, the evil inside him lending enough superhuman strength to pluck her high above his head. Holding her as if she were a grain sack in a barn, he cast her at the floor with a thud.

She lay without air in her lungs and or any feeling in her legs or arms, thinking at first that her neck may have broken, until she could wiggle her toes and fingers one by one. As the feeling in them returned, so did the pain. She would have struggled to free herself if Vinny had allowed. But instead, his hand touched the space between her legs. Swooning, she tried to pull away from his knife and certain death, only to be flattened against the floor with his weight as he traced the arteries on her throat with his knife. No longer having the strength to fight, she knew he would filet her like a boneless lamb roast.

"Your dogs will eat your parts for this!" he said, laughing like a hyena.

109
BITS O' BEN

Sounds of fierce struggling drew Ben toward the melee. Praying we would make it in time to save Catherine, he slid in his socks down the length of the hallway until he closed in on the struggle. There were no police on the grounds. Rescuing her was up to him.

Mortified by the bloody scene, Ben shouted at the killer to stop. Using his bike shoe like a fastball, he wound up a pitch, delivering the heel of it to the knife slasher's head, striking him above his eye. It bounced off.

Puziari only flinched.

"Drop the knife!" Ben roared, flashing his newfound courage. Vincent undeterred like a lion with prey, touched his knife tip to her larynx.

"Sure," Puziari said, as if he were hanging a painting. "Is this a good spot?"

Ben soared toward Puziari, ripping he and his knife from Catherine as if they were Velcro. He wanted to pound the miserable bastard until he looked like a baked manicotti.

Ben's non-stop punches threw Puziari off his game. He
staggered in small circles, dropping his rifle to the floor.
Ben kicked it under the piano. Puziari regaining his equi-
librium, retaliated without mercy, paying him back with
a knee blow to the groin and elbow chop on the jaw.
Vile curses flew one a second, until in one lucky return,
Ben flattened Vinny's Roman nose, causing all motion to
suspend for a fraction of a second. The assassin, frozen
by disbelief, drawing in a long breath, coughed slightly,
and collapsed to the floor, gripping his knife until all was
finally silent.

Catherine lay shivering in shock on the floor. Ben said
a quick prayer of thanks. "Are you alright?" he asked her
gently, dropping on one knew by her side, supporting
her waist with his arm. His eyes teared with unharnessed
emotion. He pulled her trembling body close, stroking her
head softly for comfort. Pussi's anorexic body lay lifeless
in a pool of congealing blood, her long blond wig, like
wet cotton candy. Vincent Puziari would not be going
anywhere after Ben's knockout punch.

Ben could hardly believe it himself. This time, he had
not failed. She was safe. Her fingertip touched the bruise
on his chin gently—she smiled with her beautiful blue
eyes. He cradled her head gently in both of his hands
and turned her face until their mouths almost aligned. He
wanted to touch foreheads and press his lips on hers. But
he did not.

She smiled and touched his face with her hand in a
moment of deep appreciation. "Thank you, Superman,"
she said. But suddenly, her grateful eyes blinked and

opened wide as her hand slipped away. The hair on Ben's neck and forearms bristled. Zombie Man, fueled by hatred, had risen from the dead and was yanking him in the air by his tie. He had him in a choking strangle hold and was twisting. He tossed Ben from side to side, the knife held in his teeth flashing in the moonlight.

Vincent smacked him to the floor. Ben seeing stars, tried to roll loose—one more round in the ring—but his battered head did not allow, and everything went dark.

110
ZOMBIE MAN

Vinny flashed a smile straight from *The Shining* to the missus. He liked when his victims rocked themselves back and forth, as she was doing now. Except for losing Pussi, he was pleased with the way the evening was shaping up—he felt a pang as he glanced at her corpse. On the positive side, as sore as he was, he would now have uninterrupted time with the pretty missus, the thought of which gave him a rise. There would be money in it too, he would make sure of that. But first, he was a killer with a job to do.

The guy lying unconscious on the floor was a fancy man who wore bike shorts with dress shirts, and ties with little fishing boats on them—he deserved to sink. Vinny had a brilliant thought—he would finish strangling him with his tie, before he went for a swim in the lake with Pussi. But first, he wanted to demonstrate his deftness for the missus at removing delicate body parts with a common kitchen knife. The extractions would go easy like they had with her husband, like cutting butter in the sun. Vinny glanced at Ben, and then he looked at the missus who lay whimpering on the floor in a fetal position. "Who bought him this ugly tie?" he demanded. "I thought so! And now," he announced like a game show host as he examined Ben's shrinking crotch, "for the next act, master butcher Vincent Puziari will filet another sausage for Madame's deep freeze!"

The rude pounding of galloping paws interrupted him, a savage Basset Hound, exploding on the scene. Snapping like a piranha at his kneecaps, the vicious dog leaped on him, chomping for a grip, spitting out chunks of his flesh. Screaming in pain, Vinny tried to throw it off, but the frothing animal responded with a bite in the groin. Vinny, desperate to throw the dog off, picked up Pussi's blonde wig, waving it. The Basset Hound stopped to look.

"Stupid mongrel!" Vinny seethed. He dangled the heavy dog by his choke collar, swinging it. "Say good-bye to your darling Basset Hound, Missus," he taunted, jabbing his knife at her yelping pet.

"Please, Vinny, *not my dog!*" she begged.

"Freeze!" A cop lurched through the doorway, shooting, and striking a perfect bullseye on Vinny's butt with his pistol. Impressed, he dropped to the floor, shocked to see the killer dog approach once again, its hackles menacingly up. Without warning, the crazy dog wagged his tail and pulled the dog treats from his pocket.

111

GETTING IT ON
THE THIRD RING

"Good evening, Chicago!" hollered the McCormick Center emcee in his mike. The hazy-blue stage burst into life with lights synced to the rhythm of the warm-up band. The fidgeting audience roared with enthusiasm. They were psyched for a great show, and their grueling wait was over. Bobo Doc stood behind the heavy curtain, swallowing hard, waiting for his cue. The producer was talking animatedly into his headset. He and Digger were the first act. A loud squeal and the stage went dark, something technical. He snuck a peek into the audience from behind the curtain. The auditorium was awash in harsh house lights. It was another sellout year. The stage was warm. His armpits were moist.

"Auntie Ella is out there, all right!" he told Digger as the stage lights continued to rise. Bobo Doc laughed shook his head to blow off his stage fright. He crossed and uncrossed his arms. Meanwhile, his little brother stood staring at the exit. He looked downright chalky for a dark Negro guy, even in his yellow sanitation worker costume.

He grabbed Digger's sleeve and pulled him over so that he could see their fans. Especially Auntie Ella in the front row. "She came from St. Louis to see us, thanks be to Jah!" he said, keeping an eye on the producer. They had practiced for the moment when they could finally make their special auntie and the people of Montserrat proud. "Digger, you and me, will be joining Marley and Arrow soon!"

"They're dead, Bobo," Digger reminded him as his eyes scanned the crowd. Bobo Doc needed Digger; the Dumpster Divers Trash Band was a two-person act. Digger, who looked more like a nutcracker than a professional disposal engineer, finally spotted their people and began showing signs of life, especially when he noticed the sweat stains under his costume arms and rocked back in horror. "Oh, no!" he cried, fanning his armpits with a playbill.

"Not even Auntie will see that!" Bobo Doc lied. "Don't worry—be happy." At this point, nothing could be done for it, or their dripping wet dreadlocks, mashed under their crocheted sky pieces, or the sweat channels in their pancake makeup. The show was going on—and they were going out first, which was any minute now.

"Wow," Digger said. Bobo Doc knew Digger was punchy-scared. He wiggled his hips. "Auntie Ella is a cougar in da miniskirt, Bobo!"

"And look at her shiny red boots!" Hoping to loosen Digger up, Bobo Doc broke into a spur of the moment rap, Auntie Ella believed he had a gift from above.

"Don't be a pain! We're in de fast lane"

Digger cracked a smile and Bobo Doc beamed. He hadn't been completely himself since the Big Ting. Most important, was that Digger improved every day. Tonight's song had started out as an exercise suggested by their PTS therapist. "Never let a good tragedy go to waste," she had advised.

As far as Bobo Doc's eyes could see, every row in the auditorium was filled with paying customers. Auntie was feeling much better thanks to her two generous nephews and their pile of reward money...and to Deputy Pops Peters, who was sitting next to her, bespelled by her charm.

She and the deputy had seats with double wheelchair access, closest to the stage, courtesy of Mrs. Henniger, who was talking to Mr. Williams on her left. He chuckled, feeling their joy, they were "doing it," all right, he could tell. She called him a hero for helping to set her free, but he had only done the right thing. Someday, maybe he would see them again in Montserrat. He had told Mr. Williams of his plans to look there for a wife.

Pops was taking better care of his health and feeling like a new man since having his triple bypass. His epiphany had come while in the recovery room. If he acted fast, he could still help clean up Baxter Township, and retire in glory.

Thanks to his speedy work with the nurse's call buzzer, the worst of the Baxter County's lowlifes were snagged in a bust that night of the Pole A Bare Dance Club. Thanks to Pops, thirteen nasty girls now had something warm to cover up in—identical pink, no-iron jumpsuits. The boys wore blue. Richie and Brenda Zabaglione had been hosting an investor screening of Henniger's video when the SWAT raid went down. The canine unit had cornered the couple as they scrambled into a ten-yard dumpster in the club's parking lot. Quite the catch. Pops liked that with all their jail time, that pair would be lucky if they ever saw a Gucci shoe again.

Billy Redd was in blue, too, and enjoying Mexican corn chips from the prison snack shop on days when he had bucks in his inmate trust account. On their way to back Pops up Gray and Dubrowski had apprehended Redd on Route 167, carrying $250,000 in cash, bundled in a Nehru jacket. He was sprinting away from a disabled pink, four-door Lexus on the roadside. Henniger's red '53 MG TC was hitched behind it.

Vincent Puziari was busy in the Terre Haute Pen awaiting his appeal. Word was, he had asked a female guard for her hand. She had reported him for making a verbal threat. He would be dining with plastic knives and forks a long time.

His days had been wild since the Henniger case. The media's attention had taken Pops and the department by surprise. The local stations were first to reach the hospital, followed by the networks. Within hours, even BBC International was running the story. As it turned out, he came off great by remote from his hospital bed, and they didn't even edit around the stutters. Even the nurses had named him their 'Officer of the Month.'

Jack's memorial service, with its colorful cast of characters, had been unique. Two hundred cars had filled the Star Bowling and Meeting Center lot. Catherine, anticipating a large attendance for his *bon voyage*, had chosen the spacious venue. From behind the black veil and dark glasses, she had observed the scene with numb curiosity. There were business associates and former employees; acquaintances of every description—women in all sizes and shapes; young to mature; all "best" friends with a special Jack story. Gums flapped, tales rapped for the media, who was there to record it all.

In the end, none of it mattered anymore— not Jack, or his cheating, or the scandals.

Hoping to avoid the heavy traffic, Catherine and Ben had slipped out during the teary testimonials. Mourners were invited to stay for bowling and chili dogs. As it turned out, quite a few bowled, putting a strain on the shoe rental desk. Virgil had his own shoes, purchased with the generous bonus from the missus that included Pussi's house with the picket fence.

Gerte, watching her workman's comp pennies, had decided not to stay and play.

The producer gave the one-minute signal. Ben's warm leg pressed against Catherine's thigh, which she liked. She liked her new life, too. She and he had begun to talk about a life together. She stole a glance at his wonderful masculine profile, breathing in her newfound happiness. Next to her, sat Maggie and Tiffany, happily sharing pictures of the Chicago wedding on their cell phones.

The house lights dimmed. There was movement on the stage. Behind the emcee, she could see the silhouettes of Bobo Doc and Digger, in position with their one-of-a-kind instruments. They were playing their PVC xy-

392 | DENISE LUTZ

lophone and garbage can steel drums tonight. She was grateful to the two zany guys from the exotic island for helping to set her free. She hoped someday to be able to see their paradise.

Catherine took a furtive glance left and right. Once she could determine that all eyes were on stage, she removed an object from her handbag, a surprise for Ben.

"Ladies and Gentlemen!" The emcee shouted gaily, "Again! Welcome to the Chicago McCormick Center and to the Midwest Regional Finals of Jam McMann's Star Find." The audience went wild. "You're a great crowd tonight! We're going to start the show with some spicy Caribbean talent. Get ready for a unique Rasta act from the volcanic island of Montserrat, a place where the landfill is hot, hot, *hot!*" He motioned to the judges' section, pointing. "The famous Jam McMann is sitting with our judges and smiling, you know what that means! Jam, please stand up!" The spotlight caught Jam chewing on Cheetos. She put the bag down, somewhat awkwardly, and laughed. Everyone else laughed, too, then applauded.

"Jam has given us the go-ahead, audience, so let's see *you* erupt for this unusual group, performing on homemade instruments straight from the dump, an original composition with an important message they want everyone to remember. Ladies and gentlemen, The Dumpster Diver's Trash Band, performing their original composition, 'Don't Sext and Drive!'"

The spotlights swung to Bobo Doc and Digger and the stage exploded in sound and color.

Let me tell you where dat Devil go— my friend—you

bettah think twice, and woah
If you wanna stay alive, don't sext and drive
Dey got a ring,
and dey
got a ting—
dey ought ta
know dat dey betta go slow,
With de secret tings— dey lose dey thumbs, even mo!
If you wanna stay alive, don't sext and drive
When de driver crow about havin' mo, de Devil knows
how low he can go!
If you wanna stay alive, don't sext and drive,
De Devil do bad ting
driving and jiving,
there might be no reviving!
De man has a ring, but he pick de wi-fi fling with de
fast data ting,
Why you wanna lie, make her cry?
Marriage is for matin'
but de Devil say dat it's fo datin'
Keep de weddin' ring! Put down da sexy ting!
A harmless fling…? Let it ping.
Put down da ting, avoid de swing,
you could lose de uddah ting!
If you wanna stay alive, don't sext and drive!

Their message had merit, and hit very close to home. A spotlight fanned the auditorium. Catherine slumped in her seat, hoping that no one would recognize Jack Henniger's widow in her brunette wig.

Digger did the playing, Bobo Doc sang. Together, they chimed in together on the chorus. Although, the opera board might not invite the Divers to play, *this* audience loved them. Jam McMann was swaying to the beat, laughing. The judges were amused and entertained. Even some signs popped up, brought by the Baxter County Sheriff's office, *"Don't Sext and Drive"* and *"Stay Alive!"* People clapped and hooted.

Catherine worked her hand under their mutual arm rest to Ben's inner thigh, inching as close as she could without touching. Hidden in the palm of her hand, was a pair of saucy panties, thongs, like the ones she had found in Jack's canvas beach bag. Hers were from No Virgin's Secret; black, with a little fuchsia feather for a tail. She had had fun shopping there—and had been overdue for new underwear since Gerte had boiled the last of her Carters in the washer. The dildos there had been two for the price of one. She had hesitated at first, but then thought, what the hell, and had bought Otis a few.

Bobo Doc and Digger, a huge hit, played another selection.

With one eye on the stage and the other on Ben, she pressed the panties in his palm. He shifted slightly in his seat. She felt a small flash of shame, perhaps her forwardness had embarrassed him. She had been loveless for such a long time. But was it too late to learn about love and sex? There was a lot of good living ahead.

Feeling his temperature rise through the satin, she glanced at his face, relieved to see him smiling his wonderful smile. Rushes of happiness skipped across her skin— a personal, secret moment. He put the panties in his trouser pocket, squeezed her hand and winked. He took her hand off his inner thigh and explored her fingers softly. As the Dumpster Divers completed their first appearance ever on stage, Ben gave a little tug to each of her fingers to the beat. He wiggled her thumb. She smiled and winked. It was wonderful to feel so appreciated.

Ben moved to her middle finger, fiddling with it awkwardly. Something light and scratchy was rolling on. She glanced down to see what, catching the sparkle of a pop can ring. *A ring!* Any finger would do. Or a thumb. Her eyes, welling with emotion, met his tender, direct gaze. He looked deeply in hers and squeezed her hand with utmost confidence. The spotlight fanning the auditorium stopped at the two of them and stayed. Her mouth opened in surprise.

"I love you, Cathy," he shouted over the applause. *"Marry me?"*

The Dumpster Divers concluded their piece with a roar from the crowd.

"Tell the judges if you like them!" said the emcee.

"Hah?" she yelled messing with Ben, her eyes laughing joyful tears as she rose on wobbly legs to stand with the wildly clapping audience. With a real, one hundred-percent smile that matched his, she drew him to her until their lips met for a tender kiss.

She reached her hands to the heavens, and with every finger dancing, shouted her answer to Ben, the judges, and the happy, swaying crowd.

"YES...!!"

THE END